THE UNWANTEDS

Island of Legends

LISA McMANN

THE UNWANTEDS
Island of Legends

Aladdin
NEW YORK LONDON TORONTO SYDNEY NEW DELHI

ALADDIN

An imprint of Simon & Schuster Children's Publishing Division

1230 Avenue of the Americas, New York, NY 10020

This Aladdin hardcover edition September 2014

Text copyright © 2014 by Lisa McMann

Jacket illustration copyright © 2014 by Owen Richardson

Book design by Karin Paprocki

For information about special discounts for bulk purchases, please contact Simon & Schuster Special Sales

at 1-866-506-1949 or business@simonandschuster.com.

The Simon & Schuster Speakers Bureau can bring authors to your live event.

For more information or to book an event contact the Simon & Schuster Speakers Bureau

at 1-866-248-3049 or visit our website at www.simonspeakers.com.

The text of this book was set in Truesdell Regular.

Manufactured in the United States of America 0814 FFG

2 4 6 8 10 9 7 5 3 1

Library of Congress Cataloging-in-Publication Data

McMann, Lisa, author.

Island of legends / Lisa McMann. — First Aladdin hardcover edition.

pages cm. — (The Unwanteds ; book 4)

Summary: Divided by their society into Wanted and Unwanted at thirteen, estranged twin brothers Aaron and Alex have both run into trouble—as mage of Artime, Alex must defend the island from attack, while Aaron continues to scheme to take over the islands and get rid of the Unwanteds altogether.

ISBN 9781-4814-3799-8 (prop)

ISBN 978-1-4424-9330-8 (eBook)

1. Brothers—Juvenile fiction. 2. Twins—Juvenile fiction. 3. Magic—Juvenile fiction. 4. Social problems—Juvenile fiction. [1. Brothers—Fiction. 2. Twins—Fiction. 3. Magic—Fiction. 4. Social problems—Fiction. 5. Fantasy.]

I. Title. II. Series: McMann, Lisa. Unwanteds ; book 4.

PZ7.M478757Ir 2014

813.6—dc23

2013034053

For Jackson

Acknowledgments

This series is such a joy to write thanks to you, my wonderful readers. If you've sent me a letter or e-mail, or found me on The Unwanteds Facebook page or on Twitter or Instagram (@lisa_mcmann), or gotten your friends interested in The Unwanteds, or made a book trailer, or created your own magic spells, or drawn characters from the book and sent them to me, or written your own stories, or invented something, or tried acting or singing or playing an instrument for the first time, or done science experiments, or found your own creative thing to do because of these books, then this page is for you. THANK YOU, Unwanted friend. It is because of you and your wonderful support that I can continue this story. I hope you find joy in the pages as well.

It's important for you to know that even if I continued writing the story from my house in the desert land of Quill (oops, I mean Phoenix), it wouldn't get into your hands without the help of dozens of people who know how to make magic happen. People like my agent, Michael Bourret; my editor, Liesa Abrams, and her editorial team; publisher Mara Anastas; and the shockingly wise Lauren Forte, who has hawk eyes (actual hawk eyes, I'm not kidding). She's like that teacher who catches every single one of your mistakes, but she's really nice about it—you know what I'm talking about? And because of that I learn so much and hopefully end up making fewer mistakes next time.

There are so many others at Simon & Schuster who play a huge part in putting this book together so that you can read it. You noticed the cover, I'm sure—Owen Richardson is the talented artist who draws all the Unwanteds covers, and Karin Paprocki designs them with a little help from her team. A designer figures out how to lay out everything, determines which fonts to use, and decides how the inside pages look with those giant capital letters and cool little origami dragons at each chapter. Wouldn't that be a fun job to have?

Another important part of the team is the production department. They work with the printer on getting the books printed correctly, and they make sure all the special effects on the cover are perfect.

Lucille (who gives the best hugs) and Carolyn (who tells the funniest stories) and the rest of my marketing team at S&S do a ton of awesome stuff. They're the ones who bring you cool giveaways and contests at places like KidzBop.com and Goodreads.com, and at the various S&S social media pages. They also make the bookmarks and stickers that go with this series, and they along with Matt maintain TheUnwantedsSeries.com website. And my publicity team is constantly working to send me around the country so I can do presentations at your schools and at book festivals and trade shows.

Michelle and Anthony are part of the incredible library and education team that works on this series, bringing it to the attention of your teachers and librarians. One cool thing I know you'll enjoy is the curriculum guide to the series written by Kathleen Odean. It's filled with fascinating and thought-provoking questions about what happens in the books. If you're an educator, homeschooling parent, or a super-fan of any age, you're going to want to see it. And the best part is that it's free. You can find a link to it on TheUnwantedsSeries.com or here: http://d28hgpri8am2if.cloudfront.net/tagged_assets/12838_unwanteds_cg.pdf

Reader, you would never have heard of this series if it weren't for the sales team. The sales team travels from place to place within the US and in other countries too, showing books to the bookstore people and telling them what the series is about months before the books even come out. If the people who work in the stores had never heard of The Unwanteds, they wouldn't order the books for their stores, and you wouldn't find them on the shelves. So it's pretty obvious that being on a sales team is a really crucial part of the process that many people don't even think about. (But now you know!)

And even if everyone I mentioned so far did their jobs perfectly, there is still one very necessary cog to the wheel—and that is the booksellers themselves. They are the coolest people of all (I know, because I used to be one)! They order and stock their physical and virtual shelves with books they think their customers will like. And that's where you come in—if you tell the booksellers what books you like, and if you ask them to order the books you are interested in, guess what? They will. So remember that the next time you can't find the book you want.

Finally, the last key player in the book process is you. And even though I sound like a broken record, there would be no Unwanteds series without you (or your beautiful parents) who buy the books. And just as important as you, the reader, is your friend who hasn't heard about The Unwanteds yet. Because, thanks to you, they might just find out, and then everybody wins.

I hope you enjoy *Island of Legends*. Many of you have told me that a year is just too long to wait between books, so my team and I decided to work extra hard to bring you the next three books in the series every six months. When you are finished reading *Island of Legends*, look for Book 5: *Island of Shipwrecks* in February 2015, Book 6 in September 2015, and Book 7 in February 2016.

xox
Lisa

Contents

THE UNWANTEDS

Island of Legends

Other Nasty Places

Aaron Stowe, the high priest of Quill, blinked and turned his head. It was dark as pitch. A moment before, he'd been running through the chaos in Artimé, wrists shackled in front of him. He'd stumbled up the marble staircase of the mansion and flown down the last hallway on the left, all the way to the end of it, and taken a sharp right turn into the kitchenette, which is where he'd arrived from in the first place. He'd stepped into the glass tube that had brought him here, and looked at all the buttons as the voices behind him grew louder. The tube in Haluki's office closet had only one button, but this . . . As the panic rose

LISA McMANN

to his throat, Aaron raised his hands and pressed down, hitting all the buttons at once. Instantly the light disappeared.

Had he gone back to Haluki's house? Perhaps one of the closet's double doors had swung shut. Aaron raised his arms in front of him, finding the opening in the tube so he could exit. He reached his shackled hands through it and felt nothing but air. No closet doors. Nothing solid at all.

He gingerly stepped one foot outside the tube. The surface below was uneven, not floorlike at all. In fact, it felt like dirt, but not well-packed dirt like a road in Quill. The earth beneath him had not been heavily trod upon for quite some time. Perhaps never. *Well, it couldn't be never,* Aaron reasoned. *Someone had to have put the tube here.*

He sniffed and hung on to the side of the tube's opening. He could smell dampness in the air, like Quill an hour after a rare downpour, only this was somehow richer. Earthier. The scent of mint was in the air as well, and he could hear something trickling, a brook or a stream not far away. It seemed like it could be pleasant here, but it was different and unexpected, and therefore quite frightening to someone from Quill.

"What is this place?" Aaron whispered, straining to see

something. Anything. His fingers trembled, and he gripped the edge of the tube opening even harder. He turned his head to look back inside the tube, but if there were any buttons, they weren't visible in the darkness.

Eventually his eyes adjusted enough that he could just barely make out a few shapes. Large trees loomed overhead, and the outline of an enormous rock appeared to step out of the shadows. Near the rock he could see a faint patch of light from the moon shining through the trees.

After another moment of calm, Aaron felt a bit of courage returning. It was enough for him to venture one step toward the light, and then another. A stick cracked under his foot and he froze, but nothing came of it. He glanced over his shoulder, making sure he could still see the tube, and then continued toward the light.

When he stood in the middle of the glow, he looked up through the clearing. Jungle vines hung all around from the most monstrous trees he'd ever seen. The rock nearby was much larger than he'd thought. It jutted upward into the darkness, and Aaron couldn't tell how high or deep it went.

Aaron peered at the rock. Perhaps he could slam his shackles

LISA McMANN

against it to break free. He edged closer, eyeing the shadowy crevasses, one of which looked like it could be the entrance to a cave. Tentatively he tapped the clay shackles on the rock.

Immediately two craggy yellow eyes opened and stared back at him. The cave opening changed shape, as if it were the giant rock's mouth, but it didn't speak. Aaron backed away in fright. And then, from behind him, a high-pitched noise like a woman's scream pierced his ears.

Aaron whirled around and screamed too. The screech grew louder, turning the boy's knees to liquid. He could make out a large animal shape creeping toward him. Aaron tried to run but stumbled over his feet, unable to get his legs to move properly, and then pitched forward as his foot tangled with a vine on the jungle floor. He braced his fall with his forearms and rolled onto his back, desperate to see if either the yellow-eyed rock or the screaming monster was following him.

One of them was. The screaming creature crouched nearby, its hindquarters shifting as if it were about to pounce.

Aaron rolled again, onto his front side, and scrambled up to his feet, inching sideways toward the tube and holding his only weapon—his shackled wrists—in front of him. He scooted faster now in the direction of the tube, praying not to trip, as the monster leaped and landed on the ground in the patch of light where Aaron had been.

The creature gleamed black all over, shining brighter along the curve of its back. Its face resembled that of the frightening winged statue who guarded Aaron's twin brother, Alex, and the mansion in Artimé, and its body was nearly as large. But this creature had no wings. It crept toward Aaron and screamed once more, displaying four gleaming, dripping fangs.

Aaron froze, nearly fainting with fear, paralyzed by the hideous screaming as if he were under a spell. The creature pounced, knocking Aaron to the ground and holding him there with a giant paw on his chest.

It was so startling, so uncommon, that instead of frightening Aaron, it infuriated him. He was the high priest of Quill, after all. He demanded respect. Aaron forgot his fear and sprang into action, slamming his shackles hard into the nose of the creature and crying out with all his might, "Get off, beast! Release me!"

To Aaron's astonishment, the creature stepped back. After the slightest hesitation, Aaron rolled out of reach and crawled

LISA McMANN

to the tube, his hands flailing wildly for buttons—any buttons he could find. Anything to get him out of here.

As his right hand connected and the dark jungle disappeared, Aaron realized his shackles had fallen away. His hands were free.

A Looming Attack

At the sight of a hundred lights pricking the horizon in the direction of Warbler Island, Alex Stowe, head mage of Artimé, bounded into the mansion with robes flying and leaped up the stairs three in a stride. He didn't have time to look for his awful brother, Aaron. He didn't have time to comfort his newest friends, Sky and her younger brother, Crow, who felt sure that the people of Warbler were coming to attack Artimé because of them and their escape. Alex only had time to act.

Behind him came Simber, and behind Simber came Ms.

LISA McMANN

Octavia, the octogator, nearly appearing to float through the air on her many tentacles.

Alex dashed through the no-longer-a-secret hallway, past the two mysterious doors he had not yet been able to unlock, and then past the doors to his new living quarters and the Museum of Large. He turned left into his new office at the end of the hall, by the picture window that overlooked Artimé.

Charlie the gargoyle was there already—he spent a good deal of time in this wing of the mansion, still not quite having gotten over the loss of his creator, Mr. Today, whose recent death had shaken Artimé.

"Can you ask Matilda to contact us if she sees Aaron showing up at the palace tonight?" Alex asked Charlie. "Also, find out if his wrists are still shackled."

Charlie responded with a hand signal Alex had determined to mean "yes," though Sky, who knew the sign language, had said something once about how that hand signal had a more complex meaning, like "yes" with an air of reverence, as if the gargoyle were acknowledging Alex as a king. It made Alex feel a little embarrassed to be referred to in such a manner, but Sky had said it would be insulting to Charlie if Alex asked him to stop, so the new mage reluctantly accepted it.

"Thanks," Alex said. He drummed his fingers nervously on the desk and sorted through a stack of papers, not really seeing them, just keeping his fingers busy as if to mimic the speed of the wheels turning in his head.

Simber and Ms. Octavia entered the office and took their places. Claire Morning and Gunnar Haluki, both recovered from their brushes with death, were not far behind. Tailing them was Florence, who had stayed back to be sure everyone made it safely inside the mansion to await their instructions.

Alex stood abruptly and paced the floor, distracted by a whirl-wind of thoughts and not knowing quite how or where to start preparing for an attack at home. Crow had cried out that it was the birds of Warbler coming to get them, but Alex thought it was more likely that the dots of light were from Queen Eagala's fleet of ships she'd been building for years. Sky had said there were many in various states of construction. He wondered if Warbler really could be heading to Artimé to attack.

"But of course they must be," muttered Alex. "Don't be ridiculous." He looked up when the floor shook slightly. Florence had taken her seat.

The strange party of humans, statues, and creatures glanced uneasily about, quite possibly because of Alex's strange mumblings. Not a single one in the room had been around to see Alex's forced evolution from boy to head mage back when Artimé had turned to dust, the creatures rendered lifeless and the humans nearly so from lack of food and water. And while Alex, after a number of stumbles and amid countless moments of despair, had proven to be quite worthy of taking the place of their beloved leader, Mr. Today, the team had not been there to witness the worst of the situation.

Alex looked around the room, thankful for perhaps the eighty-seven millionth time that the eyes that sought his belonged to this particular group of advisors. He opened his lips to greet them, but hesitated, both in speaking and in pacing. Instead he took a moment to really consider who sat with him at this pivotal juncture: Simber, the pristine stone winged cheetah who had almost without effort grown to be Alex's confidant and first mate. Florence, the enormous ebony statue who commanded Artimé's magical warriors. Ms. Octavia, the art instructor, one of Mr. Today's most gifted, trusted, and outspoken creations. Gunnar Haluki, the former high priest of Quill and the father of Alex's dear and valuable friends Lani and Henry. And Claire Morning, Mr. Today's daughter, a musical genius and a nurturer rather than leader, by her own proclamation. It was an incredible group—Mr. Today's own hand-picked team—and they were among the best of Artimé. Yet for Alex, something wasn't quite right. Because during their absence when Artimé had disappeared, Alex had quite desperately come to trust a few others.

Alex tapped his lips. "How much time do we have before they get here, Sim?"

"Severrral hourrrs. Likely morrre," replied the beast.

Alex nodded. "I'll be right back," he said. He strode to the rear wall of the office, uttered a spell, and went through the secret magical door that led into his private quarters.

"Clive," he called.

Alex's blackboard took on a slight glow in the dark room. A face pressed out of it. "Yes, m'lord?"

"Knock it off," Alex muttered. "I need you to summon Samheed Burkesh, Carina Holiday, and Sean Ranger. Have them come to my office at once."

"Certainly, Your Grace."

LISA McMANN

"You're going to be sorry about mocking me very soon," Alex warned. He didn't have patience for Clive's sarcastic jokes today. His eyes landed on the cabinet that held his spell components. Alex took a few seconds to top off his robe's pockets as well as the pockets of his component vest underneath, and then he returned to the office. Clive called out an old but welcome reminder not to die as Alex closed the door.

Simber stood gazing out toward the sea from the office windows. Alex muttered a spell to unlatch one of them. He opened it so Simber could sample the air to get a better sense of what was approaching. The others talked quietly, already planning.

A moment later, Alex's three breathless friends arrived and stood uncertainly in the doorway.

"Come in. Are Sky and Crow all right?" Alex asked.

"Lani and Meg are calming them down." Unconsciously Samheed touched the scars on his neck. "They're upset about what the leaders tell you at Warbler," he said. He sat down and jiggled his foot. "That Queen Eagala would come after anyone who escaped, identify them by their orange eyes, and kill them. Lani and I nearly busted up laughing the first time we heard that back in Warbler, but Crow and Sky are really afraid. And upset because of what they've brought on us by escaping and landing here. Sky is a mess over it."

"I was afraid of that." Alex sighed, but then he perked up and pointed at the empty chairs in the room. "Sit down, guys," he urged.

Samheed looked like he was full of questions, but apparently he knew enough not to ask them now.

Alex glanced at Simber, as if he wanted the giant stone cheetah's approval of the decision to invite these friends to the meeting. Simber dipped his head slightly, barely a nod, but the meaning was clear to Alex that Simber thought well of the plan.

Alex expelled a breath, trying to push his nervousness out with it, and leaned back against the desk, half sitting on the corner of it. "Hi, everyone. Thank you for coming so quickly," he said. He looked at the three new, earnest faces in the room and felt immediately assured he'd made the right choice. "Now then," he continued, clasping his hands in his lap, "let's figure this all out, shall we?"

It was the voice of a leader. A leader who, for perhaps the first time, felt and sounded quite sure of himself.

A Word from Clive

Samheed, in a minor fit of anxiety over being included as an advisor, took painstaking notes at the meeting in an effort to prove his usefulness to the intimidating group. By the end of twenty minutes, his record of the conversation looked something like this:

—*Florence to organize and prepare squads as usual. Also will assign squad placement along shore and give all info to Alex for distribution via blackboard.*

—*As fleet approaches, Haluki to sail out via Claire's boat to leader vessel and try for peaceful resolution.*

—Carina reminds us most Warblerans can't swim. How will they approach without running their ships aground? Advantage for Artimé?

—Alex suggests stationing all orange-eyed residents—me, Lani, Sky, Crow—in water for safety since Warblerans can't swim. Dumb idea, Stowe! They can still throw or shoot weapons at us. I suggest library third floor instead and adding Meg too because of thornament scars, as Lani and I believe Queen Eagala will seek revenge for her escape.

—Alex to expand hospital wing. Ms. Morning to take charge as chief healer, with Henry Haluki and other nurses as her assistants.

—Simber to monitor approach.

—We think Eagala has some kind of magic, e.g., the silence spell over nonhuman noises on Warbler, but no one's sure what is the extent of it. Lani and I did not witness inhabitants using any magic. Carina to find out if Sky and Crow have info.

—After lengthy discussion, we decided to help defend Quill if Warbler breaches the wall, but we always take care of Artiméans first.

—Our goal: defend Artimé and drive Warblerans away with as few casualties as possible.

—Artiméans should feel perfectly comfortable using any and all means of magic to protect themselves.

—Any Warblerans who truly wish to escape the tyrant Queen Eagala will find shelter within Artimé.

In addition, there were many scratched-out notes as the multitude of ideas was broken down and some discarded as being faulty. When they had run out of ideas, the team dispersed to prepare for battle in their various ways.

Alex descended the marble staircase and found Sky and Crow in the dining room with Meghan, looking glum. He checked the time and then walked over to them.

They looked up when he approached. Sky's hair was still as sleek and fashioned as it had been at the masquerade ball a few hours earlier, but she no longer wore her dress. Instead she was dressed like any other Artiméan ready for battle, with a component vest and everything.

Alex felt breathless around her whenever she looked at him, even now, but he forced himself to stay focused. He pulled a chair around, sat on it backward, and lowered his head until his chin rested on the chair back and he was face-to-face with Crow. "You okay, little guy?"

Crow nodded, but his eyes told a different story.

"I need you to hear me. Both of you," he said, glancing briefly at Sky as well. "It appears we are going to be attacked, and it'll happen in a few hours. You guys can sit here and feel terrible about it even though it is not your fault, or you can help us prepare."

"We'll help, of course," murmured Sky in her husky voice, damaged by the thorns she once wore around her neck. Crow dropped his gaze, but he nodded in agreement.

"Good," Alex said. "Because we need you."

The brief pep talk seemed to rally them, giving them new resolve.

Alex headed next to the area near the landing so he could expand the hospital wing while he waited for Florence to report back with warrior instructions. He held up his hands to the small four-bed room and concentrated, thinking about the size room he wanted, and when he felt quite confident, he whispered, "Extend and heal, size large."

The small room's walls grew, pushing back to create a larger space. They glided smoothly as the floor and ceiling hastened along with them, fixtures and workstations pressing out from the bare walls. When the room ceased to move, the beds and tables popped out and dropped neatly into place.

LISA McMANN

Alex counted the beds. There were forty in all. "More than enough, wouldn't you say?" he asked as Florence approached.

"Dear me. I certainly hope so." Florence handed over a stack of papers to Alex. "Here are the battle plans. Simber says at the speed they're moving, they won't be here before day-break."

"Thanks," Alex said, looking them over. "I'll have Clive send out the orders right away."

Alex returned to his living quarters and summoned Clive, who pushed his face through the blackboard.

"Now what?" Clive asked.

"I have a job for you. It's urgent."

"Great." Clive rolled his eyes.

"If you're not up to it, I can ask Stuart," Alex said. Stuart was Samheed's blackboard. For reasons unknown to Alex, Clive didn't seem all that fond of Stuart.

Clive frowned. "What's the job?"

"We're about to be attacked," Alex said. "You're the first to know."

Clive's eyes widened. "Me?"

"You're the head blackboard now. I need you to distribute

LISA McMANN

the orders. I need to be able to count on you. Can you do this? Or do I—"

Clive's mouth fell open. He nearly drooled before he snapped his mouth shut once more. "Yes," he said reverently. "Yes, Alex. I most certainly can." There was no trace of sarcasm in his voice now.

Alex might have smiled had the situation not been so dire. "Good. Don't mess it up. This is of the utmost importance."

Clive nodded. "You can count on me."

"I know I can," Alex said. "Here goes." Alex looked at the papers in his hand and dictated the various assignments to Clive so that Clive could send out instructions to each team in Artimé, letting them know where and when to report.

When Alex finished, Clive said in earnest, "Shall I open it with a general announcement? Something that will really get their attention?"

Alex hid a smile. "Oh, by all means. Put your heart and soul into it, Clive." A moment later he felt the floor shake—a sure sign that Simber and Florence were coming to do one last careful run through the plans. "And now I've got to go."

Clive nodded. "Thank you," he said quietly. And then he disappeared into the blackboard.

Shortly thereafter, on blackboards everywhere in Artimé, the following words appeared in stunning neon letters:

From Clive, head blackboard and confidant to our noble mage, Alex Stowe: Artimé is under attack! Please read and follow your instructions. And above all . . . DON'T DIE.

A Mass of Tubes

As it turned out, there was only one button in the jungle tube for the High Priest Aaron Stowe to push. When he opened his eyes, he was back in the kitchenette in Artimé's mansion, his hands free and his heart pounding. He peered out, wondering if it would be smarter to risk his life trying to exit Artimé on foot rather than attempt to push another button.

But the hallway outside the kitchenette was filled with voices, most notably his brother's and the growling voice of the ridiculously huge flying monster. Aaron thought that exiting the mansion now would mean certain death. He looked at the

LISA McMANN

panel before him, agonizing over which button to push. Finally he decided to start at the beginning of the row. He sucked in a deep breath to steady his nerves, and blew it out as he pressed the first one.

Instantly he was thrust into darkness again, and he feared the worst—that he was back in the horrible jungle with the screaming black creature and the enormous rock with yellow eyes. He nearly slammed his fist on the panel in search of another button, but as he lifted his hand to do so, he noticed that the smell was quite different from the musky scent he remembered. This place smelled like . . . like stale, rotting wood. The heat of this location seeped into the tube and warmed him immediately, and after a moment he put his hand out through the tube's opening.

Aaron's fingers found a solid panel. He pushed on it, and with a creak, it swung open. A bit of moonlight trickled in through a window, and soon Aaron realized where he was. He was back in Haluki's empty house.

"Oh, thank Quill," he breathed, and he stumbled out of the closet on weak legs and sank to his knees, trembling, in the very spot where Mr. Today had taken his last breath. Aaron sat there for a very long time, feeling faint every time he tried to stand. Finally he crawled out of Haluki's office, down the hallway, and into a bedroom, where he climbed onto the bed and lay there, trying very hard not to think about what he'd seen and how he'd nearly perished.

When he drifted off to sleep, he experienced rare dreams that were filled with strange, frightening creatures chasing him through a jungle. At every turn, he stumbled and the creatures devoured him. No matter how he tried to shout "Release me!" to them, he couldn't get the words to come out in time.

Aaron awoke with a start just before daybreak, unsure at first of where he was, and then remembering. He felt a wave of shame wash through him—dreaming was not allowed in Quill, and he'd had quite a night of it. He scowled defiantly as he stared at the ceiling. What did it matter now? He was the high priest. He had no obligation to tell a soul.

After a while he rose and scrounged through the Haluki pantry to see if he could find anything to eat. He made himself a meager breakfast, and it was while he was eating that he finally remembered what had happened *before* he got caught up in the crazy tubes: The explosion in the sky. The lights pricking the darkness over the sea. And the chaos that followed in Artimé.

Their island was being attacked. The palace, with its opening in the wall, was vulnerable. Quill, with its entrance into Artimé, was vulnerable. And here he sat.

Aaron froze mid-chew, and then he shoved the chair back, hurried to the door, and ran out of the house. He turned up the road and headed toward the palace. "Hurry up," he said, jiggling the portcullis impatiently as he waited for the guards to open it, and sprinting the rest of the way up the drive. He ran to the opening he'd made in the forty-foot-tall wall that surrounded Quill and peered through it, careful to hide his body in case the attackers were already closing in.

His eyes darted all around the downward slope on the other side of the wall, and then, seeing nothing on land, he swept his gaze over the sea. A dozen ships sailed not far off shore, heading around the curve of the land toward Artimé. Aaron gasped at the sight. He'd never seen anything like it. His body was frozen to the spot as he watched the vessels inch toward his brother's section of the island. They were headed to Artimé. For a rare moment, Aaron felt a pang of compassion. And for the briefest time he actually thought, *Perhaps I should help them.*

But the moment passed quickly, and Aaron realized that his first order of business was to protect Quill. He would close up the space in the wall and build a barricade in front of the entrance to Artimé.

Feverishly Aaron reached for the first block, too scared to wait for a team of Necessaries to assemble and do the work, and placed it in the opening in the wall. He hoisted a second block, and a third, pushing them tightly together, scraping his knuckles and drawing blood, muttering to himself as he filled in the space.

As he worked, Aaron realized something very important about the former ruler of Quill: The High Priest Justine had been right all along about the dangers beyond the wall. She had protected Quill for fifty years without a single incident until the Unwanteds botched things up. And she'd done that by closing off Quill to the outside world.

Now, by opening up the wall and allowing his people to mingle with the Unwanteds, Aaron had broken the very best rule Justine had made, leaving the people of Quill vulnerable.

How terribly, awfully, utterly foolish Aaron was to have doubted his hero.

Weapons of Mass Confusion

At daybreak, the entire community of Artimé assembled throughout the main floor of the mansion, in rows on the stairs, and on the balcony.

"Good morning," Alex said crisply from the front window near the door that faced the sea. "It's a bit crowded in here, but as Clive explained in your instructions, we have decided not to go outside until we know just how the people of Warbler plan to attack us.

"I'd like you all to know that an hour ago, we attempted a peacekeeping mission by sending Gunnar Haluki out to speak with the Warblerans, but they would have nothing to do with

LISA McMANN

him unless he gave up our two Warbler natives as well as Samheed, Meghan, and Lani. Of course that was out of the question. And try as he might, he was unable to get any sense of their method of attack."

A murmur arose and Alex paused, glancing at Sky. He went on. "Haluki returned to us, and we now have Simber stationed on the lawn. Please stay quiet and wait for me to give your team leaders the signal to exit the mansion and take your stations."

Alex turned his attention to the window, watching as a fleet of twelve ships approached. "At least there aren't a hundred," he remarked in a low voice to Florence. "There must have been several lights on each ship." The Warbler ships dwarfed Artimé's own pirate vessel, which Captain Ahab, the mildly insane statue, had moved to the lagoon for safekeeping.

"It seems like this could be an easy battle," Florence said. "But that's exactly what worries me. Queen Eagala is not a fool."

"And so we wait," Alex said.

The ships sat in front of Artimé for at least thirty minutes without a single thing happening. The people inside the mansion whispered and shifted and tried not to bump each other.

Sky and Crow grew more nervous as time passed. Soon Sky sidled up to Alex. "They're up to something," she murmured. "I'm sure of it."

"We're ready," he said, not taking his eyes off the ships. "We're taking it seriously. I promise." He pressed his lips together, then added, "Please do whatever it takes to keep you and Crow safe. If they come after you, take the tube to the library and then the steps up to the third floor. That's the safest place."

Sky frowned. "We want to help."

"Sky," Alex said in earnest, "it would really help me to know that you are safe. The last thing we need is to have to rescue you from Warbler again. We have other places to go and people to rescue . . . like your mother."

"I know." Sky closed her eyes for a moment and sighed. "You're right, of course. But we're still helping. We need to."

She didn't elaborate, but Alex knew she needed to help to prove that she was loyal to Artimé—even though no one doubted it.

"That's fine," Alex said. "We want you to help, but I also

LISA McMANN

need to trust you. You can fight. But do the right thing and hide if necessary."

"If necessary," Sky agreed. "Got that, Crow?"

Crow nodded.

At that moment, a large growl from outside the mansion turned into a full-on roar, making the mansion's windows vibrate. Alex's gaze darted from one ship to the next as large wooden planks quickly rose up from every deck. A dozen loud *thwapps* peppered the air, and the giant arms swung toward Artimé, releasing objects into the sky.

"Catapults!" Florence yelled. "Get back! Away from the windows!"

Alex stepped back as a multitude of *things* flew toward the mansion. "What the . . . ," he muttered. "What are they?"

In the air, the *things* sprouted parachutes, slowing them down, and as they neared the island they began to float toward the ground.

"They're people!" Alex shouted. "Warbler's first line is landing on the shore." *And they aren't very big or scary-looking,* he thought, a bit puzzled. He turned to face the Unwanteds. "Leaders, take your places outside and attack!"

LISA McMANN

The Battle with Warbler

The Artiméans streamed outside the mansion from all doors as Simber's continuous roar rendered the Warblerans unable to fight, leaving them cowering instead.

"Some of them are barely more than children," Claire Morning said, looking closely at the living arsenal coming toward them. "I wonder if Warbler's youth took to fighting by necessity, like our young Unwanteds." She prepared a spell and glanced at Mr. Appleblossom, who was standing next to her with a look of horror on his face. "What is it, Siggy?"

Mr. Appleblossom stood staring at a girl of about twelve

LISA McMANN

who was now frozen by a magical spell, a look of fear on her face. He lowered his hand and looked down. "What shame it is to see this cherub's face," Mr. Appleblossom said softly. "And cowardly of them to sacrifice their youth to take their Queen Eagala's place! I have no means in me to do *this* twice."

"They may be children, but they're attacking us!" Ms. Morning said. She regarded him thoughtfully for a moment. Her gaze swept over the young Unwanteds around them, already fighting, and wondered if anyone on Warbler felt guilty for fighting against children. She doubted it. She reached over and squeezed Mr. Appleblossom's shoulder. "I understand. You didn't hurt her, though."

"That look of fear is hurt enough, you know." Mr. Appleblossom nodded brusquely, turned, and walked back to the mansion.

Ms. Morning pressed her lips together. After a moment, watching her friend Sigfried leave over his convictions, she looked at Crow and Henry and the rest of the generation of Unwanteds who had been fighting since they were small. She continued on with the task, though she wore the dilemma on her troubled face for some time after.

LISA McMANN

By now, the other team leaders had given their orders, and the Unwanteds spouted off a plethora of freeze spells, blinding spells, and shackles. Some cleverly thought to use scatterclips, which sent Warbler fighters flying backward through the air until they hit the sides of their own ships and stuck fast just above water level, unable to be reached by those on board.

As the Unwanteds defended Artimé, the catapult arms moved slowly, skimming the sky as they returned to their initial positions.

"Prepare for round two!" Florence shouted.

Just as the last enemy was frozen, the catapults released again, sending dozens upon dozens more young Warblerans soaring through the air and coming to rest on land, only to be immediately made useless by the simplest of spells.

It was almost too easy, Alex thought. "Stay on your guard!" he warned.

Several Unwanteds stationed near the wall that separated Artimé and Quill had had none of the action thus far, and began to scoff at the efforts of Queen Eagala.

"Stay on yourrr guarrrd!" repeated Simber.

But it wasn't easy when Warbler's best efforts seemed

ridiculous. Several minutes passed as Artimé waited to see what was next. Some of the Unwanteds, tired of standing, sat down despite the warnings.

"Hold your ground," Alex commanded, and Florence repeated it so all could hear.

Finally the catapults let loose a third time . . . and another round of Warblerans sailed up into the air and down toward Artimé, their parachutes bringing them lightly to the ground, where the Unwanteds put a swift end to their movements completely.

"Is this all they have?" Alex muttered.

"I don't know," Florence replied. "If it is, we're in luck. Watch—here's another round. Maybe Eagala thinks we'll run out of spells."

"Maybe." But Alex knew his army was well stocked, and even if they ran out of the old faithful spell components, the Unwanteds were coming up with new spells all the time and were fully armed.

The *thwapp*s were heard again, and the catapult arms swung once more. The people of Artimé watched nonchalantly as the fourth round released into the air.

LISA McMANN

Simber stood on his hind legs, madly sniffing the air. "Take coverrr!" he cried. "These arrren't alive!"

But it was too late. Dozens of giant boulders flew toward Artimé with no parachutes to slow them down, bowling over rows of Unwanteds as loud thuds and the sound of breaking glass filled the air. The mansion windows had been hit.

Immediately the catapults returned to loading positions and let loose once more. Dozens of boulders even bigger than the last ones flew at the Unwanteds: Artiméans everywhere dove to get out of the way, or flew if they could fly, some managing to dodge one boulder but ending up directly in the path of another. The ground shook as the boulders hit it. Screams filled the air. Artimé was in chaos. There was no spell that would stop an attack like this. None that Alex knew, anyway.

As a third round of boulders pelted the island, enough time had passed to allow the first group of Warblerans to come back to life from their temporary frozen states. And almost as if they'd planned it, they began charging at the Unwanteds, drawing knives from their belts.

Ms. Morning reared back. "Watch out!" she cried. The children of Warbler didn't seem so innocent anymore.

"Attack!" shouted Alex, but he wasn't to be heard above the noise.

"Attack!" yelled Simber and Florence together.

Alex, narrowly dodging a boulder, fired off several rounds of scatterclips, sending half a dozen Warblerans to the sides of the ships. At the same time, the original rounds of scatterclips began to wear off, leaving those enemies dangling unceremoniously above the water by a single clip or two.

The next group of Warblerans emerged from their temporary spells, and they charged into the chaos, looking around desperately as if they were searching for someone. And of course they were.

The battle shifted. Caught off guard, Alex switched his verbal components to permanent chants and began laying Warblerans out across the shore, one by one.

"Florence, permanent spells from here on out," he said, and Florence yelled out the command. When he had a second, Alex turned around to see what had become of his people. At least a third of them were on the ground. The rest were fighting valiantly, Sky among them.

"Sky!" Alex cried. "Go! Like we talked about!"

But his voice was lost in the battle. He sought out Crow, Sam, and Lani, but they too were out of hearing.

Frustrated, Alex turned back to see the third wave of Warbler fighters come to life as their spells wore off. At the sight of the weapons, Mr. Appleblossom had returned with an apparent change of heart. He stuck by Alex's side, having pushed his way forward to assist now that so many of Artimé's front line were flattened.

"Oh, thank goodness," Alex said, seeing the eccentric theater instructor. "Let's split these up and be done, shall we? Scatterclips seem to be the answer here."

Together they fired a dozen smart rounds of scatterclips, sending all but a few of the Warblerans smacking into the sides of ships. The few whose paths were not in a direct line with a ship flew past them and kept going, out of sight.

When Alex ran out of scatterclips, he pulled out a new spell component that Meghan had created and popped it into his mouth. He blew through his lips, and a long, thin bubble emerged, taking the form of a sword. Alex grabbed the bubble sword and began swiping it at the oncoming attackers, sending them bouncing in various directions, where others could subdue them.

Mr. Appleblossom followed up with a new abstract spell, which caused the Warbler attackers' body parts to scramble, causing mass confusion.

Once the last of the Warblerans at the shoreline was rendered useless, Alex and Mr. Appleblossom turned to see who might have gotten past them. As it turned out, a great number of them had.

The two charged toward the enemy, meeting up with Sean and Carina near the entrance to Quill. "Over there!" Carina cried. "They've got Crow." She rushed off, and when she was in range, fired off a variety of spells. Crow fell to the ground. Carina scooped him up and ran inside the mansion.

"Sean," Alex said, "we've got to get Sam, Meg, and Lani into the mansion. Sky, too, if you can find her." He looked all around, knowing Sky must be outside. There was no way she would have gone to the library without Crow.

Alex ran toward Henry just as the boy was being held against a tree with a knife to his throat, and quickly put a stop to that. Then the two turned to see a concerted effort by adult Unwanteds, not known for their magical fighting abilities, who pooled some swan song spells and sent eight

LISA McMANN

Warblerans squawking and waddling in a circle all at once.

"Well done!" Alex shouted to them. "Can you do it again?"

With a few more quick blasts by each Unwanted who was still able, the remaining Warblerans were soon contained in one way or another—many of them stone-cold statues, reminding Alex a little too much of how things had looked on these grounds not so long ago.

As the noise died down, Alex, breathing hard, whirled around to assess the damage. "Be very sure you've got the attackers contained by permanent spells. Check each one over to be certain no one is faking."

The Unwanteds set out.

Alex turned to Florence and Simber. "What's happening out there at the ships?"

"Simber's going to take a look if you think it's wise."

The enormous cat stood patiently, waiting for Alex's reply.

Alex thought for a moment, worried that a boulder in a catapult could hurt the statue. "Okay," he said, his voice guarded. "But be nimble."

The cat needed no further urging. He leaped into the air and flapped his enormous wings. It took only seconds for him to soar high over the ships and release a shattering roar. Moments later, Simber didn't need to make any announcement as to what was happening. Whoever remained on the ships began pulling anchors and raising sails. Those stuck to the sides of the ships began screaming in fear, but the ships pulled away, leaving great numbers of their own people dropping into the water or frozen stiff on shore.

"Get our wounded inside!" Alex commanded the Unwanteds. "Ms. Morning, Henry, and the rest of the nurses are already heading in there. Let's go!" He paused and looked at the Warblerans in the water, knowing they probably couldn't swim. "And get a team of good swimmers and the squirrelicorns to rescue them right away." The Unwanteds jumped to action.

Alex stepped around a boulder and lifted the shoulders of a woman, her forehead bleeding. He and Mr. Appleblossom picked her up and carried her into the mansion. They placed her on a bed and turned around to go back for another, watching as the long stream of wounded limped or were carried inside.

Alex stopped when he saw Samheed stumbling toward him, carrying a girl whose hair and body were covered with a layer of dirt. She was limp in his arms.

"Stowe, make way!" Samheed barked, dodging around Alex. He set the girl on an empty bed. His voice softened and he put his hand on his friend's shoulder. "And brace yourself. This is a pretty bad scene."

Alex looked past Samheed at the girl on the bed and gasped. It was Sky.

In a Panic

O utside the palace, the High Priest Aaron took in one last glimpse of the sea, slid the final block into the hole in the wall, and stepped back. He wiped his bloody knuckles on his pants and then dabbed the sweat on his forehead with his sleeve. "There," he said, surveying his work and trying not to think about what was happening in Artimé right about now. He needed to get moving on securing the other weak wall in Quill, though he knew there was no way to do it now while there was likely a battle in progress over there. For some ridiculous reason, Aaron's hands wouldn't stop shaking.

LISA McMANN

He stepped back and drew a keen eye over the wall. It wasn't perfect, and it needed some patching, but he wondered if anyone far away could tell there had once been an opening in this spot. He concluded that it looked reasonably like the rest of the wall from a distance. Close up, one could see a few narrow slits and holes at eye level, through which tiny breezes blew. Aaron could just barely make out bits of the sea through them if he stood close, but it couldn't be helped. He frowned at the bloody scrapes on his hands, which stung, and turned to go into the palace.

At the entrance to the cold, gray structure stood Eva Fathom, arms crossed over her chest, watching Aaron.

"Secretary," Aaron muttered, using the name she'd gone by for fifty years. He didn't need her nosing around or asking questions right now.

"Welcome back," she replied. She didn't move from the doorway. "Where've you been?"

Aaron stopped in front of her. "It's none of your business. Excuse me," he said. "I have a lot to do today." He stood several inches taller than the curled old woman, but that didn't keep Aaron from being a bit apprehensive around her. He was never sure if he could fully trust her, and the two occasionally butted heads. Still, she had been Secretary to the High Priest Justine for decades before the ruler's untimely death, and Aaron was Justine's most fervent fan. Surely the former high priest had had good reason to trust Secretary. Aaron just hadn't figured out what that reason was yet.

The woman stepped aside to let Aaron in. She followed him up to his office. "How shall I assist you today?" she asked when Aaron sat down at his desk.

Aaron studied her through narrowed eyes. "Aren't you going to ask about the hole in the wall?"

Secretary's voice was smooth. "You'll tell me eventually if there is something you need me to know about it, High Priest."

"So you didn't see those big—those big jalopies on the sea?"

The woman hesitated, puzzled. "You mean ships?" she asked.

"Whatever they are. A dozen of them. Headed to Artimé."

"Oh dear." A frown passed over her face. "You should send guards over to stand in the entrance to Quill and keep intruders out. It's wide open these days, isn't it?"

LISA McMANN

"Good idea. Why don't you tell them to get over there."

Eva stepped outside the office to take care of the orders. While she was gone, Aaron picked up a dull pencil and drew a very crooked triangle on a piece of paper, for the sheer reason that he could now that he was high priest. Besides, the distraction helped him think. He drew some other shapes too. Rectangles, like the sails of the ships. Before he knew it, he was drawing lines to connect them.

Secretary cleared her throat. She'd returned, unheard.

Abruptly Aaron stopped drawing and looked up. He set down the pencil. "We need more than guards. We need to wall in the entrance to Quill," he said. "Immediately. We—*Haluki* allowed Quill to be vulnerable for too long."

Secretary's brow furrowed, the wrinkles in her forehead deepening such that they resembled tree bark.

Before she could speak, Aaron lifted a hand. "Don't even begin to argue with me," he warned. "It's my duty to keep Quill safe, and that is what I shall do. We'll need a team of Necessaries to get to work immediately—and *not* my father this time, please." He gave the woman a sour look as if his father's visit to the palace had been her fault.

"But—" Secretary began.

"Ut-tut-tut!" Aaron replied. "What did I say?"

Eva Fathom closed her icy lips.

Aaron watched her face, suddenly wondering what she was going to say but too proud to ask her now.

"Very well." She nodded. As she turned to carry out Aaron's wishes, her face wore the smuggest smile Aaron had ever seen.

Somewhere deep inside him, Aaron began to panic.

Skyfall

Alex rushed to Sky's side just as Henry came running.

"Is she breathing?" Alex cried. "Is she dead? She can't be dead!"

Henry was silent as he checked over Sky. After a moment he looked around frantically and shouted, "Ms. Morning!" He turned to Samheed and squeaked, "For Jim's sake, get Alex out of here. He's making me nervous."

Samheed pulled Alex out of the way. Alex, numb, could do nothing but watch as Henry and Ms. Morning worked feverishly over the girl. A thousand memories pummeled his brain:

Sky and Crow unconscious on the raft. Sky finally waking up on that fateful day. Sky inching away and spitting water in Alex's face. Sky stoic and silent on the roof as Alex cried. Sky bringing him the model of the mansion, helping Alex figure out how to get Artimé back. Sky on the pirate ship's stairway, startling Alex with a kiss. And Sky on a raft once more, determined to save her mother.

"She's not breathing," Alex heard somebody say.

"Oh no," he whispered, leaning heavily against the door frame of the hospital wing. "No. No." He wanted to scream it. He couldn't bear to lose her. Not now. Not after everything. He gripped his robe—the robe that Sky had hemmed for him so it wouldn't drag on the floor. He stood on his tiptoes, trying to see around the crowd of nurses, trying to see her face. If only he could see her face. . . . "Sky!" he screamed. "Your mother—you have to breathe! We need to save your mother!" Several in the room turned to look at him, their faces growing scared.

"Alex," Samheed said, his voice wretched. He gripped Alex's arm tighter. "Pull it together, man."

"Sky!" Alex yelled again, and then he stopped and shot Samheed a wild look. "Where's Crow?"

Samheed shrugged, helpless. "I don't know. I saw him, I mean . . . I think he's fine."

"Do you think she's . . . ?"

"I don't know, Al."

Alex knew that he should try to find Crow, let him know his sister was hurt. Or dying. Or . . . dead. But he couldn't move. His feet were cemented to the floor. "I can't believe this is happening."

More and more Artiméans rushed in carrying injured humans and creatures, filling up the beds.

"What are they doing to her?" Alex asked.

"It's hard to tell," Samheed said.

"She can't die. Not after everything."

Samheed looked on with Alex and nodded. "I know. It's not right."

Just then there was a flurry of activity at Sky's side.

"Roll her on her side!" Ms. Morning shouted. "Quickly!"

Alex strained to see what was happening. "Sky, please!" he cried out as his insides ached and trembled. Samheed didn't try to quiet him.

After a moment of stillness, there was another burst of

movement. Henry lifted something in the air and shouted in triumph, "Okay, Sky—now breathe!"

Another agonizing moment passed. And then Alex thought he heard a hoarse cough.

"Atta girl," Ms. Morning said. "That's it. Get it all out."

Before Alex's eyes, Sky sat up, coughing and hacking, sucking in air.

A cheer arose. Alex broke free from Samheed's grasp and ran to her bedside, squeezing past the people who surrounded her. She coughed a bit more, and when she stopped, Alex spoke her name. "Sky?"

She turned, seeing him for the first time, and smiled weakly. "Hey."

Alex flung his arms around her. There was nothing that could possibly feel better right now than her dirt-covered cheek on his, and her ragged breath against his neck.

The New
Unwanteds

While Sky was left to spend a few hours recovering in the hospital ward with the dozens of other injured, Alex and Samheed found Lani and Meghan at the shore hard at work. They and several others had all the people of Warbler lined up and shackled to keep them contained until Artimé could figure out what to do with them.

Simber and a bunch of squirrelicorns flew out over the water behind the fleet, plucking up any additional Warblerans who were falling off the sides of the ships as their spells wore off. They brought them to the shore, where Meghan took over, stripping them of their weapons, shackling their wrists, and walking them over to the others.

Almost all the newcomers were children, and they looked scared. Their ages varied, but most looked around ten or eleven, like Henry and Crow. Some a little older. They pleaded with their orange eyes. Others cried silently or looked at the ground. None of them made a sound, of course.

Alex looked them over carefully, not yet sure what he was going to do with them. They seemed harmless enough. He glanced over his shoulder at Meghan. "See if you can find Crow and ask him to come here, will you? He may still be in the library."

"Be right back." Meghan took off for the mansion.

Alex turned back to the silent prisoners. "Well, here you all are," he mused. "Abandoned." They didn't look like criminals at all. "Look," he said matter-of-factly, "when you surprised us by parachuting in, we didn't know what we were facing. We cast some spells on you to keep the situation under control, but none of them were painful. Looking back, I now under-stand that somebody probably strapped a parachute to you and put you in a catapult, and you maybe didn't have any say in that. But the reason I'm angry with you is that once you got here, you attacked us with knives and you hurt people. You did that all on your own. And I'm wondering why you'd do such a thing. Did we hurt *you* in some way when we went to Warbler to rescue our friends?"

Several Warbler children burst into silent tears. Alex couldn't look at them. He had to figure out if there was evil in these children. He needed to know if they felt bad about what they did and if he could trust them not to hurt anyone else. He took his time studying each face. By the time he had looked at them all, the entire group had dissolved into remorse.

Alex softened. "Listen, guys. We do things a little differently in Artimé." His voice grew kind. "You see, we found ourselves here because we were Unwanted and Purged from our society in Quill, which lies beyond that wall." He paused as the children of Warbler lifted their heads to look where he was pointing. "It appears your ruler has used you and left you for dead," he said. "Which I guess makes you Unwanted too."

A blond girl in the front row raised her shackled hands to her lips. A boy behind her touched her elbow. Another girl gazed across the water at the retreating ships, lip quivering.

Suddenly Alex realized they didn't understand. To him, now, being Unwanted was a good thing. But the term still held its nasty bite to the children before him, stuck in this precarious position. "First," he said hastily, "I want you to know that we consider Unwanted people to be very special. But I know—it feels terrible." He nodded solemnly and wondered about these children's parents. Did they know they'd be losing their children today? And were they as okay with it as Alex's parents were? Maybe these children actually wanted to go back to Warbler.

He frowned, trying to imagine what Mr. Today would say, and then followed his instincts. "Well, we have a few options here. Let's see. Does anyone wish to be returned to Warbler? We will get you there safely. Don't be afraid." When no one moved, Alex said, "Uh, you don't need to answer yet—let me give you all the options first." He turned when he heard footsteps coming up the path toward him.

"Ah, good," Alex said, relieved. "Crow, can you interpret for us?"

"Sure," Crow said. He scanned the group. "Hey," he said. His eyes alighted on the blond girl in the front. A look of

LISA McMANN

recognition passed between them. Crow studied her teary face for a long minute and then turned to Alex. "You can ask them the questions yourself. But they can't answer with the shackles on."

"Oh. Of course. Which—?"

"Her," Crow said, pointing to the girl. "I know her."

Alex bent down next to Crow and said in a low voice, "Do you want to try to release the shackles?"

Crow shook his head. He wasn't very good at magic. "You do it."

Alex did. The shackles fell to the ground. The girl rubbed her wrists and signed, "Thank you."

"Can you tell us . . . anything?" Alex wasn't sure where to start. "Why did they use children in the catapults? Why did they leave you all here?"

The girl's hands flew through the air. Crow watched. Sam and Lani did too, since they'd begun learning this language, but soon it was clear by the looks on their faces that they were lost. Every now and then Crow stopped her and reported her answers, and before long, the whole story came out.

"It was the parents," Crow said. "When they heard that

Queen Eagala was going to attack, and how she was going to do it with the catapults, the parents began a secret mission to send the children on shore to fight. They convinced Queen Eagala's ruling board that the catapults could fit more children because they are smaller. Their plan all along was to retreat without going back for them."

"What? That's terrible!" Lani cried.

"It's just like Quill," Samheed muttered.

"I can't believe it," Meghan said.

The girl began signing faster.

"No," Crow said. He jumped up and down, trying to get the Unwanteds' attention. "Not like Quill. Listen."

Alex held up a hand to quiet everyone and addressed Crow. "What are you saying?"

"She says the people of Warbler—their parents—convinced the ruling board to send the children to attack because their parents were trying to *save* the kids." He looked at the girl, whose hands had slowed. "Their parents did it so the children could escape Warbler for good. To give them a chance here in Artimé." He turned to Alex. "They did it out of love."

"So they're not Unwanted at all," Alex said. He tried to

LISA McMANN

imagine what it would be like to have to send your children off when you didn't actually want to, in order to save them. It was kind of like what Lani's parents did when they sent her to the Death Farm. Only she didn't know it at first.

Samheed didn't look convinced. "How do you know she's telling the truth?"

Crow shrugged. "Because I know her. But mostly because that's what parents are supposed to do."

A Journey into Quill

Later, with the nurses caring for the injured and several of Alex's trusted friends monitoring the Warbler children to be sure they weren't tricking the people of Artimé, Alex turned his thoughts back to the events of the previous night. Something had been bothering him.

He knew what it was, of course, but hadn't had a spare moment to think about it. Now that things were settling down a bit, Alex frowned, deep in thought. Anger bubbled up inside him. He slipped past the busy Artiméans and made his way with a firm step up the stairs, across the balcony, and down the last hallway on the left. At the end of it, he turned

LISA McMANN

right and entered the tube. He pressed the first button.

In an instant he was reaching through the tube opening, feeling for the closet doors in the dark. He found them and pushed them open, stepped into Haluki's stuffy office, and strode through the house to the front door, letting himself out into the overpowering desert heat of Quill. He walked up the short, dusty road to the larger main road that encircled Quill, and headed up the hill toward the palace.

As he drew near his identical twin brother's lackluster residence, portions of his angry inner rant broke through his lips like bursts of steam from a kettle. He approached the rickety old gate. Two guards stood on the other side. "Open up," he growled at the guards.

There was a moment of confusion as they looked at Alex, clearly mistaking him for Aaron but taken aback by the bright color of Alex's robe. "It's the brother," one of them muttered. "I seen 'im before, wearing one a those ugly robes. Don't let him in."

The guards stood fast.

Alex clenched his jaw. He was in no mood for an argument. "Open the gate," he said through gritted teeth, "or I'll blast you."

The guards drew their rusty metal weapons.

Alex's brain had nearly heated to a boil. With a split-second movement, he reached inside his robe, pulled out two abstract spells, and flung them at the guards. Immediately their appendages spun around their bodies to different sockets, and their eyes and ears rearranged with their noses and mouths. The guards lost their balance and stumbled about, crying out.

Alex focused on the chain and lock and muttered, "Release."

The chain fell in pieces to the dirt. Alex kicked the lock aside, opened the gate, and went up the driveway toward the palace door. Without comment, he stunned the door guard with a soliloquy. Inside the palace, Alex stood and looked around for a moment, unsure where to go. It had been a while since he'd been here, and he'd never gone upstairs before, but he had an inkling that would be where the palace chambers and offices would be.

He took the stairs two at a time. At the top, he rounded the corner and nearly ran smack into someone.

It was Eva Fathom, Carina's mother. She gasped at the sight of him, then clapped her hand to her mouth, too late to stop it.

Alex stopped short and fought the urge to turn around and

go the other way. Eva's betrayal, choosing Quill over Artimé and helping Aaron take down the magical world and its leader, still stung quite a bit. He cringed but held her gaze, and waited for her to shout a warning to Aaron that he was coming.

The two stood frozen, staring at one another in a most intense way, each wondering what the other would do next. After what seemed to Alex like the longest second in the history of time, Eva Fathom wordlessly stepped aside and pointed out the door to Aaron's office.

Confrontation at the Palace

Alex remained still a moment longer, confused and surprised, and then brusquely nodded his thanks. He turned on his heel toward the office door while Eva slipped downstairs at a frightening speed for an old woman.

Alex shoved the door open. It slammed against the wall, and a giant hinge broke off, which made a dissonant clang when it bounced on the stone floor.

The High Priest Aaron Stowe jumped out of his seat, yelling out in fright. His pencil went flying, and the paper he was doodling on slipped to the floor. "What do you want?" Aaron

LISA McMANN

demanded, once he realized it was his brother standing before him. "Secretary!"

But Eva Fathom had been just swift enough to make it outside and, arguably, out of earshot. Alex caught a glimpse of her from Aaron's window, walking along as if she hadn't heard.

Alex picked up the paper, looking at Aaron's ship drawings in disgust. He faced his brother, and the anger welled up again. He slammed the paper down on Aaron's desk and gave him a cool stare. "You're a disgusting coward."

Aaron looked on in disdain. "Please," he said with a sneer. "I'm the high priest of Quill. You'll treat me with respect." He snatched the paper and moved it out of Alex's reach.

Alex laughed bitterly. "Right. Like how you treat me?"

"I don't have to treat you with respect," Aaron said. "You're nobody."

"I see." Alex toyed with the spell components in his robe pocket. "Well, it may surprise you to realize that I am not under your command, so I don't have to respect you. Nor do I. But I'm not here to quibble about that. I'm here to call you a coward, and to inform you that if you don't do a better job of protecting *our* island, you might not remain high priest for long."

Aaron glanced out the window at the forty-foot wall around Quill. "I'm taking care of *my* island just fine. In fact, further reinforcements go into place today."

"We protected you."

"From?"

"From Warbler Island's attack. You saw the ships."

Aaron barely shifted. "They weren't attacking Quill."

"We all live on this island, Aaron. And they didn't get into Quill because we kept them at bay on our shore! We protected your people. And what did you do? You ran away and hid." Alex could feel the bile rising to his throat. "You're such a stinking coward! Next time we'll let them in and point them in the direction of your cruddy palace."

"No, actually, you won't," Aaron said coolly. "After today, there will no longer be an entrance into Quill."

"What?" Alex looked confused for a moment, and then his eyes flew to the window once more. "You filled in the hole in the wall?" he said. "Why would you want to do that?"

"And we're blocking over the space where the gate was as well. You'll have to continue fighting battles on your own. I'm not interested. Justine had it right. And I have it even more

LISA McMANN

right. There will no longer be *any* vulnerable parts to our fortress."

Alex gripped his head in frustration. "Aaron, not that I care to help you, but that's a *huge* mistake. Just because you can't *see* things happening doesn't mean they aren't happening! Besides, some of your Quillens visit—"

Aaron cut him off. "Actually, the fact that all of you exist is the huge mistake, and I do blame Justine for not being aware of what her nasty brother was doing. And I'm not stopping there. Once we've walled over the gate, I'll be blockading your magical entrance to Haluki's house. Since you haven't destroyed your evil tube in Artimé, I'm going to have to do it here. We'll never have to see each other again."

Alex seethed. "Fine. You need us more than we need you, anyway."

"Ha! Tell that to all the Unwanteds and Necessaries you starved. They're all here in Quill!"

Alex worked his jaw. "When you come to regret this, remember that you sealed your own fate—literally. If you wall off all access, it will be for forever if I have anything to say about it." He pulled himself up to his full height. "You want to cut all ties? That's completely fine with me. I don't need you in my life—you're just a cowardly, annoying fly buzzing about, being worthless." He went on, growing more stubborn and reckless by the minute. "But make no mistake. If you do it, Artimé will never, ever help you again. Never."

"As if I need help from a bunch of Unwanted losers."

Alex glared at his brother. He glanced at the drawing on Aaron's desk and shook his head, disgusted. "You could have been one of us."

"Death would've been a better option."

Alex clenched and unclenched his fists. And just before he turned to leave, he did something he knew was completely, utterly wrong. He wound up and punched Aaron smack in the jaw.

Aaron reeled, off balance, and flipped over his chair, landing hard on his back on the floor. He grunted, the wind knocked out of him.

"That's for the day in the rain when we were ten," Alex said. He shook his hand out, adjusted his robe around his neck, and set off, out of the palace.

Paying Respects

Instead of heading straight to Haluki's house to take the tube back to Artimé, after he released the spells he'd put on the guards at the gate, Alex found himself wandering through the sectors of Quill. He ignored the glances from Quillens and walked, stone-faced, in one particular direction, as though propelled there by a mystical force.

Soon he found himself in the Ancients Sector, standing in front of the burial grounds.

Alex hadn't been here in years—not since he was a little boy, spending the day helping his father dig graves. *How grotesque,* Alex thought now, about this job that could really be very meaningful. But here in Quill it was ordinary and emotionless when you knew no one cared about the dead. There was no mourning. As he thought about the grave he sought, he began to worry that Aaron had turned it into some sort of mockery, a reason to rejoice. Alex imagined a sign celebrating the death of the Death Farmer himself . . . the Death Farmer who had tricked all of Quill for dozens of years. Who had defeated Quill once already, to the High Priest Aaron's great shame. Alex wished he'd demanded to bury Mr. Today's body himself back when Aaron had delivered the mage's robe to him. But by then it had been too late. He picked up his pace, dreading what he might find.

He walked over to the small building and began to read the names of the recent dead. He scanned the list, recognizing a few surnames—Quillens who had died in the skirmish that broke out after Artimé disappeared. And then he saw it.

Marcus Today—89–25

"Eighty-nine dash twenty-five," Alex whispered. He dodged a Necessary worker and hurried over to the burial area, searching for row eighty-nine. When he found it, he swept his eyes down the row, expecting to see some sort of display taunting the death of the great mage of Artimé.

Nothing stood out. Alex made his way down the row, counting out the mounds of dirt until he came to number twenty-five. It looked like all the others—completely forgotten. He was a distant memory here, just like everyone else.

Alex knelt down, placing his hand on top of the hot dirt. He felt like he should say something, but there was nothing adequate coming from the void inside him, so he remained quiet and stared at the dirt as a bead of sweat dripped from his temple to the tip of his nose and landed on the grave.

After a time Alex rose. Heavyhearted, he turned back toward the road, but on his first step he kicked something in the dirt alongside Mr. Today's grave. He bent over and picked it up, shaking off the dust. It was a dried flower. Sort of, anyway—it wasn't like any flower in Artimé. But Alex felt like he'd seen a flower like this before somewhere.

"In Quill?" he muttered. He knew there were no flowers here. "Oh," he said after a moment. "The Favored Farm." He'd been there on a few secret excursions, stealing food when all was lost in Artimé. This flower was a blossom from a pumpkin vine.

He gave it a quizzical look, then set it on top of Mr. Today's grave. "Someone brought a flower for you," he murmured. "How strange. I wonder who it was."

After a moment, Alex rose once more and walked back toward the road, keeping his eyes low whenever he passed a Necessary at work. He knew that with his colorful robe, he couldn't help but stand out. But he didn't want to talk to anybody. Artimé, with its injured and its new inhabitants, called out to him—he had to get back.

As Alex turned out of row eighty-nine, a familiar, stooped figure caught his eye. Alex's stomach clenched and he took in a sharp breath.

The man looked up at the noise. His tired eyes widened and then flitted to Alex's robe, and a sense of recognition spread across the man's face.

"Hello, Father," Alex said.

The realization on Mr. Stowe's face turned quickly to fear. He looked around wildly, this way and that, as if he were being watched, and then darted up the steps to the burial building and disappeared inside.

Alex stood for a moment, trying to figure out what had just happened. Trying to determine what he was supposed to do

LISA McMANN

now. Go after him? Not a chance. Alex had been just fine with not seeing his parents ever again. Although, he had to admit he was curious about his new siblings. Had his mother had the babies yet? She must have, by now.

He frowned at the door to the burial building. When his father didn't return, Alex shrugged and headed down a street that cut through the heart of Quill, out of the Ancients Sector, and through the Wanted Sector. He skirted the amphitheater in the Commons where he'd been Purged and went down a row of houses in what looked to be a deserted Necessary neighborhood.

Deserted, Alex thought with a snort, *because all the Necessaries had escaped from Quill to Artimé, not the other way around.* Sure, Artimé had lost a few people, like Cole Wickett, to Quill during the tough times. Alex wondered what Cole was doing now. But the majority of the movers were moving into Artimé, not out of it.

As he pondered the whereabouts of Cole Wickett and company, Alex came across two neighboring houses with a strange, bluish-white glow coming from the windows. He looked from one house to the other, scratched his head, and looked again, wondering if the desert heat in Quill was mak-

LISA McMANN

ing him see things. After a moment he shuffled off, leaving the mystery unsolved, and pushed onward to Haluki's house.

On the step he hesitated, thinking about Aaron's plan to cut all ties. "Good-bye forever, I guess," he said to nobody. With a shrug, he went inside the house to Haluki's office, stepped into the tube, and went home.

Seeds of a New Plan

The High Priest Aaron, straining for breath as he stared at the gray ceiling of his office, muttered, "Well, I suppose I deserved that." After a moment more, he picked himself up off the floor, using the corner of his desk to pull himself up to standing. He leaned against the desk and gently fingered his cheek, then opened his mouth, gingerly testing his jaw's hinges to see if anything was broken. It was a pretty impressive punch, he had to admit. He picked up the paper from his desk and turned it over, looking at his scribbles for a long moment. Then he folded it and put it in a drawer, slipping it under his two remaining heart attack spells.

He wasn't sure why he wasn't mad at Alex for punching him. Truth be told, as much as he pretended to have it all together, Aaron had been constantly second-guessing himself lately. He'd felt driven by fear, and frankly, that bothered him some. But now going back to Justine's ways seemed right. If only he could be absolutely sure that he could protect himself and Quill from everything, he'd be able to relax a little. Because right now, after that attack on Artimé, things were way too dangerous. He just had to get the last reinforcements in place. Once Quill was stabilized, Aaron could focus on his future plans . . . taking over Artimé and getting rid of the Unwanteds once and for all.

He thought about the dark, musky-smelling jungle where he'd been last night, and fear tore through him anew. He'd been so close to getting attacked. What luck that the creature had backed off at the last moment. The night was a blur to Aaron. He still wasn't sure how he'd managed to get his shackles off.

"Secretary!" he yelled, trying to clear the jungle from his mind. "Is the opening to Artimé secure?" She didn't answer. He went to the door and shouted for her once more.

LISA McMANN

After searching all around the palace for Secretary, to no avail, Aaron finally began barking orders at the guards to arrange to have the back hallway of the palace blocked off so no one could get in through the magical passageway that Mr. Today had once used. And as long as the old hag was actually taking care of the gate to Artimé, that left only the tube . . . and Aaron would take care of that himself.

He looked around the palace, gathering tools, and made his way past the portcullis to Haluki's house. Once inside, he entered the office and opened the closet. He peered at the tube, wondering how it was attached and how to dismantle it. It seemed to be freestanding. Aaron pushed against it, trying to tip it, but it didn't budge.

He wandered through Haluki's house, looking for anything at all he could use to cover the opening in the glass. Some tin, perhaps. Or a blanket. But neither would be hard to break through.

Aaron would have to destroy the button, he supposed, which would prevent someone from going into Artimé. But would that prevent someone from arriving here? Aaron didn't know. It was a puzzling phenomenon to begin with, this magic.

Still, he didn't want Artiméans able to get into Quill to attack without him having the same advantage.

He scratched his head. Maybe he was being hasty. Was it really a bad thing that he could stage a surprise attack on his brother, right in the heart of Alex's own office? "Perhaps a lock on the closet doors," Aaron murmured. He closed the double doors to the closet and looked at the knobs, trying to imagine a way to lock them so that anyone trying to come to Quill through the tube would be stuck inside the closet.

He'd have to fashion something, he supposed. A tiny thrill ran up his spine as he thought about it—the design it would take. It reminded him of the excitement he'd felt when he'd designed the Favored Farm and when he'd thought he'd figured out how to solve the oil problem that the Quillitary was having with the vehicles using too much of their drinking water. It was like a different part of his brain woke up.

Aaron searched the house again, coming up with a thin, rusty chain attached to a yoke, which had once supported water buckets. It would have to do for now. Anything to block off the strange tube. What if that creature in the jungle figured out how to use it? It wasn't impossible that it could press a few buttons by accident and find its way into Quill.

As Aaron wound the chain around the doorknobs, he frowned. That creature had had every chance to attack Aaron. But it didn't. It was like it understood Aaron's words. Did it— could it possibly—?

"No," Aaron said, almost embarrassed to think it. But why else? "Did it somehow sense that I am the high priest of Quill?" There in Haluki's office, it sounded ridiculous. But so did a magical world called Artimé, yet that existed.

Still he wondered. The thought of creatures from other realms obeying his commands was enough to get Aaron's blood pumping. If he could command creatures like that, it would be so much easier to take over Artimé.

As he worked the chain, his fingers slowed. Aaron bit his lip. It was daylight now. Perhaps . . .

He stood there contemplating for a long moment. And then slowly, with trembling fingers, he worked the chain the other way until it slithered to the floor at his feet. The closet doors popped open, and once again, Aaron stepped inside.

Wrapping Up
Loose Ends

After making the rounds once more, checking on the injured and stopping for a meeting with Mr. Appleblossom about how to handle the new children from Warbler, Alex took the tube to the lounge. He waved to Fox and Kitten in the band, stopped to greet Earl, the lounge blackboard, and made his way over to the booth where his friends had gathered.

"Alex!" Lani exclaimed. "I thought you were too cool for this place now." She grinned. Once jealous that Mr. Today had chosen Alex over her as his successor, Lani, after all she'd been through as a prisoner on Warbler, no

LISA McMANN

longer held any animosity toward Alex about that.

"I think this place is probably too cool for me," Alex said with a laugh. "I miss this." He squeezed in next to Sky, who was feeling back to her old self now that she could breathe. She smiled and dropped her eyes as she scooted to make room.

"At least we're all together again," Meghan said, and Samheed nodded. Sean and Carina came over and pulled up chairs to join them, and, as it was crowded, Sean tapped the table and the entire booth grew a bit to accommodate them all. He signaled to the lounge server, who in no time brought out a round of creamy orange drinks for everyone.

"How are the injured?" Lani asked Carina.

"Lots of them have been fixed up and sent to their rooms already," Carina said. She leaned her head back against the seat, tired from a long day in the hospital wing. "Most had scrapes, bruises, that sort of thing. A few deep gashes, a handful of concussions, and some broken bones. But everybody is stable."

"That's good to hear," Lani said.

"Henry's really developing his skills for medicine," Carina

added. "He's keeping everybody comfortable and relatively free of pain, which is something we weren't able to do last time we had a battle, so I think we're really improving."

"That would be good," Samheed said, remembering the fight he once had with his father, when Mr. Appleblossom had come to his aid. His face had ached for days.

"Are you feeling all right, Sky?" Sean asked.

"I'm totally fine," Sky said. Her bronze cheeks deepened in color. "I just feel kind of stupid about it. I mean, what kind of idiot inhales a rock?"

The group laughed, and Meghan said, "Well, that boulder did explode into a billion pieces right in front of you as you were casting a tuba spell. How could it miss? Well done on that, by the way."

Alex glanced sidelong at Sky. "You're casting spells now?" he asked.

She shrugged. "I had the components. Figured I'd try, at least."

"She did it, too," Meghan said.

"Third attempt," Sky added.

Alex smiled. He knew not to say anything—he'd learned

LISA McMANN

79 « Island of Legends

a lot about when to shut up from Lani since they'd first found themselves here in Artimé. He knew that Sky had jumbled feelings about whether she belonged in Artimé and whether she was creative enough to do magic. As much as he and Meghan had tried to explain to her that everybody in the world was creative in their own ways, Sky had kept her distance when it came to embracing the Unwanted status. Not because she didn't feel worthy, but because she wanted to prove herself valuable without being magical. Which she had, multiple times.

"When the rocks started coming at me, I figured I ought to give it a try before getting crushed to death," Sky said agreeably. And then she added as a warning, "Don't get used to it, though. I tried it once, but I didn't really enjoy it, so I probably won't be doing that again."

"You never have to," Alex said. He sipped his orange cream, and the others fell into a pleasant silence. It was good to be together. "I saw my father today," he said. "First time since the Purge."

Meghan frowned. "On purpose? Did he come here?"

"No, I ran into him when I went into Quill to take care of

a few things." He rubbed his sore knuckles. "Aaron, for one. He's planning on walling over the gate between Artimé and Quill. He's going back to Justine's ways, and then some."

"Fear, fear, fear," Sean said, his voice angry. "And what about the people who like to go back and forth now? They have to choose one place or the other, permanently?"

Alex shrugged. "Don't get too worked up. I figure we can blast the wall down anytime we want. It's not like they'll notice—nobody in the government ever comes near the gate anymore."

"Oh," Sean said. After a moment he chuckled. "I hadn't thought of that."

Alex sniffed. "That's why I'm the mage around here."

Sean punched him lightly in the arm. "I guess that's why they pay you the big bucks."

Samheed frowned. "Huh?"

Carina waved him off. "Never mind Sean. He's been reading some of the new books that washed ashore this afternoon. That was a line from one of them. We have no idea what it means, but it seems to fit."

"New books?" Lani exclaimed. "Where?"

LISA McMANN

"They're spread out on a table in the dining room, drying."

"Where'd they come from?" Alex asked.

"Probably that thing that exploded in the sky," Meghan said, slurping the last of her drink.

"Ah," Alex said. He'd forgotten about that in all the craziness of the attack. "I suppose in the morning we ought to recover it and pull it ashore."

"The plan is already in place," Carina said. "I'm going to head it up, if that's okay."

"That's great," Alex said. "Thanks. Now I just need to figure out what to do with all the Warbler children in the long term. I talked to Mr. Appleblossom, and I think we should observe them for a while before we trust them to run around completely freely, don't you?"

Everyone but Sky nodded in agreement.

"It's not like they're in jail or anything. Mr. Appleblossom is keeping them entertained," Meghan said. "I'm helping, along with a bunch of others."

"I think they're telling the truth about their parents sending them," Sky interjected, "but I understand why you need to be careful."

Alex flashed her a sympathetic smile. "If they'd all washed ashore on rafts, it would be different."

"I know. I get it."

Alex reached under the table and squeezed Sky's hand. She squeezed back. "Good," he said. "Well, that frees me up to prepare for the next big thing." He turned to look at Sky full-on. "Are you finally ready to rescue your mother?"

"Not quite," Sky said, rolling her eyes. "Let me think of five other life-threatening things to do first." She grinned.

Alex blushed in return. Every time Sky smiled at him, he felt like he lost half his brain.

"Well, I'm ready," Samheed said, excitement building in his voice. "Ms. Octavia says we're good to go whenever you are." He was eager to be on the rescuing end of things this time.

"We should be all set to go in a day or two. I just have a few things to prepare first," Alex said, turning his focus back to their next task. "How does that sound?"

No one hesitated. They were ready.

He shoved his empty glass to the middle of the table and got to his feet. "Carina, keep me posted on that . . . that *thing* out there in the water. And Meg, let me know how it's going with the Warbler children. Make sure they have everything they need, you know, to give them comfort, or whatever." The idea of Warbler parents trying to give their children a better life still astounded Alex.

When they'd tubed back to the main entryway of the mansion and said good night, Meghan pulled Alex aside. "That must have been quite a shock, seeing your father. What did he say to you when you saw him?" she asked.

"Nothing," Alex said. "Not one thing." He thought about the strange, frightened look on his father's face. "He took one look at me and went the other way."

Meghan nodded sympathetically, both of them sorely reminded of the fact that there are some things magic can't fix.

Another Creature

In the tube in Haluki's office, Aaron hit the single button, which took him to the kitchenette in Artimé's mansion. He poked his head out of the opening in the glass to make sure no one had noticed his presence. It was deserted and quiet. Aaron turned his attention to the buttons before him, wondering which of them would take him back to the jungle. He'd forgotten about his mad dash to push them all at once, which is what had brought him there in the first place. This might not be quite as easy as he thought. He studied them, wiping his clammy hands on his pants, and then, in a moment of brilliance, he took a deep

LISA McMANN

breath and pressed them all at once, like he had done before.

In an instant he was thrust into the musky-smelling jungle. A few thin streaks of bright sunlight made their way through to the jungle floor, but most of the area surrounding Aaron was shaded by a canopy of leaves.

Aaron stood completely still, hand poised on the button that would take him back to the mansion. Only his eyes traveled as he canvassed the area, looking for anything that moved.

When his gaze passed over the ground directly in front of the tube, he saw the shackles. They were intact, not smashed. The cuffs were open, as if their locking mechanisms had been released. Cautiously Aaron crouched down, picked up the shackles, and pulled them inside the tube. They could be useful someday.

While crouched, Aaron dared a glance behind him through the glass. Nothing moved.

After a moment, Aaron stood up. He took a few steps outside the tube, ready to bolt back inside it again at the sight of anything alarming. It was then that he realized the gigantic rock was gone.

Aaron's lips parted in surprise. Where could it be? He

looked all around. Was he confused? He couldn't have imagined it. He took a few steps toward the clearing, then a few more, and peered down a path. There was no big rock anywhere to be seen.

When he heard a rustling in the leaves, Aaron whirled around, realizing how far he'd strayed from the tube. His eyes scanned the jungle floor, unsure where the rustling noise came from. He crept toward the tube, looking in every direction as he moved. "Who's there?" he called out in a loud whisper.

From a clump of brown and orange leaves, a small body emerged with exactly the same colorings as its background. He had the floppy ears of a dog and the wagging tail of a dog, and for all manner of speaking he quite probably *was* a dog, though his strange brown and orange coloring threw Aaron a bit. The dog smiled, his two perfect rows of tiny, pointy teeth fitting together like puzzle pieces.

Aaron ran for safety in the tube. The creature continued smiling pleasantly and dipped his head, almost as if to bow. His ears brushed the ground.

"D-d-do you know who I am?" Aaron asked.

The dog tilted his head.

Aaron took a step toward it. "I'm the high priest of Quill."

The creature's back end wagged, his tail slapping lightly against a sapling.

Aaron looked around. He didn't see the large black creature anywhere, so he took another step toward the friendly little thing.

The dog stepped closer to Aaron, too. Just as Aaron leaned forward to pet him, the dog leaped at him with a shriek, mouth open wide. He dug his tiny, sharp teeth into Aaron's arm.

"Ow!" Aaron yelled. He shook his arm, trying to get the dog to let go, but the dog hung on. He was much heavier than Aaron would have guessed, but Aaron didn't have the where-withal to speculate about that. His arm hurt terribly. "Let go of me!"

The dog didn't obey.

Aaron tried to kick the dog off but succeeded only in hurting his toes. The thing had to be made of cement. "Release me!" he cried.

And just like that, the creature's jaw unhinged and the dog dropped to the ground.

Aaron grabbed his throbbing, bleeding arm and held it to

his body. "What in the name of Quill is wrong with you?" He stepped back as the dog retreated, still grinning. Then the dog jumped straight into the air and bit into a tree branch. He hung there, swinging and grinning, as his body slowly changed to the solid brown color of the bark on the tree behind it.

"Evil thing," Aaron muttered. Keeping one eye on the dog in the tree, he inspected his arm. Dozens of miniature puncture wounds dotted his skin, and droplets of blood oozed from them. Aaron lifted his shirttail and carefully wrapped it around his arm, holding it tight, and wished for some water. This visit was not turning out like he'd expected.

When a shadow fell over him, Aaron turned and looked up. His mouth dropped open.

It was the rock, its cavelike mouth agape.

And on top of the rock stood the black creature, crouched low and ready to pounce.

Mountains Bow Down

Aaron gasped. "No!" he cried out. "Don't hurt me!" He scrambled toward the tube, losing his footing more than once on the uneven ground. When he reached it, he turned swiftly with a feeling of dread, fully expecting the paws and mouth of the creature to be upon him. He stretched his hand toward the button but stopped short of pushing it when he saw that the black creature hadn't moved. She stayed on top of the rock, watching Aaron.

The rock remained still, also watching Aaron. And then its cavelike mouth moved, and groaning noises emerged.

LISA McMANN

Aaron's heart thudded. He knew he should push the button. He knew he should get to safety. But he was mesmerized. Where had they been? How did the rock move? And was it . . . speaking to him?

In a rumbling voice like distant thunder, the rock spoke. "Where's Marcus?"

Aaron nearly leaped out of his own skin. "Wh-what?"

The rock repeated the words, louder this time. "Where's Marcus?"

Aaron stared. "He-he's dead."

The rock grumbled in disbelief, and the dog dropped from the tree branch and started running around howling. The panther lowered her head.

Aaron scrambled to read their reactions. "He—he was a good man. Wasn't he? I mean, don't you agree?"

"Well, of course!" boomed the rock. The dog and the panther seemed to feel the same way.

Aaron sighed inwardly in relief. He knew now where they stood. All he had to do was play this game right. "We all just . . . miss him terribly," he began. "He, ah, he put me in charge. So I'm just checking in on you like he asked me

LISA McMANN

to. I'm—I'm sorry it's been a while. There was, um, a lot to take care of. It was all very sudden, you see."

The rock regarded him, and rumbled, "So you're the boy called Alex."

It wasn't a question.

And in Aaron's mind, there was barely a moment's hesitation. If being Alex gave him an advantage, then he would be Alex once more—only here, there was no one to detect the tiny physical differences between the boys. "Yes," he said. "That's me."

The enormous rock bowed its craggy peak. "I'm sorry to hear of Marcus's death," he said. "But he told us about you."

"He, um, he didn't tell me much about you, I'm sorry to say," Aaron said. "So . . . perhaps . . . you could?"

The rock seemed to frown. "I am the caretaker of the dangerous ones," he said in his rumbling voice. "Mr. Today's imperfect creations, which are, shall we say, not to be trusted."

The panther snarled.

The rock continued. "Marcus couldn't bear to end it for any of them, so he put them here. Ol' Tater was here for a time, but that was . . . troublesome."

Aaron didn't know who Ol' Tater was, but he sounded delicious.

The rock looked at itself. "They can't hurt me, you see."

Aaron tried to look sympathetic, though he wasn't very good at it. "Do—did they hurt Mr. Today?"

"No. He had a way with them, like you. You'll do fine. It's putting them out there in Artimé with the others that causes problems."

The high priest narrowed his eyes. *A way with them? Like me? What an odd thing to say.* "Well," Aaron said, slightly unsettled, "I just wanted to check in and see if all was okay, and it appears it is, so—"

"Wait!" thundered the rock, making the nearby leaves tremble on the trees. "Panther needs your help."

The black creature nodded emphatically.

"Oh," Aaron said, a little impatiently. "Well, then. What's wrong?" He wanted these creatures to do his bidding, not add to his burdens.

"It's her tail again. She can't balance in the trees without it."

Aaron's eyes opened wide. "What?"

"Her tail. She needs you to repair it."

LISA McMANN

"Repair it? Me?"

The rock slid forward almost silently, its eyes wearing a puzzled expression. "Of course you."

The panther nimbly made her way down the rock and jumped to the ground. She snarled and hissed at Aaron, but sidled up to him, brushing against the boy's hip.

Aaron stepped back nervously, one foot in the tube. He could still run for it. Disappear forever. But what if . . . what if he really could get this jungle filled with dangerous creatures to obey him? He wouldn't need any Quillitary vehicles to take over Artimé—he'd simply turn Mr. Today's misfits against the Unwanteds, and they'd tear them to bits!

It was a brilliant plan, if only Aaron had a clue how to fix the panther's tail. Aaron looked at the panther's stubby tail and started to panic. How in Quill was he supposed to fix that?

"Where's the missing part?" he asked.

The panther shrugged and looked off into the jungle, disinterested.

Sweat broke out on Aaron's forehead as he looked around. "How . . . ?" He faltered, knowing that this moment could solidify his control over these creatures. His eyes darted this way and that.

He stared at the panther, trying to figure out what it was made of.

But it was all too impossible. Aaron had no idea where to start or what to do. The questions made his head hurt. He couldn't continue this farce any longer. It was over.

The Sky Vessel

Alex made his way into the Museum of Large, as he liked to do most evenings, leaving the door open in case Simber needed him. But now that things were under control in Artimé once more, it was time to push on to the next task—rescuing Sky and Crow's mother. It seemed impossible, and it was going to be very dangerous, too.

"Not exactly sure how we're going to do this rescue thing," Alex murmured as he worked on his favorite task of late: turning Mr. Today's whale skeleton into a beautiful sculpture. This was where Alex did his best thinking, when his hands were busy creating something new. Alex had finally gotten all the bones in their places after Ol' Tater had scattered them far and wide, only to find there was one long, spearlike bone that didn't seem to belong anywhere at all. Alex debated for a while what to do with it and then decided to stick it on the whale's forehead, because really—who wouldn't want a big bone spear jutting out of their forehead? It looked extremely cool, too. Alex sharpened the point and studded it with sparkling stones that he'd found on the beach. They shone like diamonds.

Alex mixed up a container of thick, shiny blue liquid, preparing to spread it over the whale's "skin." The skin he'd made by weaving dried, knotted seaweed in a loom, and he'd used the preserve spell on it, which made the whale virtually indestructible. It had taken the last of Alex's preserve components to cover the enormous mammal, and Alex made a note to make some more.

After a few swipes with the blue paint, Alex stepped back to analyze the color. He'd wanted to try covering the whale in a mosaic, like Jim the winged tortoise's shell, but he would have to save that for another time—it was just too ambitious a project. But the brilliant blue paint looked very good next to the silvery diamond-like stones on the spear. He began painting in broad strokes.

"You need a name, I think," Alex said after a while, finishing up the first coat. "Are you a boy or a girl?" He scratched his head. "Spike. No matter what." He thought about it for a bit and nodded to himself. "Yes, I think that's very fitting. Spike."

When Alex heard a noise, he looked up, seeing Simber and Ms. Octavia coming into the museum.

"Interrrresting," Simber remarked, nodding at the new horn adorning the whale's head. "She didn't have that beforrre."

Alex grinned and shrugged. "There was an extra bone. I couldn't figure out where it went, so I gave her an accessory." He tilted his head. "She? It's a girl, then?"

Simber rolled his eyes. "Clearrrly," he said, but he didn't elaborate.

"Well, her name is Spike," Alex said. "Spike . . . Furious." He grinned, pleased with the way the name came to him so easily.

Ms. Octavia snorted. "Don't get carried away. But I admit, it has a ring to it. And with the faux-diamond treatment to the horn, she needs a name just as grand to go with it. Spike Furious sounds very commanding." She turned a more critical, art instructor eye to the project. "You've done a beautiful job painting her."

"Thanks," Alex said, beginning the second coat. "Want to help finish?" He tossed a handful of paintbrushes to Ms. Octavia, who seemed pleased to be asked.

"It's too bad more of your friends can't see her," Ms. Octavia said, digging into the job.

"That's for sure." Alex was thinking particularly of Sky, who would probably really like Spike. And Lani and Meg, too, of course. But they couldn't get into this wing. He'd have to paint a rendition for them, which was hardly the same as seeing Spike's gloriousness in person.

There was a noise at the door, bringing Alex back to the moment.

"Ah, herrre they arrre," Simber said. "We've rrrecoverrred the sky vessel frrrom the sea. Florrrence, Carrrina, Sean, and Samheed arrre brrringing the pieces up now. We thought they could go in herrre with the otherrrs. Is that all rrright?"

"Yes, that's perfect," Alex said. He looked around. "They can set them right there, where the pirate ship was."

A moment later the floor quivered and Florence entered the museum, carrying a large piece of the vessel. Following her were the others with smaller broken pieces, some salvaged equipment, and other curious-looking goods. Alex and Ms. Octavia put down their brushes and hurried over to observe the contents.

"What about the passengers?" Alex asked gently.

"Buried at sea," Carina said, setting her things down. "Three of them."

"We found a lot of interesting stuff," Samheed said. "Papers and more books and clothing, and other things we're not quite sure about." He and Florence spread the goods out across the floor. "Some of it needs to dry out a bit. Mr. Appleblossom is taking care of the papers and books—he's done this before and knows the best way to care for them without ruining everything."

Alex studied the pieces, walking around them to get a full view. He pictured how the pieces fit together to make the vessel. It was larger than he had imagined. There was a long cockpit made of glass and some other strange white material. The cockpit was shaped a little bit like one of Artimé's tubes lying on its side. Inside were four seats and an instrument panel that looked somewhat like a blackboard, with lots of buttons and gauges and letters on it. Some of the glass was broken, but the rest of the vessel seemed like it was in decent shape—just a few dents. There was one long wing jutting out, and another piece that looked like a second wing that had broken off.

At the nose of the vessel there were several blades attached, like a pinwheel, and a few more loose blades, bent and broken, that had been recovered from the ocean floor. Simber loped over to other pieces in the museum that had been collected years before to compare.

"They look similarrr," he said.

"That's what Mr. Appleblossom said too," Samheed remarked. "He said he did some research in the library, and he thinks this is something called an airplane. I guess there was a manual in the stack of books we found."

Alex tapped his lips, deep in thought. "Interesting. So it's supposed to stay in the air? Like, it flies? How does it ever land safely without crashing? Do you think people just live in these things forever?"

"No," Sean said. "Sigfried also said that they are like ships—they just transport people from one place to another. Like riding on Simber's back, I suppose."

"Except I would neverrr crrrash," Simber muttered.

LISA McMANN

"Easy there, cat. I've seen you crash," Alex reminded him. "You might not remember it, but it happened." He held his hand to his forehead dramatically. "I'm still traumatized." He was only partly joking. He still had regular nightmares about Simber's frozen body crashing into the sea.

Simber frowned and walked back to the others. "That won't happen again."

"If it does, I may not survive my grief." Alex reached out and let his hand rest on the cat's neck in a rare show of the deep affection between the two. He thought he could feel Simber purring just the slightest bit, but he wasn't sure.

"Harrrumph! Anyway. Wherrre do you suppose the airrr-plane came frrrom? And what made it crrrash?"

Alex was as mystified as everyone else. "No idea." He looked at the pieces again and shrugged. "I guess we just store these here until we can think of something useful to do with them. I wonder if we can restore it. Make it fly again." He looked side-long at Simber. "You know, in case Simber ever *does* take another nosedive into the sea and we need some air transportation."

The cat growled. "We have morrre imporrrtant things to do," he said.

"Good point," said Ms. Octavia. "And we'll be ready to go soon. Alex, do you have a finalized list of who will be accompanying us?"

"I will by tomorrow."

"Perfect."

Later, when everyone had left, Alex stood alone with the whale once more, doing some final touch-ups with the paint and thinking about the upcoming rescue, and the reverse aquarium full of pirates and their captives underneath the strangely disappearing fiery volcanic island. "You know, Spike," he said as he finished, "we could really use somebody like you on this trip." He sighed, imagining it. "If only I knew how to make you come alive."

Certain Death

The High Priest Aaron stood with one toe inside the tube and wiped the sweat from his forehead, commanding himself to pull it together. How was he supposed to fix the panther's tail? He had to do something—if he just turned and escaped through the tube, he'd lose all hope of having these creatures on his side. And at this point, with the Quillitary still not very keen on Aaron because of his role in Justine's death, the high priest could really use these creatures to take over Artimé. How would that be for giving the Artiméans a taste of their own medicine? Aaron was practically drooling over the idea.

LISA McMANN

But all hope would be lost if he failed to fix the tail, he argued with himself. Unless he could stall them. "I . . . um . . . ," he began.

The dog barked and started sniffing around in the undergrowth. He barked a few more times, then backed out from under a bush, pulling something in his mouth.

"Did you find the tail?" the giant rock rumbled, rolling closer to the dog and nudging Aaron away from the tube.

Aaron stumbled forward. The dog kept tugging as Aaron's hopes sank. Eventually the dog pulled hard enough to reveal the source of his endeavors. It was a vine.

"There," said the rock.

The panther looked on with disdain that slowly turned to interest. After a moment she leaped over to the dog's side, snapping at it until the dog retreated. Then the panther bit hard on the vine, severing it in two places to form the right length. She turned and screamed at Aaron, startling him.

His nerves frayed, Aaron jumped to pick up the vine as the panther circled him, edging him even farther away from the tube. Aaron knew now that there was no way out of this. The panther was sure to attack him if he tried to run. Aaron had no choice. He was about to get eaten, or at least ripped to shreds. It was only a matter of time. Once they figured out he was a phony, it would be all over.

The thought of confessing briefly came to mind, but Aaron dismissed it. He wouldn't want to live after showing such cowardice.

Bravely he examined the stretch of vine. He bent down and picked up a sharp stone to try to streamline the tip of it. "For better balance," he said, but he was only buying time. Death was inevitable.

The panther paced between Aaron and the tube, swishing the stub of her tail in awkward, jerky movements that chronicled her growing impatience. It was becoming extremely clear to Aaron why these creatures were kept away from everyone else. They were living, breathing, percolating claw-and-tooth fests just waiting to explode.

Finally, with shaking hands, Aaron beckoned to the panther. "Come here, then," he said, his voice squeaking. He felt the blood drain from his head and hoped that, once the creature attacked, he'd simply pass out before the pain took hold.

The panther darted to Aaron's side, hissing wide-mouthed

in some bizarre, backward show of appreciation . . . or maybe just to show Aaron her dripping fangs. Aaron wobbled as he squatted next to the creature, and he put his hand on the panther's back to steady himself. "Breathe," he whispered, angry about his fear. "Calm down." He took in a few breaths. "Okay," he said, louder. "Hold still, Panther."

The creature obeyed.

Aaron gripped the panther's shortened tail in one hand and the vine in the other, knowing all he could do now was wish for the impossible. He pressed the thick end of the vine to the broken end of the panther's tail, wishing and imagining with all his might that a miracle would take place. "Please," he begged under his breath as drops of sweat fell from the dark ringlets framing his face.

He closed his eyes, knowing it was only a matter of seconds before they'd all realize it was a scam, and only a minute or so after that he'd be dead. He swallowed hard and gripped the two parts in his sweat-damp hand. "Come on," he said. "Heal up. Just please magically heal."

Aaron wanted it so badly he could almost feel the two pieces meld into one inside his grip. But he knew it was impossible, and he couldn't bear to look at his failure. Soon the strain of the silent anticipation and tension grew so unbearable that slowly he let go. Crippled and faint with fear, Aaron dropped backward onto the jungle floor and bared his neck, giving up. He hoped only for a merciful kill.

The panther's scream chilled Aaron's blood, and he knew his wait was over. Everything went black.

When Aaron opened his eyes, the panther's face was right in front of him, her ivory teeth just inches from his neck. Slimy drool dripped from the panther's jaws. Aaron emitted a blood-curdling cry, choking from the dryness in his throat.

The panther jumped back.

Aaron screamed again, and then, when he realized he wasn't dead, lurched wildly to his feet and lunged, disoriented, in the wrong direction, running smack into the corner of the giant rock and falling flat on his face. Stunned, he got to his feet and tried again, the rock moving out of his way just in time. Aaron tripped over a vine and fell, and then, after finally locating the tube, he resorted to scrambling on hands and knees toward it.

The rock, panther, and dog all began to shout and howl.

The panther charged after Aaron. As Aaron dove into the tube, he turned and looked at his pursuer, and as he reached for the button, he noticed one very interesting thing.

The panther's tail.

Long and supple, the tail swished back and forth as the panther bounded past Aaron, around the tube, and up the nearby tree to test out her balance.

Aaron stared from his sprawled-out position at the bottom of the tube, his chest heaving, sweat pouring off him. He wiped his eyes to see better, and it was true. Somehow he'd done it.

Without any components, without uttering any magical chants or spells, Aaron had turned a vine into a tail. As the howling and yelling around him subsided, as the realization of what he'd just done took hold, and as a new surge of power coursed through his veins, Aaron Stowe closed his eyes and leaned his head against the glass, thinking, *I'm going to take over the world.*

The Book

Alex stared at Spike. He couldn't get the thought out of his mind.

Later, when he was walking along the shore with Sky, looking at the beautiful orange moonlight that matched her eyes, his mind kept returning to it. What if Spike really could come to life? He thought back to the day in Mr. Today's office when he'd told the old mage he didn't want to take over Artimé.

"If only I had told him I wanted the job . . . ," he muttered. "If only I hadn't been so selfish, I could have found out how

LISA McMANN

to do it. But no, I refused the job, and he refused to teach me. And now it's too late."

Sky looked at him. "You're doing that thing again. Mage problems?"

Alex startled, then laughed under his breath. "Yeah."

"What is it this time?" Her voice rang curious and not at all annoyed, which reminded Alex just how much he liked Sky. She no longer seemed to resent the time he spent preoccupied with his other thoughts. She had plenty of her own thoughts to be busy with, so they made a good pair.

Alex picked up a stick, sat down, and began to sketch the whale in the sand as he talked. "I made this whale out of the old bones in the Museum of Large. It started out as a project to clean up the museum after the Ol' Tater incident, but once I had all the bones in place, I covered the skeleton with layers of woven seaweed to give it a body. Then I preserved it and painted it, and earlier I realized she would really come in handy if she could swim along with us to Pirate Island."

"Cool. Wish I could see her." She sat down in the sand next to Alex.

LISA McMANN

"Me too."

"Can't you just bring her to life like Mr. Today did with Jim and Florence and Simber and all the statues?"

"I wish I knew how."

Sky wrinkled up her nose, thinking. "What about the book Mr. Today left you? The one with the restore spell—I remember how disgusted you were that he'd left it out for you just a little too late to be useful when we lost Artimé."

Alex frowned. "I don't think that spell will bring the whale sculpture to life if it wasn't living before."

"Yeah, probably not, or else the mansion and the fountains would all be alive now, I suppose." She grinned and leaned against Alex.

He loved it when she did that. "Wouldn't that be creepy?" He slipped his arm around her shoulders, and they sat in silence for a few minutes, lost in thought again. Then Alex scrambled to his feet. "Wait a second," he said. "That book!" He started running for the mansion, then stopped abruptly to turn around and run back to Sky. "I've got to go," he said, grabbing her hand and pulling her to her feet. "I think there's a living type of spell in that book! It was called *The Triad* something or other. I think 'Live' was one of the sections."

Sky laughed. "See? I knew you'd figure it out. Go on, then!" she said, shooing him away. "Don't come back until you have a real, live whale."

"I won't," Alex said, but he didn't move. He just looked at her, his stomach flipping all over the place. "You're kind of brilliant, you know that?"

Sky tilted her head, a smile playing on her lips. "I know," she said.

It reminded Alex of the time they were on the roof of the shack together, figuring out Mr. Today's riddle. His skin tingled, and a rush of good feelings surged through him. And she didn't look away. Without thinking, Alex reached his hand out to touch her cheek, and then he leaned in and kissed her.

"Thanks," he said, grinning when he pulled back and saw the startled look on her face. He turned away and ran toward the mansion, leaving Sky blushing alone in the moonlight.

Alex found the book on the dresser in his room. *The Triad: Live, Hide, Restore.* He'd been meaning to read it ever since Simber

LISA McMANN

showed it to him, but it wasn't like Alex had a lot of spare time lately. Now it felt like he didn't have time *not* to read it. He climbed into bed and paged to the first section.

LIVE

HISTORY: It is with a heavy heart that I begin this book. When one thinks about life, one hopes for a good one. Simber, Florence, and Ms. Octavia, among others, are the epitome of successful creations. Creatures with good lives. Unfortunately, I have also given a less-than-perfect life to a number of creatures, and I wish to chronicle their evolutions here, so that my successor is able to learn from my mistakes and, hopefully, not repeat them.

All my longings, my needs, my desires, went into Simber. I was lonely, in need of a companion, and as I created him I thought about all that was missing in my life. It was with love that I first breathed life into Simber, and he took on the very essence of my thoughts and dreams.

As Simber was my first creature, I thought I was

quite perfect at bringing creatures to life. Excited and enthused, I began a series of creatures in quick succession, thinking that if Simber was this wonderful, wouldn't a dozen more creatures be a dozen times more wonderful?

But it was not to be.

I made a little dog, but he attacked without provocation. I have the teeth mark scars to prove it. Then a panther—yes, a wonderful, beautiful creature. I designed her as a friend for Simber, but while she could understand me, she refused to speak. She was violent and grew to resent Simber for his closeness with me, and she became a threat.

I created a scorpion that for reasons unknown grew to an enormous size, and a few other creatures, just trying to re-create what I had with Simber. But I had used all of my heart at that time for the cheetah, I'm afraid. It took me too long to realize it and to admit that my creatures were failures. When I finally realized what had to come from inside me in order to make a successful life, I had a dozen monsters on my hands, including Ol' Tater, who terrorized the other terrorists, making everyone miserable, even himself, and eventually he asked to be put to sleep.

But truly none of them were safe to be around. So for their protection and my own, I had to isolate them, which I did with a heavy heart. They now live in the deepest part of the jungle—so deep that only their caretaker and one other know the way out.

That jungle is one of the places where the tube in the kitchenette will take you. Because of the danger, I didn't wish for anyone to accidentally find himself in the jungle, so to visit there, you must push all the buttons at once.

Be warned—the creatures are dangerous. If they know you are visiting with my blessing, there is a chance they will not attack, for I have been kind and they've grown to love me . . . at least a little bit, I think. And if you use your magic to hold them back, you will fare well.

As dangerous as it is, I'd like you to visit now and then to see if anyone needs anything. There's a good chance

Panther will have lost her tail—a vine will do the trick.

MAGIC: The live and restore spells have one thing in common: both can be found in the dot art that hangs in my office. The art is intuitive. What I mean is that if the world needs to be restored, the dots in the pictures in the mansion model (found in a kitchen cupboard in the gray shack) contain the magical words "breathe," "commence," etc. (see Restore section). But if Artimé exists, the art on my office walls hides the magical words for the live spell. So all you need to do is study the art from right to left (or as the setting sun, opposite from the restore spell), and you'll see the words you need to bring a creature to life: "initiate," "invigorate," "instill," "improve."

Here, there was some writing in the margins. Alex turned the book sideways to read the words.

Part Two: For best success regarding the "improve" portion, add: "comfort," "happiness," "peace," "success."

LISA McMANN

And a final line in a shakier hand, which looked like it had been written late in Mr. Today's life.

Part Three: "loyalty," "devotion," "zeal," "intensity," ~~"fury."~~

And in the tiniest print next to the crossed-out word:

No! Passion. Use "passion" instead.

The Live Spell

It was amazing how much more complicated the live spell was compared to the restore spell. But when Alex thought about it, it all made sense. He finished reading the section, noting that Mr. Today recommended bringing a creature to life in a safe, enclosed space and to alert anyone nearby to his actions so they could take cover if necessary.

Mr. Today went on to explain that just like the other Triad spells, the words should be concentrated on and thought deeply about, while wearing the robe, of course. Oh—and the mage should lay his hand on the side of the creature when performing the spell, or it wouldn't work at all.

LISA McMANN

Alex took the book into the Museum of Large. He looked at the whale and then back at the book. He reread the passage extra carefully this time. And then he looked at the whale once more.

"I can do this, I think," he said. His knees quivered and he felt a little light-headed. "I mean, of course I can. I already did one of the Triad spells, and I didn't even have the book for it. So . . ." He let his hand slide across the belly of the whale. A bit of still-damp paint came away on his fingers and shone in the light of the museum. Alex's heart pounded. Could he do what Mr. Today said to do? Could he put that much of himself, his dreams, into this creature? He wasn't sure.

But Alex was no longer a frightened boy. Alex was a mage now, who had taken on the end of his world and almost single-handedly brought it back to life. Surely he could handle bringing one creature to life for the first time. And now Sky was counting on him to do this. A silly grin crossed his face as he thought about kissing her. But he knew he had to focus on this spell if he was going to do it right.

He studied the instructions again, took a deep breath, and placed his hand on the whale's side. And then, trying hard to push thoughts of Sky far from his mind, he began.

"Initiate," he said, thinking about the word and what it meant. Starting something for the first time—that was definitely something he was doing here with Spike. When Alex felt he had focused on "initiate" long enough, he moved on to "invigorate." He closed his eyes, thinking invigorating thoughts that might transfer through his hand to give life and vigor to the whale. He could almost feel the power pulse through his fingertips. And then he moved on to "instill," softening the pressure against the whale's side a bit, trying to think of every good thing he had inside himself that he could transfer into the creature. Things like the wisdom he had gained since coming to Artimé, and the experience of deepest sorrow, which can only come from deepest love. Alex wanted the whale to have the ability to reach both . . . even though he knew that both at times could be quite painful.

Alex wanted to instill a sense of right and wrong in the creature, and so he focused his thoughts for a moment on kindness, tolerance, and selflessness, which Alex associated with making good and right choices. And he wanted the whale to be brave and strong and intelligent, so he thought about those things too.

It took quite a long time to get through the first three words

LISA McMANN

of the live spell, and Alex was already tired by the time he got to the word "improve." Still, he pressed on, now focusing his attention on improving the things he'd already cast upon the sculpture. He wasn't exactly sure how to do that, but in his mind he imagined the most perfect creature companion, and ideas came pouring out. *Let Spike speak and understand any human or creature. And be able to send messages through sonar!* he thought, and then added, feeling a bit panicky about all the gifts and abilities he was bestowing on this creature, *But only for good. And . . . to benefit others.* Alex could only guess that unbridled magical abilities could cause extremely bad problems. And even though there were times when he wished he could do everything magically, he knew that ultimately he wouldn't want the burden of it. It was hard enough just being mage now and having people clamoring for him to fix every little thing they couldn't fix on their own.

When Alex could think of no more ways to improve on the initial phase of the live spell, he took a deep breath and opened his eyes so he could review the second phase. Spike seemed slightly brighter in color than before, and her skin seemed warmer. But her eyes remained closed.

"Let's get on with it, then," Alex murmured, as if to assure the whale that he would continue.

He spoke the words in turn, concentrating very seriously on each. "Comfort," he said, picturing not only physical comfort for the whale, but also sort of a spiritual, emotional comfort that would emerge in times of distress. "Happiness," he added, and then "peace," thinking about how much he wanted both for himself as well, and emitting an extra burst of concentration in those areas as the thoughts pulsed through his fingertips into the beast. "Success." Alex thought about the whale overcoming any obstacle and leading other sea creatures to victory.

Immediately he rolled into the third phase. "Loyalty," Alex said, thinking of Simber. "Devotion." He pictured the girrinos, most especially Arija, who had given her life for the safety of Artimé. "Zeal," Alex said, not quite positive what the word meant, but thinking it had something to do with really liking to eat, since a cook in the mansion's kitchen had used the word once in talking about all the food Samheed had on his tray. So Alex pictured Spike with a real love for food.

He was getting a little dizzy with all the concentrating. Bringing life to a creature was no light task. He moved on.

"Intensity," he said, thinking of Ms. Octavia and her abilities, and then going off script as he sometimes had a tendency to do in Actors' Studio, he added "speed," and pictured the whale positively flying through the sea.

Alex moved on. "Passion." *Yes*, Alex thought. *Passion is what must take the place of fury. Passion makes us want to live another day, to try to do the right thing. Passion contains love and fear and anger and motivation. Passion keeps you fighting when you want to give up.* It was, Alex reflected later, something you could even work to improve inside yourself.

As he neared the end, Alex was tempted to add "fury" despite Mr. Today's crossing it out. But Alex didn't want to mess with Mr. Today's obviously well-thought-out spell. Having "Furious" in her name would have to do. And really, Spike Furious was probably the best name a creature could have.

Alex turned the page, keeping one hand on the whale.

Finally, address your new creature by name, urging him or her to take a breath.

Don't forget to step back and give your creature some room to breathe and move about.

Alex put the book down and placed his other hand on the whale. He took a deep breath and said, "Spike Furious, you are alive! Take your first breath!"

There was a hum, a buzz in the air, and the whale began to shimmer. Alex stumbled backward so he could watch, taking it all in. "Spike," he breathed again, unable to contain his excitement. "Breathe!"

The enormous creature opened her milky eyes, which expressed immediate surprise in a most beautiful way.

Her blowhole pulsed and her tail flapped.

She breathed once, twice.

And then her body began to slump and sag.

Her eyes became pinpricks of fear, and her gorgeous blue skin turned a sickening shade of gray.

The Short, Uneventful Life of Spike Furious

Alex paled. His hands rose to his forehead, his fingers threading through and gripping his hair. "What is it, Spike? What's wrong?"

Spike's eyes rolled back and her lids closed. Her sides heaved, and a moan came from somewhere deep inside her.

In an instant Alex realized that he had made a horrendous mistake.

He ran to her side and placed his hand on the whale, struggling to think of the term he needed. "Um, Im-Improve!" he shouted. "Be able to live on land!" He jiggled the heaving creature's side, which had become very hot. "Stay alive," he cried. But it was no use. The spell had been enacted, and there was no way to go back and fix it.

Wildly Alex looked around for water, but there was nothing here—he'd have to run all the way to the kitchenette, and even then he had only teacups with which to transport it. "No!" he cried as the memory flooded back—the memory of Mr. Today talking about how he had found this whale on the shore, and how he had watched it die because it couldn't get back into the water. Now Alex had brought it to life only to watch it die again. It was the most horrible thing he could imagine. And he had done it to the poor creature. Guilt raked his insides.

"Water!" Alex yelled, pointing at a book, trying to create it. But nothing happened. He'd never been able to do it—Lani was the only one he knew of who could turn things into soup, and as far as he knew, putting the whale into soup wouldn't exactly solve the problem. He needed to get the whale into water. He needed to get the whale into the sea.

An idea sprang to Alex's mind. The transport spell! He'd transport the whale to the sea. But what if she swam away? Alex whipped his head around, looking for any other option

LISA McMANN

that would assure him that Spike would live, but there was none. All he knew was that he couldn't let this whale die. Alex put his hands on Spike's side once more.

He screwed up his face, clenching his jaw and squeezing his eyes shut, as he pictured the sea of Artimé, just off shore but in deep enough water that the whale could be fully immersed. And even though he was exhausted from creating the beast, he mustered up his strongest concentration, picturing the location where he wanted to transport her.

When he was sure he had focused sufficiently, he muttered, "Transport."

He waited a moment, but he could still feel the creature struggling under his touch. He peeked at her, then shut his eyes once more. "Transport," he said, louder and more desperately this time.

But the whale didn't disappear.

"Ugh!" Alex had no idea why it wasn't working. "Come on!" He tried a third time, to no avail.

"I'm so sorry!" he cried, clinging to Spike. "I don't know what to do! Why won't it work?" Alex turned away, slumped to the floor in agony, and buried his head in his hands. He would have to stay until it was over, that much he knew. The whale's gasps and moans, her shuddering flank—all of it was the most horrendous thing Alex could imagine. And he was the cause of it. No wonder Mr. Today had stopped making creatures. It was too painful when you made a mistake.

When Alex looked up, he found himself staring at the statue of Ol' Tater and remembering his conversation with Mr. Today about the transport spell. And soon the words came back to Alex. Ol' Tater had been transported to the Museum of Large with a transport spell, but that was *after* Mr. Today had put him to sleep. "It doesn't work with humans or living creatures," Mr. Today had said.

Alex looked up at Spike in horror. That was why it didn't work. Spike was a living creature. At least for a few more minutes. It was agonizing. Would he even be able to bring back a creature who had died? Ol' Tater hadn't died—Mr. Today had put him to sleep. Was there a difference? Alex jumped to his feet. He couldn't stand it—Spike was in misery. He looked at Ol' Tater once more, and then, slowly, Alex turned toward the whale and began singing, his mind searching desperately for the words and changing the ones that mattered:

"Spikey girl, Spikey girl,

Too much sadness, no repeats.

I am sorry, more than sorry,

But it's time for you to sleep."

Immediately the whale ceased her struggles, and her body turned back into the materials Alex had used to make her.

The new mage checked her over carefully and emitted a long sigh. At least he had put her out of her misery. But he was still very sorry to have made her suffer so much first. It had been a mistake. A big one. And it had been made on someone else's life. Alex knew he would most certainly never forget it as long as he lived.

Still shaking, Alex touched the whale's side once more, eager now to right his wrongs. "Let's get you into the water," he said. "Ready?" He sucked in a deep breath and let it out. "Okay."

Alex closed his eyes and once again pictured the sea, just off shore but deep enough for the whale to be fully immersed. He concentrated on the spot in his mind for a long time. And then he whispered, "Transport."

The whale disappeared.

Alex's eyes flew open. He stared at the empty spot. And then he ran out of the Museum of Large and through the hall to the balcony, tripped down the steps and around the few residents who remained awake at this hour, raced past dozing statues Simber and Florence, and flung open the front door, which immediately woke Simber.

Before Simber could speak, Alex, still running, yelled, "Going for a late-night dip in the sea!"

At the edge of the water he kicked off his shoes and fought his way out of his pants, but kept his robe on, and then dashed out to the water, running and splashing until it became too deep, and dove in.

Pulling a blinding highlighter from his robe pocket while he swam, he aimed it at the ocean floor, trying to find the lifeless Spike. He knew she'd be at the bottom, like Simber had been. But where exactly? Alex also knew the transport spell wasn't entirely accurate.

The effects of Ms. Octavia's underwater breathing class became evident as Alex searched. It was loads easier to hold his breath underwater now, using the oxygen in his blood to

LISA McMANN

keep him going, and he could easily stay underwater for six or seven minutes without coming up to the surface.

He needed those six or seven minutes now. In the murky water, magically coaxing the blinding highlighter to hold a steady, not-blinding light rather than flashing quickly and fading away, Alex pushed himself along the ocean floor. As he searched for the large body, he realized he didn't remember all of the live spell—he hadn't memorized it. Perhaps he should go back to shore and get the book.

But then he shook his head. He didn't need the live spell—that's not what had brought Ol' Tater back to life. He needed to use the restore spell.

Frantically he tried to recall the words from that spell and the order they went in. It started with "imagine." Could he remember the rest? It seemed like years ago that he'd restored Artimé, even though it had only been a matter of months. He pictured Sky at his side like she had been back then, and that seemed to calm his mind as he recalled her patient hand signals to help him remember the words: "imagine," "believe," "whisper" . . . He hesitated, knowing that the next word was the one he always forgot, and today was no different. He closed his eyes to concentrate for a moment, and pictured Sky, pressing on his chest. He smiled and opened his eyes, letting the seawater sting them once more. Of course—the one thing he'd forgotten to do then and couldn't exactly do now. It was "breathe." And then, finally, the word that would trigger rebirth: "commence."

Oh, Sky, he thought. Maybe if he hadn't been so googly-eyed about kissing her, he wouldn't have made such a stupid mistake, and he wouldn't be in this predicament right now. He frowned. Now wasn't a good time to be thinking about her either. All Alex really needed to do was find the whale. Which was turning out to be impossible. His lungs began to burn. It was time to surface.

He pushed himself upward and broke the surface, taking in deep breaths of the cool night air. He looked around to see where the lights of Artimé lay and found himself a good bit offshore. Had he missed Spike somewhere? Perhaps he should double back. He saw Simber, backlit by the mansion lights, licking a paw and then yawning at the edge of the water, and waved to him. Simber nodded in return. Alex was secretly proud that the cat hadn't come out over the water to see what Alex was up to. That meant Simber trusted Alex not to drown. It was a positive step, Alex thought.

Once he had his wind back again, Alex dove down and resumed his search, this time swimming laps parallel to the shore, drawing closer and closer to shore until he could nearly touch the bottom. Since the whale was quite a bit taller than he, she would stick out above the waves, so she couldn't be here. Alex had to keep searching.

After about an hour, he caught sight of the whale a good thousand feet on the other side of the mansion, where no one liked to swim because of the big rocks and sharp edges of the reef. The very tip of Spike's tail stuck out of the water just slightly, as she was lodged on the reef, head pointed down at the ocean floor.

"Finally," Alex grumbled. "That transport spell needs a bit of work, if you ask me." But no one was there to ask him, so all Alex could do was continue on. Once he had his breath, he stood cautiously on the reef and reached down under the water to touch the whale's side. His sopping-wet robe stuck to his shivering body, but once again that night Alex concentrated and began to utter a very important spell. One that he knew he should never forget.

"Imagine," he whispered, imagining the whale alive again.

"Believe." Oh boy, did he believe it. He'd seen it happen before, and he didn't need anybody to convince him that this spell would work. "Whisper," he said, knowing he'd be whispering all along, his magic and his energy giving life to the whale.

Without hesitation this time, Alex uttered the next word. "Breathe." *However you do it best, Spike, you must do it now.* And with that, he ended it. "Commence." He repeated the words two more times, and then he waited.

When he felt something electric pulsing through his fingers, Alex opened his eyes. The whale's tail was moving the slightest bit. "Spike!" he shouted. "Spike Furious, you're alive!"

The water was charged with the great creature's presence. Alex could feel the life around him—the rebirth of this creature, the return to her natural habitat. And then he felt the slap—the really extremely hard slap—of her tail on the side of his face, and he felt his body being lifted out of the water and thrown ten feet aside.

When Alex resurfaced, sputtering, and came to his senses, Spike was gone.

Overwhelmed

Aaron Stowe, covered in leaves and dirt, got up from the bottom of the jungle tube. He brushed himself off and watched as the panther jumped from tree to tree, the little dog following along, yipping from the ground below and then hopping up to grab a branch with his teeth and swinging from branch to branch by the grip of his mouth. Aaron didn't know what to think. All he knew was that he needed to get out of here before something else went wrong.

He wiped the dirt off his clothing and looked at the rock. "Okay, well, good-bye then." He hesitated. Now that the danger was over, he felt strangely drawn to this place.

The rock moved closer. "We shall see you again soon, I hope," it rumbled.

"Ahh . . . right. Of course. I shall come by again soon to make sure everything is working as it should." He looked over his shoulder at the tube's button, as if that would help him leave more quickly. "By the way," he said, "how many creatures are out here?"

"A dozen or so. Some of them I haven't seen in . . . well, in years, I suppose. I think about them, though. They know how to find me if . . . if they need me."

Aaron frowned. The rock's voice had turned wistful, and Aaron didn't know how to process that. And frankly, he didn't want to know. Not today. He'd had enough for today. He nodded and said another awkward good-bye. And then he pressed the button.

Spending less than a second in the tube in his brother's mansion, Aaron pushed the first button, which would take him to Haluki's. When he arrived there, he felt a cool draft, colder than any temperature he'd ever felt in Quill before. His heart pounded. Had he hit the wrong button by mistake? He pushed his hand out of the tube and found the familiar closet doors.

Cautiously he opened it and stepped into Haluki's office. His shoes squished on the wet floor.

What in Quill? Aaron wondered, stepping gingerly across the room. It was almost chilly in there. The walls were wet. The ceiling dripped with water. And the floor was soaked. It was more water than he'd seen in one place before, if you didn't count Artimé. And he didn't.

He dipped a finger into a small pool of water and tasted it. He'd never felt something so cold on his tongue before. And it tasted good. He cupped his hands and drank some more, glad for it but feeling like he was in a strange dream. Why was it here?

Puzzled, he wandered through the house, still in a daze from the jungle experience. It was the same everywhere— water dripping from the tables and chairs, standing in the sink, soaking into the wooden floorboards. And in the center of the dining table was a small white puck of something strange. Aaron reached out and touched it. "Ouch!" he cried. It had felt good at first, but then it made his fingers burn. He dropped the puck, watched it skate across the floor, and pressed his fingertips to his cheek. They were cold.

Aaron could feel a strange, anxious feeling welling up inside him. It was all too much for him to process after what he'd just been through. He couldn't make sense of anything tonight. It was all he could do to keep his legs from collapsing under him as he made his way to the palace. What Aaron needed more than anything right now, he decided, was to forget everything weird that had happened and go to sleep for a week. Then he could figure out just how to handle this new, secret part of his life.

Staggering back home to the palace, Aaron didn't even notice Secretary on the side of the road, hiding in the shadow of the wall, talking quietly with a friend . . . or perhaps it was an enemy.

But Eva Fathom saw him.

"He's up to something," Eva said in the shadows after Aaron was out of sight. "I can feel it."

"Well, you'll have to hold him off for a while."

"I'll try. He's a bit of a coward, so it shouldn't be difficult. Be safe."

"You too."

The two—friends or enemies, perhaps not even they knew for sure—clasped hands and then parted ways.

LISA McMANN

The List

By morning, preparations were in full swing for the rescue, and Alex didn't have time to lament the loss of his first creature. He'd been preoccupied, had acted hastily, and hadn't thought things out, which had resulted in several obvious mistakes. Perhaps that was why Mr. Today had never tried to re-create the whale. There was no place to keep it and train it, or simply talk to it.

It was a bit embarrassing, actually, now that the fear of Spike's dying was over. Alex was glad he hadn't brought an audience around to witness it—especially Sky. What if she was disappointed in him? He hoped she wouldn't ask about it. Though maybe if he'd included her more in the planning, she might have had some better ideas. She was known for that, after all. But the truth was, whenever Sky was around, Alex felt like he wasn't concentrating enough on being the leader of Artimé. And it was when he wasn't concentrating enough that mistakes were made. It was a serious problem.

"Blurgh," he muttered, thinking not for the first time that maybe mages just weren't cut out for having relationships—not romantic ones, anyway. Alex hoped Sky wasn't hurt that he hadn't asked her to help. He decided that if he just didn't mention the whale and acted really busy and focused on the quest to rescue Sky's mother, all these awkward feelings about Sky, and about his mistakes with Spike, would go away soon enough.

Simber had witnessed the entire Spike saga from shore, of course. Eventually he'd been joined by Sean, who'd gone out for a late-night walk, as he often did. Simber tried to explain to Sean what was happening to Alex, but he didn't actually know all the details, so he made them up, much to Sean's delight. The two had waited patiently on shore as Alex swam back alone. The giant cat had held his tongue, hard as it sometimes was, so at least Alex had that relief. Sean just laughed once he

LISA McMANN

knew the whale was all right, and he promised not to say anything to embarrass Alex.

In spite of the darkness, Alex had remained on the shore, watching out over the water. At first he had thought the whale might come back, but after several hours reality set in, and eventually Alex had stopped looking out to sea to watch for his shiny creation. He'd gotten up and gone inside to bed.

It was so strange how much Alex cared about the whale, even felt he knew the whale personally, but the whale knew little or nothing of her own creator, or how much work he'd put into her to make her just so. Would she even know him if they met again? Alex doubted it.

But there was plenty of work to be done to distract Alex from Spike's short life in Artimé. It was time to pack up the pirate ship and get everybody on board with the plan.

Alex walked down the boys' hallway to Samheed's room and knocked.

Samheed opened the door to let Alex inside.

"Hello, Alex Stowe," said Samheed's blackboard, Stuart. "It's especially nice to see you."

"Nice to see you, too, Stu," Alex said. "Clive says hello."

Clive hadn't said hello, but Alex knew Clive would be annoyed by Alex's saying it, so he did.

Stuart looked suspicious. "Oh, really?" He pressed his face out a little farther to get a better look at Alex.

"Oh, yes," Alex said. "He thinks you're pretty neat. He told me the other day how much he admires you."

At this, Stuart looked almost frightened. "Oh. Dear me. I have to go." He slid back and disappeared into the blackboard.

Samheed raised an eyebrow and whispered, "Clive didn't say any of that, did he?"

"Nope."

"What is it with those two?"

Alex shrugged. "No idea. Maybe they're too alike to be friends."

"Unlike us."

Alex laughed. "Right." He flopped onto Samheed's couch and pulled the list of Artiméans from his robe pocket. "Okay, see what you think." He handed it to Samheed.

Sam sat in the chair, put his feet on the coffee table, and picked up a pen. His brow furrowed and he chewed on the end of the pen as he read.

When he was finished, he looked up. "So Mr. Appleblossom and Ms. Morning are staying here to keep watch over the Warbler kids. Are they going to take off their neck things?"

"I thought it would be fine to do that. What do you think?"

"Oh, yeah, totally fine. I don't think those kids have any secret plan at all to do anything to us. I believe what they say about their parents tricking Eagala. Problem is, she won't make that mistake again."

"Yeah." Alex jiggled his foot. "I worry that she'll attack again to get the children back. What if she comes when we're gone?"

"We can't sit around waiting for an attack."

"True."

"Besides, she probably doesn't know what to do next. Maybe she'll figure she should cut her losses."

"Maybe," Alex said. He pointed to the paper. "Any other comments?"

Samheed looked at the list again. "Any squirrelicorns?"

"Rufus and five others."

"No Fox or Kitten on this one?"

Alex pursed his lips. "Can you think of a use for them?"

"Well, there's always comic relief." Samheed smiled. "Besides, Fox can swim. Probably forever—he's made out of driftwood, isn't he?"

Alex sat back and tapped his lips thoughtfully. "I suppose they don't weigh much, so they wouldn't slow the ship down."

"And you never know about Kitten. She can get into some really small spaces that nobody else can. I say she's pretty valuable to have."

"I'm just afraid of losing her or having her get swept away."

"Yeah," Samheed agreed, "good point. But Henry's pretty good about keeping her in his pocket." He studied the list again. "Wait. Where's Florence? You're not taking her? Are you crazy?"

"Nope. I was just trying to think about who would be most useful for an underwater fight and rescue, if it comes to that. Plus, she weighs a ton, and the ship is always tipping—"

"I think she'd be useful in smashing the crud out of some glass walls."

"Well, that's true."

"She's good at pretty much everything."

"Except maybe hiding."

LISA McMANN

Samheed laughed. "Fair enough. And what about Meg?"

"She asked to stay back if we could spare her. She really likes spending time with the Warbler kids and thinks she can help them adjust to Artimé. Besides, she knows how to get the thornaments off."

They lapsed into silence as Alex reconsidered his choices for the journey. He took the list back from Samheed and added Florence, Fox, and Kitten to it. "All right, I think we've got a team." He stood up. "I'll go run it past Ms. Octavia and Simber and then send out a blackboard announcement."

At the word blackboard, Stuart's face pushed out. "You rang?"

"No, I was just talking about Clive. I'll be sending out an announcement later."

Stuart frowned. "You know, if Clive ever has a problem living up to his duties—"

"Easy there, Stu," Samheed said. "What, you'd leave me just like that?"

"Oh, heck yes," Stuart said. "No offense, but you're kind of difficult."

Samheed laughed. "What? I'm totally offended! That was only when I first got here. I'm cool now."

"Eh," Stuart said, looking away.

Samheed shook his head and grinned at Alex. "You see what I have to deal with?"

Alex grinned back. "I'm with Stuart. You were a real pain in the neck back then. It was really great here when you and Lani were missing. So quiet, no drama . . ."

Samheed punched Alex in the arm and they left the room together, laughing and shoving each other like they had no problems to worry about, not noticing Stuart's longing glance following Alex out the door.

Another Journey Begins

In the morning, as Captain Ahab brought the ship around from the lagoon, the warriors lined up on the shore. They were a determined bunch. Next to them were stacks of crates full of supplies. They weren't sure how long they'd be gone.

"Charlie knows you're in charge," Alex said to Ms. Morning. "If he hears from Matilda that anything strange is happening in Quill, he'll go straight to you."

Charlie moved to stand at Ms. Morning's side and gave three thumbs up.

"And you can use a seek spell to reach me," Ms. Morning said.

She presented Alex with a small piccolo charm. "Here," she said. "I made this when I was about your age. Now it's my gift to you. You can use it to let me know if you have an emergency, and if you're not too far away, I'll send squirrelicorns out to see what's happening. I've got Meghan here too, to help Mr. Appleblossom and me with the Warbler children, so I think we'll be all right."

Alex nodded. He handed Ms. Morning a gift as well—a tiny stone that he'd painted to look like a spider. "And you can use this to send a seek spell to me." He also handed her the Triad spell book. "Take good care of this, and don't forget to wear a robe while I'm gone."

Ms. Morning smiled. She looked healthy again, and happy, too, though there was a hint of sorrow still in her eyes. She put her hand on Alex's arm. "I feel like we have come a long way, don't you? Like we can handle things now . . . without him. I mean, I know you did it all alone, but now it just feels . . . I don't know. Easier somehow."

Alex smiled. "I know what you mean. We still have a lot to figure out, but we just know more now. I don't think he expected any of it, or he would have prepared us."

"He would have, Alex, I'm sure of it. He tried with me, you

know. He was getting anxious about training someone, just in case, and of course he trusted me. But I was always too busy with my music or my classes, or simply not interested. . . . I'm sorry for that. I'm sorry I wasn't more help."

"I'll try to get you back for that," Alex teased.

"I believe you will." Ms. Morning grinned at him.

Alex held out his hand. "We'll see you when we see you, Ms. Morning."

Ms. Morning took it. "Claire," she said.

"Claire," Alex repeated. He felt like a grown-up.

"Take care, Alex. Make wise choices and you'll be fine."

Alex nodded, surprised by the welling of emotion in his chest. It made him think of his father . . . and the Warbler children . . . and how Claire's words were something a parent should say. Words Alex had never heard from his own parents. "Thanks," he said, turning away.

He looked at the lineup of the crew. "My, we are a motley bunch," he said, making a joke to chase away the lump in his throat. From giant Florence to tiny Kitten, from gruff Simber to a half-dozen rigid squirrelicorns, from crazy Captain Ahab fresh from the prop closet to efficient Ms. Octavia and her flying appendages, and from Unwanted boy-mage Alex to brave-hearted Sky and Crow, the Artiméan army came in all shapes and sizes and colors and origins. But they were the strongest assembled crew Alex had ever seen. It occurred to him that he should tell them that.

He looked at each person and creature, really looked at them, thinking about their strengths. And then he addressed them in a strong, steady voice. "You make me feel safe," he said. "You bring honor to Artimé and to those who are in need of our help." He scanned the group, all of whom stood in silent reverence as they listened to their mage. He noticed a tear slipping down Sky's cheek, and it almost made him choke up once more. He cleared his throat and continued. "There's no place I'd rather be than on a rescue adventure with you." He paused. "We have a hard journey ahead, and we don't know what will happen. We'll face lots of trouble, I'm sure—it seems to follow us, doesn't it? But I won't despair if you don't." He smiled and brought his fist to his chest.

The others, even the statues, did the same.

"Any questions?"

There was silence.

Alex nodded. "Well then, crew, all aboard."

A New Energy in the Palace

When Aaron woke, safe in the palace despite his nightmares, it felt like his brain had sorted out a dozen things for him. As if an instruction book had been handed to him overnight, Aaron knew what he had to do. It was so clear!

He propped himself up in bed, took a piece of paper and a pencil from his bedside table, and let the pencil roam over the paper like he'd done before, drawing bloblike circles and crooked triangles and squares. It helped him think.

And that's exactly what he needed—to think just a little bit differently, like he'd done when he came up with the plan for the Favored Farm. Only this time, Aaron needed to realize all of the potential that was right in front of him. To be clear, he knew that following Justine's ways in Quill was still the best plan. And he would continue following that. But Aaron had a new element to consider, which Justine never could have dreamed of. And being the strong, intelligent Wanted that he was, his very own mind had come up with it. Aaron needed to be in that jungle, winning over and training that army of misfits. That was all there was to it. Those creatures were his secret weapons, and he would tell no one about them.

But he couldn't neglect Quill, because his people needed some direction too, and definitely some nudging and motivation to get them ready for the ultimate fight. So while Aaron was out training the jungle creatures, somebody had to be in the palace to watch over things in Quill—to slowly mold the Wanteds and Necessaries into a stronger, more loyal society and to get them angry again. They needed to build up their anger to an intensity to want to fight, like before. It might take a while, but with perseverance and a solid plan that included Aaron's secret weapons of the jungle, all of Quill would one day come together for a major attack on Artimé from all directions. The Unwanteds wouldn't

LISA McMANN

know what hit them. It was absolutely, utterly the most perfect plan in the history of Quill.

Aaron set his scribblings aside and got out of bed. He hurried to wash and dress, and he headed straight to his office.

"Breakfast!" he barked at a passing maid, and then, "Secretary!"

Eva Fathom was in earshot. She hurried over to Aaron's doorway. "Yes?"

"Has the work begun on the opening to Artimé?"

"Yes," Eva said. "People are moving as quickly as they can. We had to assemble—"

"I need you to halt the work immediately."

Eva's mouth hung open. Slowly she closed her lips. "May I ask why?"

Aaron leaned back in his chair. "I've decided that while it's important to close off Quill completely from outside aggressors, we need to deal with the ones encroaching on our own island first. Obviously we can't take over Artimé if we don't have access to it. Once we have control of their property and we do away with all the Unwanteds, we'll build a new length of wall to enclose everything, including that mansion, within Quill." He folded his arms, pleased by his own cleverness.

Eva blinked. "That makes a lot of sense," she said evenly. "Do you mean to take over the mansion? It's quite stunning inside."

"Perhaps I will. Seems a shame to let it go to ruin outside the wall." Aaron knew well enough what it looked like, but Secretary didn't need to know that.

Secretary hesitated. "I'll stop the workers right away."

"Have them take down whatever they've put up so far."

"Right." She turned to go.

"Wait. Tell me—who of the former governors was most loyal to Justine?"

Eva thought for a moment. "Strang, of course."

Aaron nodded. "That's my thought too. Please invite him for dinner."

"Tonight?"

"Tomorrow. Also, who from our Restorers might be interested in a government job? Bethesda or Liam, perhaps?"

"You sent them to the Ancients Sector, sir."

Aaron tapped his lips. "Ah, yes. So I did. I've forgotten why."

Eva Fathom remained quiet as he pondered. She was not

about to remind him. "I could see if they're still alive," she said, "though it's been quite a while, so it's doubtful."

"Yes, do that. If they're still biding their time, order the sector overseer to hand them over to you."

"If you're sure."

"Of course I am."

The maid came in with a tray of breakfast for Aaron, set it on his desk, and left. Eva waited at the door to see if there was anything else.

Aaron picked up a spoon and stirred something mushy in a bowl. He tasted it and made a face. "Also, Gondoleery Rattrapp."

Eva narrowed her eyes. "What about her?"

"Invite her to dinner as well."

Eva pursed her lips but said nothing. She'd told Aaron that Gondoleery was up to something strange. But she couldn't force the high priest to make wise choices. "Very well," she said. "Anyone else?" She refrained from suggesting every ridiculous thought that came to her head now that Gondoleery had been brought into the picture. *Claire Morning, perhaps? How about Alex Stowe?*

"No, that'll do for now. If you do find Bethesda or Liam alive, invite them as well."

"For dinner tomorrow."

"Yes."

"With Governor Strang and Gondoleery." Eva couldn't imagine a more dreadful grouping of guests.

Aaron was beginning to look annoyed. "Yes." He shoved a spoonful of gruel into his mouth. "And get some decent food from the Favored Farm, since our kitchen staff doesn't seem to understand what good food tastes like. This is disgusting."

Eva Fathom began with the easiest task—lugging armloads of fruits and vegetables from the Favored Farm to the Quillitary vehicle and then stopping for chickens as well. It wasn't her job to get the food, but she didn't trust the kitchen staff to know ripe from rotten, so it was easier to do it herself.

Next her driver took her to former governor Strang's house. He still lived in the governor housing, but he hadn't been seen much since Aaron had taken over. No one knew, or seemed to care, what he was doing after he got fired. Eva walked up to the front door and knocked.

LISA McMANN

No one answered, so she knocked again. This time she heard a noise inside, and soon the door opened a crack. "Who is it?" came Strang's familiar voice. It sounded duller than usual, if that were possible.

"It's Eva Fathom. Secretary, that is." Eva tried to peek through the crack in the door without appearing to be nosy.

"What do you want?"

"The High Priest Aaron Stowe would like to invite you to dinner tomorrow evening."

The door opened farther and Strang stuck his head out. Eva Fathom tried hard not to stare, for the young man's appearance was quite different from before. His hair was long and unkempt, his face unshaven. His eyes were blood-shot, and he had gained quite a large girth since Eva had seen him last.

"What for?" Strang asked.

"I'm not exactly sure," Eva said. "Something about a job in the government. He knows you were loyal to Justine, and he'd like to talk with you."

Former Governor Strang narrowed his eyes. "What time?"

"Eight o'clock."

Strang hesitated. "Fine." He nodded once and shut the door in Eva's face.

Eva smiled condescendingly at the door and went back to the vehicle. "To the Ancients Sector, please," she told the driver.

At the Ancients Sector, Eva hesitated before she went inside. She had been very close to being sent here by Justine, and Eva didn't look at this place with any amount of warmth, that was for sure. No one did.

She waited at the small rundown gray table for someone to notice her.

A worker looked up. "Time's up, eh? Who sent you?"

"No, no," Secretary said. "I'm not checking in or out just yet. I'm on an errand for the high priest."

"Sure," the woman said.

"No, truly I am. I'm to inquire after two individuals. Bethesda Dia Gloria and Liam Healy. Are they still housed here, or are they . . . not?"

The woman stood. "Bethesda's gone and buried. Liam's heading to the sleep chamber today." She looked out the window. "He's standing there now, waiting to go in."

Eva stepped to the window. "Oh dear. Well, by order of the high priest, you'll need to put a halt to it. I'm to collect him and his things and take him to the palace."

The worker narrowed her eyes. "What proof do you have?"

Eva's lips quivered. She looked at her wrinkled hands resting on the window frame. And then she closed her eyes and used the code phrase that Justine had given to her that would overrule any other measure put in place, her voice quiet so as not to be overheard. "In the name of Quill, and upon your life and mine, it *shall* be done."

The worker was quiet. "Apologies," she said.

Eva turned to look at her. "Get going, then, before they kill him."

The woman nodded, flustered, and nearly tripped over the chair leg on her way out.

Eva hesitated, then followed. Liam was certain to be overwhelmingly grateful. And she was determined to be on the receiving end of the gratitude when he was.

A Visit to Gondoleery's

Liam sat down in the backseat of the Quillitary vehicle next to Eva Fathom. He leaned forward, elbows on his knees, and put his face in his hands. He shook while Eva instructed the driver, he shook as they drove off, and he even shook as Eva patted his shoulder a few minutes later.

Finally he took in a deep breath, sat back, and looked at her. "I don't know how to thank you for this," he said in a low voice.

Eva smiled. "One day you will know exactly how to thank me," she said. "All you need to do now is go along with whatever

LISA McMANN

Aaron says." She looked out her window. "If you want to stay out of the Ancients Sector, I mean."

Liam regarded her. "But I—after the mage—and Claire Morning, and that pantry—I just can't . . ."

Eva turned toward him. "Listen to me," she said, softly enough that the driver couldn't hear. "You can say things with your lips that your heart doesn't feel. And for now you will. You must."

Liam's lips parted. He faced forward and closed them again. "Oh. Of course. In that case. Is that what you—?"

"Good." She looked straight ahead. "Good. We'll talk again another time."

The driver stopped outside Gondoleery Rattrapp's house. Eva got out of the vehicle, and then she bent down and looked in. "I think you should come with me."

Liam fumbled with the handle and got out, and together they walked up the path to the door.

The last time Eva was here, the house had glowed blue. But this time there was a faint orange glow coming from behind the curtains. "Do you see that?" she whispered.

Liam nodded, eyes wide.

Eva knocked on the door. "Pay close attention to everything."

Scuttling noises came from inside. Eva knocked again.

When at last Gondoleery opened the door, a rush of hot air blew over Eva and Liam. Eva disguised the surprise on her face at the sight of their old Restorer, but Liam stared.

"What do you want?" Gondoleery asked. Her face was red and blistered in spots, her wild gray hair was blown back, and her knuckles were covered in burns. She pulled a thin blanket around her shoulders and gripped it tightly around her neck as if she were cold.

Eva smiled politely. "Aaron—I mean the high priest—is wondering if you will come to the palace for dinner tomorrow night. Eight o'clock."

"What for?"

The questions were sounding familiar. "I'm not sure exactly," Eva said. "Something about a possible government job. Strang will be there, and Liam, too. And me, of course." Eva knitted her brows thoughtfully. "I think."

Gondoleery stared. "Why in Quill would I ever want or need to spend time with that arrogant snot?"

Eva smiled. "I wouldn't know." She realized something else

that looked so strange about Gondoleery—her eyebrows were gone. Eva glanced over Gondoleery's shoulder, trying to look inside. She could smell wood or something else burning. "But you're invited, nevertheless, and I do hope to see you. It'll be nice to catch up again."

Liam slowly rose up on the balls of his feet, trying to see into the house.

Gondoleery sneered. "Don't count on it." She closed the door swiftly.

"All right, then," Eva said, smiling brightly at the closed door. She turned to Liam and muttered, "Let's go."

They walked back to the vehicle.

Gondoleery's front door opened again. "What time did you say?"

"Eight o'clock." Eva smiled and got in the jalopy as Gondoleery slammed her front door.

Liam climbed in beside her. "Great Quill," he said. "That was—"

Eva pressed her fingertips on his arm. "Save it," she murmured. She leaned forward to speak to the driver. "Back to the palace, if you please, sir."

They drove in strained silence the short distance to the palace. When they got out, Eva slipped the driver a sack full of fruits and vegetables she had picked up that morning from the Favored Farm. "Here, take these," she told him. "And give my best to your family."

"Th-thanks," the driver said, dubious. "Thanks a lot—my wife will be very grateful."

"Just as I am grateful for you," Eva said. "I shall call on you again when my business takes me into Quill."

The driver bowed his head. "I am at your service, madam."

She waved him off, and the two watched him drive away.

"What is going on here?" Liam asked under his breath. "I'm not quite sure I understand . . . you."

Eva tilted her head and opened the door to the palace. "Hmm?" she said. "Whatever do you mean?"

The Team

Once the ship had sailed and everyone had stowed their things, Alex gathered them on deck. "Do any of you know what 'sports' are?" he asked.

Lani, who had been studying a wrinkled piece of paper, folded it quickly and put it in her pocket, then lifted her hand in the air, along with a few others. "I read about it. It's kind of like having a battle. Everybody on your side has a job to do, and if everybody does their thing right, you can win against the other team. People do it for fun. I don't get why you'd want to have a battle just for the fun of it, but whatever."

Samheed and Carina Holiday exchanged a grin. They both

loved a good battle and would probably choose to do it for fun every day if they could.

"I saw that," Lani said.

"Anyway," Alex interrupted, "that's the kind of mission this is. Those of us who have been training with Ms. Octavia will have certain parts to play in the rescue, and everyone else will have different roles. If we do it right, it'll work perfectly and no one will even notice we've stolen Sky and Crow's mother away. That's what we're going for. A rescue without a fight."

Carina looked disappointed. She was still a bit mad about the last battle on Warbler, where she and Sean had been knocked out at the very beginning by sleep darts.

Alex continued laying out the plan. "Ideally, it'll be simple," he said. "We'll wait for Sky and Crow's mother by the skylight. Her name is Copper, by the way, which is also the same color as her hair, so that will help you identify her." Alex glanced at Sky to make sure he'd gotten the details correct.

Sky nodded. "Her hair is long and a little bit lighter than mine," she said. "She wears scarves over it, or at least she did. And she has the golden-orange eyes and thorn necklace as well."

"Sounds like she's not hard to miss," Sean said. "Right, Crow?" He'd taken quite a liking to the quiet Warbler boy.

Crow nodded. "She's beautiful," he said.

Carina's hand flitted to her mouth and her eyes glistened. "It's settled, then," she declared, patting the boy on the knee. "We shall save her." Carina had a young son of her own and was no doubt thinking of him. She gave Sky's shoulders a squeeze.

"Once we've spotted her and alerted her to our presence, we'll communicate a time for her to sneak out the fishing hatch, and we'll take her from there. And if she's unable to access that hatch or too afraid because she can't swim, we'll have her return to the spot by the skylight. Florence can smash in the window, and we'll lower a rope and pull her out that way."

Samheed yawned. "Sounds easy enough. You probably won't even need us."

"Well, that's where phase two comes in."

Carina perked up her ears. "Phase two? I'm listening."

"Remember the animals? The sea creatures caged underwater on the other side of the reverse aquarium? Some of us saw them the first time we were there."

Sky, Crow, Simber, and Carina nodded.

"Are we going to set them free?" Crow asked, excited.

Alex grinned. "Yes. At least we'll try. They shouldn't be trapped like that. I can't stop thinking about them." He also couldn't stop thinking about Spike, but that was another matter.

"Cool, so we'll figure out how to release them," Samheed said. He narrowed his eyes. "Wait. What kind of creatures are we talking about?"

"I'm not sure," Alex admitted. "We didn't get a good look."

"So they could attack us."

"I suppose they could."

Henry frowned. "I'm not sure I have any medicine to treat injuries from sea creatures," he muttered.

Simber glanced at Ms. Octavia. "Can you communicate with waterrr crrreaturrres, Octavia?"

"I've never done it before, but I can try," the art instructor answered. "I won't know until we get there."

The team began to buzz with excitement. Alex let them talk it out. He was glad to see their enthusiasm. But Sky's face wore a look of dismay. Alex studied her, and then walked over and knelt on the deck by her side. "What's wrong?"

LISA McMANN

She looked at him. "You all seem more excited about saving the creatures than saving my mother."

Alex touched her arm. "Only because they didn't know about the creatures. It's a new development—one I'd only been thinking about recently. They've known all along we were going to save your mother. And, I should add, they all volunteered their time to train for this rescue because of you and your mother, not because of sea creatures. They committed to weeks and weeks of intense training—you know more than anyone how hard we've worked." He smiled, remembering the time she'd tried to leave on a raft to rescue her mother on her own before she even knew how to swim. Impulsively he took her hand. "The entire team will be on backup in case something goes wrong with your mother. Believe me, it's our first priority."

Sky squeezed his hand. "You're right," she said. "I'm sorry. I guess I'm just anxious about it. I really am grateful."

Alex smiled. Reluctantly he pulled his hand away and stood up. "I'm glad you believe me. And now I'm going to make sure everybody else feels the same as we do about the mission."

"Thanks, Alex," Sky said sheepishly. Then she leaned in

and whispered, "Was it your whale that got you so interested in the sea creatures?"

Alex froze. "Um . . . no," he said. "I . . . um . . . I've got to . . ." He whirled around and pointed his thumbs at the group, indicating he had things to do. He flashed an apologetic smile and stepped away to address the others, leaving Sky looking confused.

"It was just a question," she muttered. But he was already out of range.

"Okay, okay," Alex said, waving his hands to get the team's attention. "Quiet down. And let's not forget that our goal here is saving Copper. We'll help the creatures if we can, but only after we've got Copper safe and sound. Clear?"

"Absolutely clearrr," Simber said.

The others nodded. "Of course!" "That's what we're here for." Their voices rang out full of enthusiasm, which eased Alex's mind. He looked at Sky, eyebrows raised.

She put her thumbs up and smiled. "Thank you."

Alex breathed a sigh of relief that the crisis was averted. But he had some jumbled feelings churning inside him that he couldn't seem to straighten out. In addition to his frustration over his

LISA McMANN

inability to concentrate, and his embarrassment over his failures with Spike, Alex couldn't help but feel a bit guilty—because he, too, was more than a little excited to rescue the sea creatures. Perhaps one of them would be so grateful to be free that it would become Alex's special water creature. Fully devoted . . . one who would replace the spot in his heart left cold and empty by his terrible mistake with Spike Furious.

Watching and Waiting

Interspersed with cries of "Thar she blows!" from Captain Ahab, mews in triplicate from Kitten, and the occasional rumblings from Florence or Simber, the conversations on board the pirate ship were mostly earnest and thoughtful as the day progressed into night. And conversations between Alex and Sky were virtually nonexistent as Alex strove to avoid all mention of Spike. Though the longer he kept the secret, the more he began wanting to confess everything to her so he could get it off his chest.

Sky wasn't quite sure what to make of it. After the kiss on

LISA McMANN

the beach, the last thing she expected was for Alex to grow more distant. She had thought the opposite would happen. But she had plenty else on her mind to focus on right now, like rescuing her mother. Everyone on board was trying to focus on the mission, Sky most of all. So she didn't give Alex's behavior much thought.

As they sailed past Warbler Island, the captain kept the ship far from shore at Alex's command—they didn't want Warbler to mistake them as coming to attack, and they kept the ship dark until they were well past the island. It was better not to let them know they had left Artimé vulnerable.

Fox, Kitten, Ahab, Simber, and Florence made up the statue brigade. Ms. Octavia and a handful of squirrelicorns represented the creatures, and Alex, Lani, Samheed, Carina, Sean, Henry, Sky, and Crow were the human factor. It was almost perfect. It would have been nice to have Meghan with them, but she was one of only a few who knew and could handle performing the dissipate spell, which would remove the thorn necklaces from the Warbler children. Alex knew from experience that it was such a painstaking spell, and so dangerous, that a person could only do a few of them a day without tempting great error. The tiniest shaking of a hand could cause irreparable damage—or make someone completely disappear, as had happened quite tragically to Gremily the squirrelicorn during the battle on Warbler.

Alex missed having Meg on this trip. While he and Meghan hadn't spent a lot of time together lately because of all the things they were busy with, he still considered her one of his best friends. Alex walked to the stern of the ship and looked back toward home. The island of Quill was there, he knew, even though it was dark.

Above his head, Simber flapped his wings now and then, but mostly he soared with them outstretched, riding the breeze. The ship moved slowly during the dark hours so that they wouldn't reach Pirate Island until daylight. Since Pirate Island could erupt or sink under the water without notice, Alex didn't want to be too close, and he wanted to be able to see.

"When we get close, you'll make surrre someone looks afterrr the kitten?"

Alex smiled in the dark. "Yes. Henry will take her." They were silent for a bit, and then Alex asked, "Can the captain swim?"

LISA McMANN

"I don't know. It won't help to ask him, so I'll keep an eye on him. I would imagine he'd sink like a rrrock."

"Everybody else can swim," Alex said. "I was careful about that when I was first choosing this group."

"It may not matterrr, if we get sucked into the volcano," Simber said dryly.

"That's not going to happen," Alex said. He hoped very much he was right. But there was no telling when the fiery island would suddenly decide to plunge underwater.

"Have you considerrred anchorrring the ship a distance away and taking a smallerrr crrrew on my back to save the woman?"

"I have," Alex mused. "But you can't possibly carry Florence, can you? We may need her."

The cat growled. "No, you'rrre rrright. I could prrrobably hold herrr a shorrrt amount of time, but not morrre than a few seconds."

"And I don't like having the others so far away if something goes wrong."

Simber nodded. "I agrrree."

"So I guess we just have to wait off shore for the island to sink and resurface, and risk it."

LISA McMANN

"It's underrrwaterrr now," Simber said, his eyes trained on the spot where the island should be. "It's been down forrr quite a while."

"Oh. Well, that's good, then. We'll try our rescue when it comes up and the volcano fire dies down."

"I'll keep you inforrrmed." Simber looked down at Alex. "You should rrrest while you can."

Alex nodded. "I'm headed that way now. Thanks, Sim."

Simber growled in response, which Alex knew was the statue's way of saying "You're welcome."

Everyone slept restlessly as they waited for daybreak. When Sky awoke, she sat at the bow of the ship, gazing forward, occupied with her thoughts. Alex left her alone. His mind was filled with preparations and plans for the rescue. And as much as he longed to sit with her and talk through his failures with Spike, he had to let that go and focus on the rescue.

As it turned out, Alex didn't need Simber to tell him when Pirate Island resurfaced. The captain made it quite clear.

"Thar she blows!" he cried. "Blasted creature. Wretched, elusive sack!" Captain Ahab seemed to think the island was the whale he'd been chasing for years, and no one could convince him otherwise. "Aye, the whale will be the death of us all!"

"There's really no need to be so dramatic," Alex muttered, forgetting the statue was a theater prop and so was inclined to drama. He sat up to watch. He could barely see the volcano outlined against the sky.

Water shot from the mouth of the volcano, followed by fire-balls and enormous flames lighting up the sky. The Artiméans could hear the slap of the water hitting the sea, and the roar and hiss of the volcano spewing molten lava.

They were far enough away that the big wave that rolled toward them was manageable, so they stood at the railing to observe. It was a most spectacular, thrilling, and frightening sight to see.

As the entire ship watched in awe, no one, not even Simber, noticed the slithering creature rise up from the murky water behind them, blinking its electric eyes.

In over Her Head

While everyone else watched the lavaworks display, Simber sampled the air and snapped to attention, looking all around. "Something's wrrrong," he growled.

Alex turned sharply. "What is it?"

Screams and shouts rang out as the head of an enormous electric eel rose out of the water. It bumped against the ship, making the decks shudder.

"Everybody get below!" Florence shouted. "Giant eel!"

The Artiméans fled in all directions. The eel began wrapping itself around the ship, slipping its tail end up and over the

LISA McMANN

port side railing while its head slithered up the starboard side and onto the deck.

Florence lunged for the head, tipping the ship precariously. Everyone on deck tumbled to the side, unable to go anywhere of their own free will.

Simber torpedoed through the air to assist, grabbing the eel's tail end in his jaws, but the slippery creature slid free and slapped Simber with a powerful blast to his head, knocking the cat off balance and sending him careening toward the water. He soared back up, shaking the nonsense from his head after the blow.

"No!" Alex cried, coming to his senses and staggering to his feet. "Come on, guys. Attack!" He rummaged for a spell, shooting off blinding highlighters at the eel's eyes. Its eyes sparked with fire, and Florence cried out. She released her grip on the eel's head as its tail lashed this way and that, seeking its next victim.

"Look out!" Sean cried as the eel wrapped its tail around Carina.

Carina began firing off every spell she knew, even using heart attack spells at the creature, but nothing seemed strong enough for such a beast. The eel lifted her into the air and flung her overboard, into the sea.

Florence let out a war cry like nothing any of them had ever heard before. She rolled to the other side of the deck, sending every human and creature on the ship tumbling again as she reached for the eel's tail.

Simber, back in the air above the ship, went after Carina as the slithering beast grabbed the fox next, flinging him far across the water in the opposite direction.

"Mewmewmew!" screamed Kitten from somewhere on the ship.

"Hang on, everybody!" Florence yelled. And then to Simber, "I've got this, Sim! You take care of everybody else!" She lunged once more, sending Henry and Samheed flying overboard into the water. Simber zoomed overhead, depositing Carina onto the deck once the ship righted itself again and going after Fox. Florence closed a two-handed grip around the tip of the giant eel's tail.

The eel jerked wildly, trying to escape from Florence's grip. It hissed as Florence dug her iron fingers into the creature and began to pull the eel by the tail. It writhed and twisted all the way around the hull of the ship, and it clamped its mouth

LISA McMANN

onto the ship's railing to stop Florence from pulling it any far-ther. Captain Ahab, carrying his wooden leg, which had been knocked loose in all the commotion, began to slam the eel over the head with it. From the ropes, Ms. Octavia unleashed an arsenal of magical spells on the creature that half the humans had never heard of before.

The eel let out a scream as Florence yanked it, and then its mouth let go of the railing and its head jerked down below the water. Florence scrambled to her feet, balancing precipitously with one foot on each side of the ship, and began coiling the eel. Simber soared in and dropped Fox onto the ship. "Arrre you surrre you've got this?" Simber roared at Florence.

"Would I lie to you?" Florence shouted back.

"Simber!" Alex yelled. "Over there!" He pointed out Henry and Samheed.

Simber glanced at the boys bobbing in the water, looked back at Florence, and hesitated in the air. Then he followed Alex's instructions and flew over the sea to rescue the boys.

Just then the eel's body twisted in Florence's hands. Its tail sprang loose from her grip and lashed out, slapping her across one cheek and then the other. Electric sparks shot up and arced like fireworks raining down on the ship. Florence lunged and staggered as the head of the eel rose up and struck at the giant statue. The ship rocked. The eel twisted itself around Florence in jerks and spasms. Florence stumbled, her arms pinned to her chest and her stride shortened by the eel's grasp. She lost her balance, fell backward, and sat down hard, crashing through the deck, her backside coming to rest on the deck ten feet below.

The eel screamed and lurched wildly to the port side. With a mighty twist, it lifted Florence's body up and out of the hole as if she weighed nothing at all. The eel wound around the ebony warrior like a bandage, and then, as a unit, they rolled to one side. Florence, arms tied to her chest by the eel, managed to loosen a hand from the creature's grasp. She flailed blindly, grabbed the railing, and shouted a muffled, "Everybody hang on!"

Simber reached the boys in the water and turned to see what had happened. "Arrre you okay for a bit?" he asked them.

They nodded.

"I'll be rrright back," he growled, and barreled back toward the ship.

Before he could reach it, the ship groaned and tilted precipitously, throwing everyone off their feet once more. With one last lunge against the railing, the eel flipped Florence and drove her over the side, but she wouldn't let go of her grip on it. The eel smashed its head against Florence's hand, forcing her to loosen her grip. Florence hung on for a breathless second, her mummy-wrapped body dangling over the water. "Simber," she called, sounding oddly calm, "as it turns out, I may need a little help after all." Her hand slipped the slightest bit, giving the entire ship a tiny jolt.

Simber roared. He reached his front legs toward her, dodging the waving tail of the eel. Stone clinked against stone as Simber's paws encircled Florence's forearm. When her fingers let go of the railing, Simber beat his wings with all his might, pulling up toward the sky.

But Florence, wrapped in a giant eel, was too heavy. And Simber was too late to do anything else. With a sickening scrape, Florence's arm slid through Simber's grasp. And with an enormous smack, Florence and the eel hit the water and disappeared.

Like a catapult, the ship snapped back, throwing everybody

on board into the sea in the opposite direction. One by one, the shouts and cries of the airborne stopped abruptly as the Artiméans hit the water.

Only Simber's roar never ceased.

When the ship had righted itself, it was clear there was nothing anyone could do about Florence except hope for her to gain the upper hand against the eel and fight her way back up.

Simber turned sharply and shouted for Alex.

"I'm here—I'm fine," Alex called out, a short distance from the ship. "Does anybody have Kitten?"

"She's in my pocket!" Henry yelled from the other side of the ship. He reached down and pulled her out, lifting her above the water's surface. "Is everybody okay?"

"Fine," groaned Carina, who had been flung into the sea twice now. "All the humans are accounted for. Creatures? Statues?"

"Yes, we're all here," Ms. Octavia said. "I'm going after Florence." She dove below the surface and disappeared.

"Blast it!" cried Captain Ahab, who had entangled himself in a rope for safety and was the only one to remain on board. "My leg—I've lost it again." His shout ended with a hiccup and a sob. "Oh, you shimmering beast. You wear a facade, but I know 'tis you, you simmering barrel of blubber!"

"But what can Ms. Octavia do about Florence?" Sky called out. "Even her magic wasn't working against the eel." She paused, then added, "Can Florence swim? How will she get back?"

Simber, silent now, lowered himself to hover just above the water. Alex grabbed a wing on its way down and vaulted onto Simber's back. Crow followed, and Simber flew to assist the others. He began rumbling under his breath.

"Florence!" Alex called, the others joining in. "Florence?" He scanned the water, silently begging Florence to surface. Soon everybody was back on board the ship and craning their necks over the sides, looking for any sign of their Magical Warrior instructor.

"Simber," Alex said quietly, fear creeping up to his throat, "do you know if Florence knows how to swim?"

"What?" Simber looked at him, alarmed. "You told me everrrybody on boarrrd but Kitten and Ahab could swim."

Everybody turned to look at Alex.

"I—I guess I forgot about Florence," Alex said in a small

voice. "I wasn't going to bring her on this journey initially, so when I was reviewing the list, I must have just . . . gotten distracted. And forgotten to ask her like I asked everybody else." He looked down. "And in all my planning, I never pictured something like *this* happening. I mean, did you? Besides," he said, feeling increasingly defensive, "Florence is . . . she's . . . she's supposed to be invincible."

"Invincible!" Simber looked sharply at Alex. "You mean just like Mrrr. Today?" he asked. His voice grew even louder. "Just like me? What's wrrrong with you, Alex? Think, boy!" He plucked Ahab's wooden leg from the water, dropped it to the deck with a clatter, and soared high overhead, circling the ship, peering down at the water as the first sliver of the sun came up and the last belches of fire lit up the sky.

The others shuffled their feet, throwing uneasy glances Alex's way. No one liked to be yelled at by Simber. But Simber yelling at Alex, the head mage? It was mortifying.

There was nothing worse than Simber's disappointment, except perhaps his silence. Alex stood at the railing near the gaping hole in the deck created by Florence's backside, his pride and confidence stinging from the public verbal slap from his closest confidant. He wished he could disappear. Simber had never spoken to Mr. Today like that. Not in front of anyone, at least. It made Alex feel like a child.

He didn't see Lani looking on with sympathy, or Sean and Carina in a heated conversation with Samheed in the corner, or the captain crawling over to retrieve his wooden leg.

What could Alex do? If she couldn't swim, Florence was most certainly at the bottom of the sea by now. Ms. Octavia couldn't bring her back to the surface any better than Alex could. He was tempted to jump in heroically in an attempt to rescue Florence, but that was something the younger Alex might have done, and it would only cause more trouble in the end.

The only question Alex couldn't face was the one that plagued his thoughts now. Sure, Simber had survived weeks stuck at the bottom of the sea, but that was when he was essentially put to sleep—the magic had been pulled out of him. His world didn't exist. But what happened if a creature or statue was alive when it happened? Did statues breathe? And if so . . . could they drown?

An Unsettling Rift

Many intense minutes passed as the reality of the situation hit them—Florence, whom no one ever thought to worry about, was gone, and she didn't seem to be coming back. Sunk to the bottom of the sea, possibly drowned by a giant sparking eel.

Finally Ms. Octavia burst through the surface and sucked in a long breath, and another.

"Did you find her?" Alex shouted. "Is she okay?"

Ms. Octavia held up a tentacle until she could speak. "She's gone," the octogator said finally.

LISA McMANN

"Gone?" Lani gasped. "Like . . . dead?"

"No—sorry. I mean she's not nearby. The eel dragged her away. I caught a glimpse of them heading in that direction at top speed." Ms. Octavia pointed to the west, beyond the fiery island. "I followed for a bit, but the eel was going much faster than I could ever go, and soon they were out of sight." She paused to cover her face for a moment.

Alex thought he heard a sob. But then Ms. Octavia dipped her face down into the water again and wiped it off with a big sigh. She reached for a rope and scrabbled up the side of the ship. When Simber swooped down to help, Ms. Octavia waved him away, as if she couldn't bear the sight of him. Once on board, she began to construct a new leg for the captain like she always did, not realizing Simber had found the old one this time.

Alex looked at Sky, needing desperately to talk about this latest disaster. This was too big for him to handle alone. She held his gaze, and they walked carefully around the hole in the deck to meet at a quiet spot, all awkwardness between them immediately pushed aside.

"Look, Alex, it's not your fault," Sky said. "Florence isn't a child. She's a grown woman. Um, statue. Whatever. She knew the risks of being on a ship. Plus, she *told* Simber she could handle it."

"And besides that," Alex said, "nobody could have predicted that there was anything powerful enough to wrestle Florence off a ship and into the sea." He was still stunned that such a sea creature existed, let alone one so unaffected by their magic.

"Exactly."

"But," Alex went on, "I still feel responsible. I'm in charge. And like Simber said . . . I should've known if she could swim or not. Because maybe Simber would have been able to do something different, or sooner, if he'd known."

"It's not like Simber was just sitting around—he was doing some pretty important things too," Sky reminded him.

But Alex pounded his forehead in frustration. "Another stupid mistake," he said, thinking about Spike. "What are we going to do without Florence?"

Sky rested a cool hand on the back of his neck. "You're being too hard on yourself," she said.

He pulled away. "You don't know the half of it."

LISA McMANN

Sky's hand jerked back like she'd been stung. "Wow. Sorry."

Alex sighed. "No, no, I'm sorry. You were being awesome. As usual," he said, feeling totally miserable. "I'm just mad . . . at myself." He looked past her, over the water. "I don't know what's wrong with me these days."

Sky pressed her lips together and stood there awkwardly, not knowing what to say. She didn't want to make things worse, so she said nothing at all.

Simber kept his distance, aloof, mourning in his own way.

Samheed approached Alex and Sky, his hair wild and standing every which way from the dousing. "It's my fault, Al," he said. "I told you to add Florence to the list at the last minute. I didn't think—"

"Thanks, Sam—I really appreciate it. But it's not your job to think," Alex said, knowing he sounded like a jerk but unable to stop himself. He raised his voice, wanting to be sure Simber picked up on it. "It's my job to think of everything. Didn't you hear? Didn't *everyone* hear?"

Samheed opened his mouth to shoot off a retort, but Sky caught his eye and her look stopped him. She took Samheed by the arm and led him a few steps away, whispering, "He's upset about Simber, not you. And Florence, of course. Any chance you can let this one slide?"

Samheed frowned, but then shrugged. "I guess I could let one dumbhead remark go. Just this once."

Alex, gazing off over the water, turned abruptly and went down the stairs to the deck below to get away from the cat and nurse his wounds—to his pride, and also to his heart from the loss of their beloved Florence.

The Quest
Continues

There was little time to mourn.

After a while, Alex realized the captain was waiting for instructions. And since the volcanic activity had halted and Pirate Island stood quiet, he knew they needed to make their approach before it was too late. Florence would have wanted them to continue with the quest—Alex knew that well enough. He made his way back to the top deck. "To the island, Captain," Alex said.

The ship, sturdy and strong as ever in spite of the hole in the main deck, was soon sailing along at a fast pace, and the subdued passengers tried to forget their shock and sad-

LISA McMANN

ness by cleaning up the mess made by the rocking ship.

Alex ignored Simber, even though he was dying to ask him if he knew anything more about Florence—like did she breathe? But he couldn't bear to be publicly rebuffed again, for failing to find out if everyone on his team breathed or not. Who even thinks about such things? Besides, finding out the answer now didn't matter. She was either dead or alive somewhere in this vast sea, and either way they'd probably never see her again.

Simber flew out ahead of the ship now, perhaps so that no one could see his face. "Not that I care," Alex muttered rather incoherently. He needed a new plan now that they didn't have Florence.

It was with great pain to his soul that he realized they didn't actually need Florence to punch a hole through the glass sky-light. Simber could do it just as easily. So she could have stayed safe in Artimé after all. Of course, then it would have been someone else getting dragged off by the eel. Probably Simber. "Not that I care," he muttered again, louder.

Ms. Octavia looked at him. "When people say that," she said, "they usually mean the opposite. And I suspect you care a great deal about whatever it is you're struggling with." The

LISA McMANN

octogator swished over to Alex. "Did I miss something?"

Alex laughed bitterly. "Yeah, you could say that."

"Do you want to talk about it?"

Alex looked at Simber. He was sure the cat could hear. The cat hears all and knows all—Alex had that ingrained in his memory well enough by now. "No, thank you."

Ms. Octavia followed Alex's gaze. "Ah. I see." She put a tentacle on Alex's arm. "He's feeling guilty, thinking he should have saved her. They were very close friends. You know," she said, turning to look at Alex, "I just realized how alike you two are. No wonder you've finally clashed."

Alex turned toward Ms. Octavia and studied her for a moment. "You've lost your glasses," he said finally.

"Yes," she said with a rueful smile. "They're at the bottom of the sea now. Siggy will find me another pair from his costume box once we get home, I suppose."

Alex's chest tightened. Tears sprang to his eyes. He remembered the last time Ms. Octavia had lost her glasses—on the day Artimé came back to life. Alex had picked them up for her, overjoyed at the sight of her yet still heartbroken because he had to tell her the news that Mr. Today was dead.

Now, with Florence gone and Simber mad, he leaned forward, elbows on the railing, and buried his face in his hands. "I'm so sorry," he choked out.

Ms. Octavia patted Alex's back. "There, there," she said. "It's just a pair of glasses! And I'll tell you a secret—they were purely for vanity. I assure you I can see perfectly."

Alex sighed and breathed in and out. "I know," he said. He kept his face covered. "Mr. Today told me."

"Oh, that Marcus, what a stinker! He wasn't supposed to tell," Ms. Octavia said with a laugh, but her eyes shone, and soon she was weeping openly. "And now Florence. Oh, dear Alex. You've been thoroughly wrung out in ways most of us will never understand."

Alex couldn't speak. After a few minutes, as Captain Ahab guided the ship to the south side of Pirate Island, Alex squeezed the end of one of Ms. Octavia's tentacles and patted the top of it. "Thank you," he said.

And then he sniffed, composed himself, and took his place at the bow of the ship to address the fractured team, for it was also his job to bring them all together once more.

The Bird's-Eye View

It was back to business, and the first team was off to Pirate Island. Alex shoved his feelings aside, more determined than ever not to let anything get in the way of this mission. He could not mess up again.

"Do you see anyone?" he whispered a short while later.

"Not on the upper level," Sky said. She leaned over the skylight of the reverse aquarium—the glassed-in, undersea island habitat that was built around a volcano. She scooped water and sand out of the shallow window well to get a clearer look. Crow pushed in beside her, and Carina, who had seen Copper briefly on their last visit and knew what she looked like, crouched on the other side of the glass. Next to her was a large coil of rope, just in case they had a chance to make a fast rescue.

Simber crouched on the rocks nearby. He ignored the others and stared to the west, sampling the air now and then.

It was a long day with little activity on the upper level. Just the occasional man or woman in dark trousers and bright-colored or white flouncy shirts. Some of the shirts were adorned with gold bars or symbols, and others were plain. Some of the men and women sported tattoos and scars, making them look quite dangerous.

Now and then they saw women in elegant dresses, complete with petticoats and feathered hats that would make Mr. Appleblossom sigh in delight. But there was no sign of Copper in her dingy brown slave clothing.

At nightfall, Simber carried Crow to the ship so he could sleep, but Sky refused to go, so Carina and Alex stayed with her. Their muscles ached from crouching all day.

It was actually easier to see into the reverse aquarium in the dark. And now they could lean over the skylight without fear of casting a shadow and being discovered. The place was lit up, though Alex wasn't exactly sure how. He could see vertical tubes here and there that contained bubbling, glowing lava, but he wasn't sure if they were casting much light or if their primary purpose was for warmth. The constant, slow movement of the globs of lava was quite relaxing and pleasant to watch. Almost too relaxing. Alex felt himself dozing off once or twice but immediately forced himself to stay alert—he couldn't afford any more mistakes. He studied the layout.

The top level, a good distance below them, was simply a suspended, wood-planked walkway around the perimeter of the glass, leading to a single set of large doors. It wasn't well traveled at all. That's where they'd seen Sky and Crow's mother the last time, when she'd told them through Warbleran hand signals that she was a slave. They'd watched her get taken away by a man with gold bars on his shirt.

"What if they killed her?" Sky asked eventually. It had taken her all day to say it out loud, even though Alex knew she'd been worried about that ever since they'd seen her.

No one knew the answer. Instead they tried to memorize the layout of the open areas far below, where large, leafy plants, vegetables, fruit trees, and flowers grew. And there was grass, too, with benches all around. People bustled about

LISA McMANN

the common area, some strolling as if they were enjoying the scenery, others stopping to pick up fruit that had fallen to the ground, still others looking like they were headed somewhere important.

"It's like they think they're outside," Carina mused. "I wonder how often they get out of this cage."

Alex shook his head. "I don't know. I can't imagine they get out very often, except to fish."

"Oh," Carina said, pointing, "there goes somebody out the fishing hatch now. See—one glass door slides open to let them into the holding space. When that inside door closes, the outside door slides open and water pours in over them, but they can hold on to a bar so they don't get swept away. And they've got masks of some sort to help them breathe."

"Shh," Alex warned. He turned and looked expectantly at the shore nearest them. "He's right below the ground over there."

"I don't think he can hear us if he's underwater," Sky said.

Alex felt the blood rise to his cheeks. "I know. I meant in case he swims up to the surface or something."

Sky elbowed him to let him know she was only teasing.

She didn't like the tension between them. But Alex just gave an absentminded smile and stayed focused on the scene below.

"There's that playground where we saw all the children," he said. That glass room was dark now.

The rocks below them shuddered, making everyone tense up. The person who had gone out the fishing hatch came back inside and quickly took off his gear as other people sprang into action inside the island. "I think that's our cue. We should go," Alex said. "Now."

Nobody questioned him.

"Captain, head out to sea immediately! We'll catch up," Alex called, knowing his voice would carry nicely over the water at night.

Within seconds, Ahab, who was standing ready, had the ship pulling away from the volcano. The ground shook again, and Alex, Sky, and Carina hopped onto Simber's back. He took off into the air, and as they passed over the skylight, Alex could see people below scurrying to the walls, where seats dropped down. The people sat down and strapped in, helping children first, then themselves.

"So that's how they don't get hurt with all the plunging

and resurfacing," Alex said, pointing. "They feel the warning shivers just like we did, and they strap in for safety."

Simber started heading for the ship. "Wait a second, please," Alex said, a bit stiffly. It was uncomfortable speaking to Simber, as it still felt like they were fighting, but Alex couldn't dwell on that now. "How do you feel about hovering over the volcano while it sinks? Maybe we can see what happens?"

"Yes!" Carina said. "What do you think, Simber? Is it safe?"

Sky looked on with interest. Everybody wanted to know more about the workings of the strange island.

"As long as no firrre shoots out when it descends, we should be safe and hidden frrrom view."

"And," Alex said, "we'll be able to see down into the hole because it's all lit up. At least until the water covers it. Plus, we've never thought to fly over the top to see where that fire comes from." He grew more excited. "I don't think it spews any fire at all when it goes down, does it, guys?"

Carina and Sky shook their heads. "I don't think so," Sky said. "Only when it comes back up, almost as if the heat inside builds up with the pressure of the water over it, and"—she paused, thinking—"maybe that's what raises the island. The

LISA McMANN

fire under the surface builds up until it lifts the volcano. It explodes and stays above the surface until it cools sufficiently, and then it goes back down again, where the process starts over."

Alex, forgetting himself for a moment, gave her an admiring glance. "Wow," he said, a little breathless. Even if she turned out to be wrong, she sounded really smart.

"That's a good theory," Carina said.

"Thank you," Sky said. "Let's watch."

Simber flew up above the top of the volcano. From here, everyone could see the rectangle of light coming from the sky-light where they had been stationed, and because it was dark out, they could see a few other skylights as well-hidden around the volcano.

"Look!" Alex said, pointing them out. "Over there—that's near where the sea creatures are."

Simber flew above a skylight on the opposite side of the island and dropped down a bit so they could get a better look, but soon the volcano rumbled once more and Simber pulled away. Still, the Artiméans could see, almost like look-ing through a porthole, an entire vat of sea beasts swimming around one another in very tight quarters.

For once the small group was stunned silent. An entire quarter of the glass cage was taken up by a giant squid with wistful eyes the size of Artimé's largest serving platters, and long, beefy tentacles splayed against the glass, as if there was a chance he might will himself through to the other side. If he sat upon the mansion in Artimé, his long tentacles might reach the ground.

In another corner was a beautiful, long-necked sea monster with stout legs and flipperlike feet. As she moved, several humps along her back rose and fell in a rippling pattern.

There were some smaller creatures too, swimming or floating about.

Alex, Carina, Sky, and Simber all stared.

Suddenly light flickered near the aquarium and the creatures inside all startled and moved away from one side of their prison. A familiar shape came into view just as the volcano shuddered harder, threatening to plunge beneath the sea.

It was the giant eel, curled up like a bedspring outside the aquarium. With a touch of its electric tail to a switch on the glass, a door slid open. In one swift motion the eel unfurled, and a new creature torpedoed into the cage. The door slid

LISA McMANN

closed and the eel shot out of sight, leaving the captured crea-tures to marvel over their new cellmate.

Carina gasped. It was Florence.

Her ebony body sank to the bottom of the glass cage, and she didn't move.

Alex shouted, Simber growled, and the volcano groaned. Shaking violently, the entire island and all its inhabitants and attachments plunged into the sea.

A Most Peculiar Dinner

Aaron Stowe waited impatiently for his guests to arrive. After his near epiphany the other night and his newfound powers in the jungle, Aaron was more eager than ever to have other people help him reorganize, reenergize, and rebuild Quill into something much more powerful than it had ever been before. He was anxious to take control of Artimé once and for all.

He knew he had many of the Necessaries on his side—he'd seen to that by giving them food incentives from the Favored Farm. But Aaron could feel the Wanteds distancing themselves. They hadn't gotten much extra attention when the Necessaries

LISA McMANN

did—only a few Unwanteds to use as slaves, which they had to share. And they hadn't had any personal interaction with the government in a while. It was time to bring them back into the fold and remind them how awful it was that Artimé existed. Once Aaron had them back to full devotion, he could slowly reel in the Quillitary once more. When he had everyone's support, combined with the ferocious jungle animals, Aaron would be invincible. He'd take over Artimé, and maybe even the island where those ships had come from.

He even dared picture himself living luxuriously in the mansion in Artimé, ruling over everything. . . . It felt wrong and good at the same time. How would he justify that to the others? It might take some convincing to get them to see that it wasn't the mansion they took issue with—it was the people inside it.

Eva Fathom cleared her throat. Aaron looked up to find her standing in the doorway to his office.

"What is it?"

"It's nearly eight. Shall I summon Liam Healy for dinner?" Eva asked. Liam's home in Quill had been taken over when he went to the Ancients Sector, so Eva had found a small room for him at the top of the palace tower. She'd chosen it for Liam because it had an interesting view overlooking all of Quill, including a close-up view of the barbed-wire ceiling, since the tower helped support it. The room held a few of Justine's things: a dressing table and chair, a few moth-eaten black robes, and a bucket that had once contained a plant.

Aaron shoved his chair back and went to the window to look down over the driveway. "Is anyone else here?"

"No."

Aaron's eyes strayed to the outer wall, where the window to the sea had been. He frowned at the cement blocks and tapped his fingers on the windowsill. "Let's wait. I thought you said they'd be coming."

"No, I said there was a chance."

"How did you invite them? Were you polite?"

"More polite than you would have been," Eva said.

Aaron strained to look down the drive toward the portcullis. "Someone's coming, I think," he said. He could feel a tiny shred of excitement building up, and he didn't try to stop it. How long had it been since he'd had any company at all? Besides grumpy old Eva Fathom, of course. "Call Liam."

"Am I to join you for dinner?" Eva asked.

Aaron turned around to look at her. He stared for a moment. "I suppose. I hadn't thought about you."

Eva offered a thin smile. "Of course you hadn't." Whatever sarcasm was in her voice went undetected. "Please accompany yourself to the dining room in five minutes."

Aaron nodded and turned back to the window. "Perhaps six minutes so I don't appear too eager."

"Oh, just make it ten, then." Eva whisked down the hallway, shaking her head.

Liam and Eva arrived in the dining room just as former governor Strang was ushered in. He had cleaned up quite well—his hair was cut short, his mustache shaved, and his beard trimmed neatly. He wore fresh clothing, though his protruding belly threatened to burst the buttons on his jacket. He almost looked like a fine young man in his early twenties once more, rather than a middle-aged slob who had given up on life.

"Good evening, Secretary," Strang said nervously as Eva and Liam entered. He held his hand out to Liam. "Hello. I'm Septimus Strang."

"Of course, Governor," Liam said. "Liam Healy, at your service."

LISA McMANN

Strang laughed uneasily. "Former. Ah, governor . . . that is." He pulled a wrinkled hankie from his pocket and wiped his forehead.

"As you wish. Well met, sir," Liam said.

"Certainly." Strang looked at Eva with a pained expression. "Is it just us tonight, then?"

"No, no. The high priest will be along presently. He's had a very busy day and is running a bit behind. Help yourself." Eva pointed to a table, where a tray with a pitcher of water and some glasses rested. "There may be one more guest as well. I'm not sure."

Strang hurried over to the table, poured a glass of water with a shaky hand, and gulped it down. He poured a second glass and held on to it.

Liam looked around the room. The palace was a bit fancier than anything he'd seen in Quill before, but it was just as colorless and uninviting. After catching a glimpse of Artimé, everything here looked bland.

A moment later Aaron entered the room wearing one of Justine's black robes. He looked to Eva.

Eva withheld the urge to laugh at how ridiculous he looked,

and announced, "May I please present the High Priest Aaron? High Priest, I believe you are well acquainted with former Governor Strang and Liam Healy."

Aaron held a limp hand out to the others as Justine had done when he'd first dined with her.

Strang hesitated and then awkwardly bowed over Aaron's hand without actually touching it. "May Quill prevail with all I have in me," he said. He'd taught that very mantra to Aaron when the boy first went to university.

Liam frowned but followed Strang's lead. "May Quill prevail . . . ," he said, and left it at that.

There was a noise at the palace entry. Eva looked at Aaron and raised her eyebrow. Aaron lifted his chin and strained to hear. They didn't have to wait long to discover that Gondoleery Rattrapp had arrived.

The guard at the door tried to accompany her, but the eccentric old woman pushed ahead and burst into the room, wearing a bright orange cape over her drab Quill clothing. Her hair stood on end, and her face was as red and blistery as it had been the day before—perhaps even more so. There were several fresh burn marks on her forearms and fingers.

"Hello," she said. Aaron held his hand out so Gondoleery could give the proper greeting, but she breezed past and went over to the tray to pour herself some water. She dipped her burned fingers into the glass.

Aaron gaped and put his limp hand down. He hadn't seen Gondoleery since before the Restorers attacked Artimé. She'd changed quite a bit from their days of plotting outside the palace gate.

"Good evening, Gondoleery," Eva said. "What a shocking cape you're wearing. Wherever did you find something so . . . colorful?"

"I used orange and red peppers from the Favored Farm as a dye," she said. "They stained my fingers, so I figured they would stain cloth as well."

Aaron frowned and glanced at Strang, who was appropriately frowning too. Aaron held his tongue, but he knew Justine would not approve of color like that in clothing. And neither would he.

Soon they were all seated around the table, and kitchen workers brought the food in and placed it before the guests. Aaron nodded at Secretary in approval—it was a fine-looking meal, for once.

Gondoleery attacked her food as if the chicken on her plate were still alive and running wild. Liam tried not to scarf his down, but he hadn't been eating well at the Ancients Sector and it showed in his thin body—he was hungry.

Strang savored his food. "This is a lot better than when Justine was high priest," he said to no one in particular, but then gave Aaron a fearful look. "I hope it's all right for me to say that. I mean no disrespect to her. I think it must be so delicious because of your Favored Farm."

"I'm always pleased to hear about how our people are enjoying the improvements in Quill," Aaron said. The forks and knives resumed clinking and clanking. After a moment Aaron turned to Gondoleery. "How did you hurt your hands?"

"I didn't," Gondoleery said. She stabbed at a potato and missed.

Aaron looked at the woman's burns. "Are you sure?"

"Quite sure." She looked at him, fork poised to stab the potato once more. "So, High Priest, how do you plan to keep Quill from being attacked now that the idiots in Artimé have been attracting visitors?"

"I have plans," Aaron said. "But I'm curious, how would you do it?"

"It's not my problem now, is it?" Gondoleery skewered the potato, popped it in her mouth, and set down her fork as she chewed.

"Well, that's what I'd like to talk to you all about," Aaron said. "I've invited you here because I'm looking to bring back governors to the ruling board in Quill. I need people who will appeal to the Wanteds yet keep the Necessaries from revolt." He looked around the table, from Liam to Gondoleery to Strang. "I'd like you to be my governors, and I hope you will consider it."

"What's in it for us?" Gondoleery asked, picking her teeth with a charred fingernail. "Besides work?"

Aaron smiled. *At last*, he thought. He pushed back his plate, set his utensils down, and folded his hands in front of him. "My dear Gondoleery, I'm so very glad you asked."

Breathe to Survive

Florence!" Alex shouted. But there was no chance Florence could hear him. She was stuck inside the glass cage, plunging farther and farther beneath the sea.

Simber circled above the water, with Alex, Carina, and Sky all straining to see below the surface. It was no use.

"Shall we go down after her?" Carina said, ready to jump.

Alex put a hand on her arm. "Wait," he said. "Let's just think this through. The eel's down there."

Carina bit her lip. "Right," she said, somewhat reluctantly.

Finally Alex directed Simber back to the ship. "We need a

LISA McMANN

plan. Let's go talk this through with the others." He knew that if Florence was alive, she could stay alive in that cage, and at least they knew where she was now. And if she was dead . . . well, then staying down there wouldn't change that, either. So it was best to be cautious.

When Simber and his passengers reached the ship, Alex called a meeting and shared everything they had witnessed.

"I think we should take a team underwater to explore," Sean said. "See how far down the island goes."

"No way. Not with that eel slinking around," Ms. Octavia said. "We don't need any more of us trapped in an underwater cage. Not even I can survive more than an hour or so without air."

Simber circled overhead, having no place to land. Fox and Kitten chattered in a corner, and Captain Ahab sat calmly on a bench, saying nothing for now.

"So *you* brrreathe," Simber said abruptly.

Alex looked up. "What?"

"Ms. Octavia, I mean. You cannot surrrvive without airrr?"

Ms. Octavia looked up too and regarded him. "Why, yes, of course. Don't you breathe?"

LISA McMANN

"I can smell things. But I don't need to brrreathe to surrr-vive." Simber swooped to the other end of the ship. "Kitten," he said, "do you brrreathe to surrrvive?"

"Mewmewmew!" said Kitten.

Fox stepped up to interpret as usual. "She says that she loves breathing, and breathing is a very important part of her day, one of her very favorite parts, in fact—"

"Quiet!" Simber said, startling everyone but staring at Fox. "Fox, *I* underrrstand quite well what Kitten is saying, thank you, and it's *neverrr* what you think. In case you didn't rrrealize, like Kitten I am also a cat. And you, you little piece of terrrmite bait, arrre not. You arrre a fox, the smallest memberrr of the Vulpini trrribe of the Canidae family; to wit, you arrre a *dog*. By the law of the land, you and cats would not be frrriends. Not everrr. And while Kitten may cerrrtainly decide forrr herrrself that she wants to be frrriends with you, though I can't imagine why, I am telling you rrright now forrr the firrrst and only time: Neverrr, everrr trrry to tell me what Kitten says again. Because you arrre always dead wrrrong. Is that clearrr?"

Fox stood frozen in fear. After a long moment he licked his lips and said in a very small voice, "D-d-did you j-j-just say . . .

I m-m-mean, that is to say, um . . . Aw, nuts." He looked down at the deck and was quiet.

"Mewmewmew," Kitten said to Simber.

Simber paused mid-flap, a look of pure disbelief on his face. "What do you mean, Fox thought he was a cat?"

"Mewmewmew!"

"A cat whose name is Fox? Now I've hearrrd everrrything. Good grrracious." The giant feline began flapping his wings once more so as not to go plunging into the ocean. "Well then, I'm surrre this rrrevelation has come as a bit of a shock," he grumbled, softening his tone a bit. "Therrre now, you prrre-posterrrous little rrratbeast. None of us wants to hearrr that sorrrt of news, I suppose."

He frowned and circled the ship. "Back to my question, which is of grrrave imporrrtance. Kitten, you said you do not need to brrreathe to surrrvive, you only like to sniff things. Quite underrrstandable forrr a cat." Simber looked around. "What about you, Fox?"

Fox flattened himself on the deck and put his paws over his eyes. "This cannot be happening," he moaned. "This cannot be happening."

LISA McMANN

Simber sighed and looked at Kitten. "Any chance you know the answerrr?"

"Mewmewmew," said Kitten.

Simber's face brightened. "So he doesn't need to brrreathe eitherrr." He turned to Captain Ahab. "What about you?"

"Aye. Whither lives the briny beast, so too live I."

Simber rolled his eyes. "Okay, so that's a yes forrr you and yourrr imaginarrry whale. You both need to brrreathe to surrrvive."

"Aye," said the captain.

Alex bit his lip and looked down, thinking of Spike, who, like Ms. Octavia, had definitely been breathing.

Simber frowned, still looking at Ahab. After a while, he said in a quiet voice, "That's quite trrroubling, indeed." He flew off toward the water that covered the volcano, flying low, as if it would bring back his comrade.

Alex leaned over toward Lani, wanting to make sure he wasn't mistaking what Simber was saying. "He's asking because of Florence, right?"

"I guess so," Lani said. She moved over so that Samheed could join them. "So far, it seems like all the statues except

LISA McMANN

Ahab can stay alive without breathing. I think he was trying to guess if Florence could possibly be alive."

"But apparently there's no rule," Alex said, pondering. "Some breathe, some don't."

"Unless you account for the fact that Florence and Ahab are human statues. Ahab needs to breathe. Ms. Octavia needs to breathe, but she's not a statue, she's a . . . a creature, I guess."

"Like Spike," Alex murmured.

"Who?"

"Never mind."

"Anyway, the point is that Ahab is a statue who needs to breathe. And the other statues who don't need to breathe, like Simber and Kitten and Fox, are not human."

Alex looked at Lani with alarm. "Oh. So is Florence like Ahab? Or like Simber?"

"I hope she's like Simber," Lani said. "But I'm afraid she might be like Ahab." She turned toward him. "So now there's a question that Simber probably wants to ask you. But since you're both being ridiculous, he can't get up the nerve to be all vulnerable or whatever. So I'll ask it for him: If we can rescue

LISA McMANN

Florence, and if she's dead, do you think you can bring her back to life?"

Alex didn't know. He grew intensely thoughtful, not noticing that the others had gathered now too, some in the shadows, to hear his answer.

He knew he could re-create the world of Artimé if it disappeared. He could put statues and creatures to "sleep," and the restore spell would bring them back to life. But what if they died? *Could* they die? He'd never seen a creature or statue die. Well, except for Gremily, but she didn't die, she disappeared, which wasn't the same. But Alex was quite certain that the whale he'd brought to life was on its last gasp before he put her to sleep, so he was pretty sure that creatures could die. But what about Florence? And if she could die, would the live spell work on her to bring her back to life? And if it would work on Florence, would it work on anything or anyone who had died?

At last he rubbed his temples and said, "If Florence is not a breathing statue, then she should be just fine no matter how long she is underwater. However, I think that if a statue or creature relies on breath to live, they must also be capable of dying. So if Florence is a breathing statue, I'm sure she is dead now."

He was quiet for a moment as that assessment sank in. "I also think, as with humans, if creatures or statues die, their death is final. There is no spell that would bring anyone who breathes back from death—not human, statue, or creature. Or we would most certainly have used it by now."

Aaron Strikes a Deal

My goal," Aaron said as dessert was being served, "is to be rid of the Unwanteds once and for all. However—and this may sound a bit shocking, but I hope you'll give me a chance to explain—as much as I despise the Unwanteds and their devious, dangerous ways, I admit I rather like the world they've constructed. I'd hate to see it go to waste. Think about it—just because we are accustomed to living with so little here in Quill doesn't mean we have to continue to do so. It seems a waste to destroy their mansion and fountains when ours are falling apart and water is scarce. Winning wars and taking over

LISA McMANN

territories should come with rewards, don't you think?"

He looked around at the skeptical faces, but he wasn't worried. He guessed that they, like him, had been secretly curious about the way things worked in Artimé. "Before I tell you what's in it for you, I want you to know it's okay if you'd like to think about it, and you may of course say no if you are not at all interested. But my plan for our mutual reward is to split the magical property four ways. Not equally, quite, but you would each get a small portion of Artimé if you were to commit to helping me."

Eva looked hard at a spot on the table.

"I count five of us," Gondoleery said.

Aaron looked around, confused. "No," he said. "You, Liam, Strang, and me. Four."

Gondoleery leaned forward. "What about Eva? Is she a ghost? Don't you see her sitting next to you?"

"Who?" Aaron asked, looking first to the wrong side, and then at Eva. "Oh, you mean Secretary? Well, I'll take her with me, of course. She'll be allowed to live in the mansion in one of my rooms."

Gondoleery frowned and picked her teeth.

Liam picked up the questioning. "I realize I don't really have much of a choice to make, since it's either this or back to the Ancients Sector, but I'd like to say that I'm in favor of this plan." He glanced at Eva, but she remained still, not looking at him.

"Excellent," Aaron said. "Strang? Any questions?"

"I—I'm not sure how the High Priest Justine would have felt about living in such a colorful place. It could be very distracting." He scratched his head. "It doesn't feel right when everything we hate about the creative people would be so evident and, ah, in our faces. I mean, the flowers and trees, and I can only imagine what the inside of that dreadful place must look like. . . ." He trailed off.

"I can assure you," Aaron said, "if only Justine had been given time to take over Artimé before she was expelled from this life, she would have made that mansion hers. She would have thought it a waste to tear down a structure so useful. And while the decor is ridiculous, it could be toned down to a nice shade of gray and we could get rid of all the useless things. And let's not forget how Justine was decorating this palace. She had plants. *Indoors*." He shook his head.

Strang wiped his forehead.

Gondoleery leaned toward Aaron. "But wait," she said. "You're assuming Justine would have been able to keep the magic going. Don't forget what happened when Marcus Today was killed. How are you going to keep Artimé if there aren't any Unwanteds running the magical world? We'd need some-one who at least knows a little bit about magic." She batted her eyelashes innocently and glanced at Eva. "Because clearly none of us can do a thing."

Eva's mouth twitched. She glanced at Liam, saw he was watching Gondoleery, and dropped her eyes to the table.

Aaron's expression barely flickered, but he wondered now just what the extent of his abilities was—if he could make a living statue's tail from a vine and release shackles from his wrists, maybe he could do more. Maybe *he* could run the magic in Quill. He hadn't even begun to explore the boundaries of his abilities. "I'm still working out the details," he said coolly, "but I won't be disclosing my solutions until I know who is interested in helping me take Quill to a stronger, more pow-erful level."

Strang shifted uncomfortably. "High Priest, if I may." He

coughed and took a sip of water. "I—I would like to be a governor again, if for the pure reason of making Quill stronger. But I don't need any colorful world or mansion to live in. I need no reward at all."

"Suit yourself," Aaron said matter-of-factly. He smiled, pleased. "So that's two fine governors so far." He turned to Gondoleery. "Need more time to think? Or shall I look for someone else to take the spot I've been holding for you?"

Gondoleery fingered a dried-up scab on her wrist. "Oh, I'll take the job, all right," she said. She stood abruptly. "When do we start?"

Aaron held back a smile. "Now. Your first task, each of you, is to figure out ways to create distrust and unrest between our people and the people of Artimé. I don't mean physical altercations in Artimé like you've done in the past, Liam. What we need to do is get all of Quill to begin banking their rage once more—building up their anger toward Artimé the way Justine did it when she was high priest, through words and ideas. Through thoughts." He hesitated. "And I suppose a few faked incidents of injustice to our people would help speed things up. After all, I don't want to spend fifty years getting there. And," he added, "I'd maybe even like to give the people of Artimé a little hint of whom they are dealing with." He studied the faces before him to see their reactions.

Eva Fathom frowned. Strang stared at the table, his leg jiggling nervously. Liam studied Aaron, tapping his lips. And Aaron could see by the look in Gondoleery's eyes that her thoughts were far, far away.

Later, after Strang and Gondoleery had left, Aaron turned to Eva and Liam. "It's time for a speech from the beloved high priest," he said. "Prepare for a gathering in the Commons." He gave a curt nod good night and headed to his bedroom.

Eva walked with Liam to the stairs that would take him up to his room.

"He's dangerous on a small scale," Eva whispered once Aaron was out of earshot. "Gondoleery's the one we need to watch."

"Forgive me—I still don't quite understand what's going on," Liam said.

Eva pressed her lips together, debating. Should she tell him what she suspected? What she knew and remembered to be

LISA McMANN

true? If Gondoleery had mastered ice, and was now covered in burns, it wouldn't be long before Quill would be swirling in dust. And Eva wasn't strong enough to take on Aaron *and* Gondoleery single-handedly. She had to risk it.

She leaned forward. "I've known Marcus, Justine, and Gondoleery since we were young children," she said. "And when I was a child, I could make it rain."

The Story of Eva Fathom

Eva's eyes darted down the hallway to make sure the high priest hadn't returned. "Can I trust you?"

Liam whispered, "You know you can, and I think you already do. You've known where I stood ever since you tested me in Haluki's house. Are you saying what I think you're saying? That you and I are on the same side—*against* him?"

Eva peered at him in the shadows. "I tested you, yes. I suggested the prisoners should be killed. You couldn't respond. That was the moment I knew—you're absolutely right."

"I couldn't kill Claire or anyone. Eva, I buried the mage of

Artimé. I feel sick about it still. What he—what Aaron was doing . . ." Liam's face was desperate. "It was wrong, Eva. I know that now. I'd rather be sent back to the Ancients Sector than do anything like that again. And now I'm living this farce. . . ."

Eva regarded Liam for a long moment. "I have no choice but to trust you. I need your eyes."

"You have them. All I can do is promise and hope you'll take me at my word, but you know already where my allegiance lies or you wouldn't have brought me with you to Gondoleery's door. You wouldn't have given the driver that food in front of me if you didn't trust me. And now I'm here, living in the palace, when there are dozens of Necessary homes I could live in. . . . You want me here. Don't you?"

"I do," Eva admitted.

"And do you . . ." He hesitated. "Do you know why I wasn't put to death right away? Do you know why they kept me alive and not Bethesda?"

Eva pursed her lips. "Yes, Liam. I do."

Liam's eyes widened. He swallowed hard and passed his hand over his face. He whispered in a shaky voice, "You did it? You kept me alive?"

She stared at him for a long moment and then nodded. "But what matters now," she said with urgency, "is that you do the right thing with your second chance. And I believe you will. I need you to. Before things get even more out of hand."

Liam reached out and put his hand on Eva's shoulder, a look of earnest truth and respect in his deep blue eyes. "My mind and heart have left the fog of Quill. I'll do the right thing now. I'll help you in any way I can. You can trust me."

Eva shook Liam's hand. "Then we shall ride this risky road together. We have two tracks. In the short term, Aaron seems restless and eager to do something to antagonize Artimé. I don't know what it is yet, but he does things in haste, and he's sure to make a mistake. And . . ." She hesitated, unsure she wanted to share such delicate information, but then went on. "Many of the leadership in Artimé are away for a time, but no one must know that. I need to keep Aaron from doing something stupid while Artimé is vulnerable."

Liam nodded. "And the other track . . . the long term?"

"Yes. That's Gondoleery. She'll be stealthy and deliberate. But when she strikes, she'll take us all down."

"Strikes? With what? What power does she have?"

LISA McMANN

"She'll have more power than anyone if she figures out how to use it." Eva lost herself in memories for a few moments. She sank to sit on the steps. "I have a story to tell."

"Then tell it, please."

Eva nodded and then began in a faraway voice. "When I was a child, I could make rain, ice, and fire."

"What's ice?" Liam asked. He sat down on the step next to her.

"Ice is frozen water, hardened like a rock, and so cold it hurts to hold it."

Liam wore a quizzical look, finding the explanation hard to follow, but he remained silent so she could explain.

"Gondoleery Rattrapp could make rain, but not ice or fire. Marcus could do any elemental magic he put his mind to, but he preferred to leave the weather alone—he was so much more creative than that. And Justine couldn't do any elemental magic at all, and not much other magic either. But she made a good bully." Eva's eyes narrowed, remembering.

She went on. "When we came to Quill, and Justine—through Marcus—made the original Quillens forget our pasts, we forgot our magic. But not long ago, Marcus gave

Gondoleery and me our memories back. Now Gondoleery is relearning all her magic, and I think she's plotting to do something horrible with it. That's why she's got burns all over her hands. She's already been successful at making ice—I saw it with my own eyes. And now she's trying to figure out how to throw fire."

Liam stared at Eva in alarm. "That's horrible! What is the high priest doing about it?"

Eva pressed her lips together. "I've told him that something strange is going on with Gondoleery. His response is apparently to celebrate it by putting her in charge of the government." Eva sighed in frustration. "I haven't told him about the fire part of it yet—that was the first I've seen of it from her, when I was with you yesterday. Before I say anything, I want to see if she manages to do more than give herself a few burns. She couldn't throw fire when we were children. I find it hard to believe she can master it now."

"Maybe Aaron asked her to be governor so he could keep an eye on her."

Eva shrugged. "If that's the reason, it would be the single smartest thing that obnoxious boy has done so far. But I don't see it. He's too arrogant to think anybody could possibly have more power than him."

Liam looked troubled. "What do you want me to do?"

"Keep your eyes open. Watch everything. Check on the vacant homes in the Necessary quadrant to see if you find anything strange happening, like the orange glowing we saw from Gondoleery's window, or possibly blue, which would be ice. But above all, keep an eye on Aaron. Gain his trust. Do what he's asking you to do . . . and if you can't, fake it."

"And what about Gondoleery?"

"I'm trying to keep up with her, magicwise. I need a new place to practice, because Aaron nearly caught me making ice and then melting it all with fire in Haluki's house. But I'm changing tack after what Aaron said tonight about letting Artimé know whom they're dealing with. I'm going to focus on him at least until Alex, Simber, and Florence get back to Artimé. Because if Aaron goes in there now to show his muscles, there's a very good chance somebody could get hurt."

Eva Fathom and Liam Healy talked long into the night, Eva filling him in on the original plan she'd had with Marcus and how everything had gone wrong. Liam was brimming with questions, but there were two that pestered him most, and finally he asked, "How do you know so much about what's happening in Artimé? Don't you have a daughter there?"

Eva shook her head. "That's one secret I need to keep for now."

Liam nodded and was silent, too scared to ask the question that had plagued him all the time he'd languished in the Ancients Sector. He was well aware that he didn't deserve to know the answer. But the guilt never let up, and his mind never let go. *Is Claire okay?*

A Sighting

By morning word spread that Florence had been seen but no one had been able to tell if she was alive or dead. All the Artiméans could do while the island was underwater was go over their newly revised plan and wait for the volcano to surface again.

Alex laid down the logic. "We can't release the creatures and rescue Florence until after we have Sky and Crow's mother, or else the pirates will know we're here and it'll ruin everything. So we've got to get Copper first and then immediately be ready to break into the aquarium and get Florence. Simber," Alex said, not looking at him, "I may need you to break the glass skylight. We'll try the route through the fishing hatch first, of course. Obviously we don't want the whole population to drown if the volcano sinks and water starts pouring in the hole, but hopefully I'd have time to repair it with a glass spell before they'd go down again."

"I can brrreak glass, as you well know."

Alex frowned. He knew, all right. Simber had had to shatter a glass wall spell in Justine's palace once, long ago. "Well, good. Is everybody clear on the plan?"

They were clear.

"Let's take the ship out a little farther, Captain," Alex said. "And batten down the hatches, or whatever. We're going to have another giant wave when the island comes up."

The captain gave the order to nobody in particular. Sean and Lani took over the battening, and soon everyone was making sure their things were secure. "At least this time we can all swim," Sean said.

"I'm still climbing up the ropes," Sky muttered. She was a bit on edge due to all the waiting. It was hard, wondering whether her mother was even alive, not to mention where she could possibly be in that . . . that giant terrarium. Add in Alex's

LISA McMANN

recent weird behavior, and it was enough to unsettle anybody.

She stood with Crow at the back of the ship, staring in the
direction of where the island should be, as Ahab maneuvered
the ship away. Alex joined them.

"Hey," he said. "I'm just checking in. Are you guys doing
all right?" He kept his eyes trained on Crow, only flitting to
Sky for a split second now and then.

Crow shrugged. "Yeah."

Sky gave Alex a grim smile and lied. "I guess." They were
quiet for a moment. "What if she never passes underneath
that skylight again?"

There were so many what-ifs. Alex had a lot of ideas about
what to do. Dangerous ones. He didn't want to have to carry
any of them out. Now he met Sky's gaze. "We'll find her," he
said, and he meant it. "We'll man the other skylights too, now
that we know where they are. We're not leaving here until we
have your mother with us."

Sky looked up at Alex, her eyes glistening. Maybe she had
imagined the growing distance between them. She popped up
on her tiptoes and planted a kiss on Alex's cheek.

He closed his eyes briefly, as if in pain, and then smiled, but when he lifted his lids again, the distance was back in his eyes.

They slept in shifts throughout the day, watching. Waiting. Talking. Playing games to pass the time. Sleeping some more. Henry taught Crow, Sean, and Fox about the different ingredients he used in his medicines. Lani pulled the wrinkled, ragged-edged paper from her bag once more, smoothed it, and studied it for hours before she got tired of it and put it away. Sky kept to herself.

It wasn't long before every one of them went from eager to on edge. They tried not to let the close quarters and anxiety lead to arguing and short tempers, but it didn't always work. Alex and Simber's short bits of communication remained strained. And during the quiet times when Alex allowed himself to get lost in his thoughts, he worried quite a bit that things would never be the same between him and the stone cheetah and that their relationship was permanently damaged. It was painful, but it also made him mad, like he wanted to punch somebody in the face. Worse, he didn't know how to fix it, and that scared him. A lot.

And then there was Sky. Alex kept having to push her face from his mind. He couldn't deal with those feelings on top of everything else. And he couldn't mess this up. He wouldn't. Being mage, performing a successful mission—it was way more important than anything.

When Pirate Island finally came shooting up out of the water and it blew its stack, everyone jumped into action. The wave came on strong, and Captain Ahab steered the ship into it. The wall of water hit them, washing a few of them overboard despite their preparations, but Simber plucked them out of the water as usual, and other than a few bumps and bruises, everyone was all right. Even Captain Ahab managed to keep his wooden leg, which gave the statue nothing to moan about afterward, so the entire course of events went along rather ho-hummedly.

For the next length of time, they watched the fiery lava sputter and hiss in the water as Captain Ahab brought them a bit closer to the island. When the volcano stopped steaming and it appeared safe to go ashore, the team disembarked. This time, knowing there would be warning tremors when the island was about to sink, Alex ordered small groups to the other skylights they'd found, and he assigned Sky, Crow, and Carina each with a different group so they'd have a better chance of spotting Copper.

Just as dusk was falling, a shout rang out. Sky, Fox, Ms. Octavia, and Alex scrambled to their feet. A second later, Simber came soaring toward them and landed. They hopped onto his back as he explained.

"Crrrow spotted herrr," he said. "She hasn't noticed them yet."

Sky nearly leaped from Simber's back as he was still attempting to land. She joined her brother. "Where?" she demanded.

"There, with the brown dress. She's carrying a bucket and a mop. See?"

Sky strained against the daylight just as the interior lights of the underwater island began to turn on. "I see her!" she cried. "Oh, that's her, all right." She rubbed Crow's back. "She's alive! Good job, Crow. We can't let her out of our sight."

Ms. Octavia and Fox took a good look at the woman. "We'll head back to our skylight," Ms. Octavia said, "so we can watch if she visits that side of the island."

"Sim, will you take me to the third skylight?" Alex asked. "I can recognize her now."

Simber nodded brusquely and Alex climbed on. They traveled to the third spot in silence.

Alex slid off and joined the small group that huddled there, filling them in on what was happening. "Have the squirrelicorns come out here," he said to Simber, "and post them two per skylight so they can spread the word if we have to act fast. And they can help get us back to the ship if the island sinks."

Soon six squirrelicorns could be seen circling their posts, while everyone else remained still and on the watch for Copper.

From time to time, when there were few pirates moving about, Alex's glance moved to the distant glass cage where the sea creatures were kept. Florence lay in the same position as before, unmoving. Alex's gut twisted.

As the evening progressed, colorfully dressed pirates emerged through the set of large doors on the upper floor and mingled with each other, leaning over the sides of the walkway and looking out at the sea creatures in the glass cage. Or they appeared briefly, barking out orders to other, younger pirates or to the few in drab brown clothing like Copper. Not one of them looked up at the skylights, but the Artiméans were also careful not to attract any attention.

Lani gasped once, and nearly fell onto the glass when she was observing two pirates talking to each other as they unrolled a scroll and studied it.

"What is it?" Samheed asked. "Did something happen?"

Lani stared at the scene below. "That scroll—those two pirates are looking at it. The drawing on it looks . . . interesting. Like maybe I've seen something like it before."

"Oh, brother," Samheed said. "You're supposed to be watching Copper, remember?"

Lani scowled and didn't respond. She strained her eyes to get a better look, but just then one of the pirates glanced around, so she had to duck to keep from being seen. When she dared to look again, they had gone down to the lower floor. They opened a glass display case near the stairs, unrolled the scroll, and pinned it inside. Then they closed the case once more and looked down into it at their drawing.

"What are they doing?" she whispered.

Samheed turned to look at her. "Will you focus, please?"

LISA McMANN

Lani felt like arguing—she was definitely focused. But not on Copper. Reluctantly she held her tongue. "I guess it was nothing," she said.

Copper stayed in view below, scrubbing the wood-plank walkway near a young man who was washing the glass walls. For the most part, the pirates ignored them.

Eventually the top level of the underwater island quieted, and more people made their way down the stairs. On the lower floor, they went individually through smaller doors.

"It looks like the upper floor is where some of them work, and the lower floor is where they live," Alex noted. "Plus, there's a stairway that goes down another flight." He couldn't see anything down there.

Soon Copper stood up straight and stretched, wiping her forehead with her sleeve. She signaled to the window washer, using Warbleran sign language.

"Do you think he's from Warbler too?" Ms. Octavia asked.

"Yes," said Fox. "I'm sure of it."

Alex couldn't help but glance at Simber to see the cat's reaction, but when Simber did the same to Alex, both quickly looked away. Alex frowned and concentrated on Copper and the man below.

The man nodded. The two of them packed up their cleaning supplies and made their way down a sweeping spiral staircase to the terrarium floor, where the pirates had gone. But Copper and the man kept going down the stairs to the floor below that. Soon their heads disappeared from sight.

When Alex heard a sound behind him, he looked up. It was Sky and Lani.

"Alex," Lani said, "we need a meeting. You, me, Henry, Sky, and Ms. Octavia. Sky has an idea."

Sky's Plan

I noticed something interesting about the pirates," Lani began. "Henry noticed it too. They look like us."

Alex knit his brow. "Like us?" He didn't understand. "You mean like Unwanteds? I didn't know we had a look."

"No," Lani said. "Like Henry and me. Most of them have our skin color, and, well, they just look like us."

"A lot of the kids down there have straight black hair, like Lani and me," Henry explained. "And many of the pirates we can see have blue eyes, like us. You know what I mean? Like they could be in our family."

"Okay . . . ," Alex said, still unsure why they needed to have a meeting about this. "Do you think you have relatives here too, who need rescuing? Is that what you're saying?" If so, Alex was getting a bit tired of this rescue game.

"I—" Lani started to say, then paused, considering Alex's question for a moment. "Well, I don't know about that, but I just noticed the resemblance, and I said something to Sky about it. And she came up with a remarkable plan. Tell him, Sky."

Sky's orange eyes lit up. "Well, I was thinking, if Lani and Henry were willing, and if you didn't think it was too danger-ous, that maybe they could go inside disguised as some of the people who live here. They could find my mother and explain who they are and then plot an escape out the fishing hatch."

Alex pondered the idea. "Yes," he said slowly, "and they could help her with the underwater part. I've been very worried about that—I assume your mother is like other Warblerans and never learned to swim?"

"Right. She can't," Sky said. She flashed a grateful smile at Alex.

"Henry and I can take her right through it and swim her to

the surface fast," Lani said. "She'll be fine, right, Henry?"

Henry nodded.

"But how are you going to get inside?" Ms. Octavia asked. "You'll be soaking wet if you just dive down and go in. The pirates use waterproof suits and helmets when they go out to fish. I've been watching."

"I'm going to sneak in through the hatch and borrow them," Sky said. Her voice held an edge to it, as if daring Alex to say no.

Alex stared at the water, lost in thought. He didn't say no. He thought it was a great idea, actually. "Fine. I'll go with you. We'll get two suits in one trip—that'll be the best way."

"But then there's the matter of our clothes," Lani said. "Once we get in there and get the suits off, we won't look like pirates. Our clothing will make us stand out."

"I can sew," Sky said. "I did it all the time on Warbler. We've got to have some clothes packed on the ship that I can fashion into something similar to what the pirates wear—bright, solid-colored shirts, gray or black pants. It won't be hard once we have the materials to work with."

"I can help you with the sewing," Ms. Octavia said. "I'm

quite good. And rather fast." She waved four or five tentacles as proof.

Sky grinned. "Then let's not waste any more time here. Everyone's gone to bed anyway, it seems."

"I was just about to say that," Alex said. "Let's see what we can do. I haven't felt any tremors at all, have you? Maybe we can get in and out of there before it sinks. I saw Copper head down the spiral stairs to somewhere below that main floor where the trees and plants are. At night would be an even better time to sneak in and rescue her, wouldn't it?"

"Yes," Henry said. "Let's do it. I'm tired of sitting around this stupid volcano all day."

With that, Simber delivered Ms. Octavia, Sky, Lani, and Henry to the ship so they could get started right away, and the rest of the crew so they could get some sleep.

Five hours later, when sunrise was still a long way off, Sky shook Alex awake. "We're ready," she whispered.

He flashed a sleepy smile at her—there was no better face to wake up to. And then he remembered. *Focus, Stowe.* The smile slipped away, and he scrambled to his feet, serious once more.

LISA McMANN

Alex, Sky, Lani, Henry, and Ms. Octavia climbed onto Simber's back, and they soared out into the night. Simber first circled the skylight to see if anyone was strapped into the wall seats. Seeing only a few pirates meandering about, Simber landed on the island, directly above the fishing hatch. He stood there for a few minutes to check for tremors, and when he was satisfied that all was well, he gave the go-ahead for the group to pile off.

"You guys totally look like pirates," Alex said to Lani and Henry. "We'll be back soon with the suits." He turned to Sky but didn't look her in the eye. "Ready?"

Sky nodded. "Ready." Her fear of the water was long gone, and she could swim with the best of them. Plus, she was so eager to finally get this rescue started that it didn't really matter how Alex was acting.

Alex turned to Ms. Octavia. "You're the lifeguard in case something goes wrong, okay?"

"Of course," Ms. Octavia said.

Then Alex took off his robe and draped it over Simber's shoulders. "And you're the mage," he said.

"We know how well that'll worrrk out if we lose Arrrtimé,"

the cat said dryly. But he held Alex's gaze for the first time since they'd lost Florence. "So be carrreful."

Ms. Octavia nodded. "Yes. And watch out for eels."

"Believe me, we will," Alex said. He hesitated, then held out his hand to Sky. She took it, and together, on three, they dove into the water.

They swam to one side of the hatch first, staying out of the light that came through the glass walls of the reverse aquarium. It was an interesting though slightly distorted view, looking in through the side rather than from above.

When all looked clear, Alex signaled to Sky, and they went toward the sliding hatch door. Alex moved his hand up and down the side, looking for the button that would open it and let them into the small drainage room. Finally, fumbling along a side panel, he hit it. The door slid open. There was already water in the holding place, so instead of getting whooshed into the open space by a wall of water under extreme pressure, he and Sky merely swam into the box.

The outer door slid closed behind them, and the door in front of them opened. The water in their box rushed out and fell through a grate in the floor. Alex and Sky landed haphazardly on top of the grate. "Looks like there's probably an art to this," Sky said, laughing under her breath as she got to her feet.

Alex grinned, and all the reasons he liked Sky rushed through his mind along with a dull ache. He *had* to focus. "Okay," he whispered. "No mistakes. Let's get the stuff. Coast is clear."

They each grabbed a suit and a helmet and rolled the suits up carefully so they wouldn't get wet inside when they went back out. Sky pressed the button. The inner door opened to the now waterless holding space. They stepped in, and the door closed behind them. "Stand back and hang on," Sky muttered. "Here comes a wall of water."

She cringed and pressed the second door's button, bracing herself. But this time the door opened very slowly, letting the water in at a manageable speed. "Very sciency," Alex remarked as the water level reached his neck. "Here we go."

They took deep breaths and held them. Once Sky and Alex were completely submerged and the water had reached the top of the box, the door opened all the way. They exited and swam the distance to the surface, eventually popping up out of the water directly in front of Lani and Henry, who had leaned over the edge of the island, trying to see.

LISA McMANN

"Here you go," Alex said, flinging his helmet and suit up over the edge. Sky did the same. They hauled themselves up with a little help and stood before their friends, dripping. "Nice and easy," Alex said. He took off his shirt, squeezed the water out of it, and put it back on. "No problems. Nobody saw us."

Sky explained how the doors worked while Lani and Henry put on the suits.

"You guys okay? You know where you're going?" Alex asked.

"Of course, you dolt," Lani said.

He smiled. "Just . . . don't get caught here, okay? Your dad will kill me if anything else happens to you."

"We won't. In fact, Henry calculated it, and he thinks we'll be back in ten minutes or so—if we can find the right room for Copper."

"That's a big if," Alex muttered. He was definitely nervous about Operation Copper working as planned. So many things could go wrong.

"Oh!" Sky said. She rummaged through her wet pocket and pulled out a thin gold chain bracelet. "Show her this so she'll know it's safe to go with you. She'll recognize it."

Lani took it and, since she couldn't reach her pockets with the suit on, slipped it on her wrist. "Got it."

"Let's go," Henry said, bouncing a bit.

Alex gave them both a quick embrace. "Best of luck, you two," he said. "Be smart and be careful. You can do this."

"We know," Lani and Henry said together, both wearing smug smiles. And with that, the Haluki children dove into the sea.

Shiver Shake
Volcano Quake

Alex, Sky, and Ms. Octavia climbed up the volcano to the skylight to get a glimpse of Lani and Henry. It didn't take the sister and brother long to figure out the doors. Soon they were tumbling onto the grate. They shed their suits and helmets and hung them up on the pegs where they belonged. Then they set out in search of Sky and Crow's mother, looking exactly like they belonged there.

Lani wore a purple shirt and gray pants. Henry wore a red shirt and black pants. If someone looked closely, they'd find a very odd-looking seam in Henry's pants where several pieces of

LISA McMANN

clothing had been sewn together to make it work, but it wasn't visible at first glance—at least not from the skylight.

"They're heading to the spiral staircase," Alex relayed to Simber, who was resting his wings nearby. "They're going down— Nope, false alarm. Lani's stopping and looking at something inside a glass case next to the stairs. Henry's keeping watch. What the heck— Okay, now he's tugging at her to hurry up." He laughed nervously under his breath. "It's probably a bunch of books or something. She can't resist them. Come on, Lani." He paused, jiggling his foot. "Okay, finally. Now they're going down."

Simber growled. "Ten minutes. Surrre."

A moment later, Alex looked up. "They're out of sight." He blew out a breath. "I hope they find her." He was more worried than he'd let on before. Who knew what these pirates would do if they found two kids who didn't seem to belong to anyone?

As they waited Alex fidgeted. He and Sky both shivered, having brought nothing dry to change into. After a while, Alex retrieved his robe from Simber and held it out to Sky. "Here," he said gruffly.

She took it and thanked him just as tersely, though she wasn't quite sure why. They sat back against some rocks, not talking, and watched the scene below.

Nothing bad happened. No one walked by. It appeared to be the easiest maneuver any Unwanteds had ever undertaken. Alex clenched and unclenched his fists, wanting desperately for it to stay that way.

Across from Alex and Sky sat Ms. Octavia, looking down through the skylight at a very different angle and seeing a different scene—the glass cage full of sea creatures. "Florence looks just the same," she remarked, more to give Simber an update than anyone else. Simber didn't answer. Soon Ms. Octavia's eyes drooped with fatigue. Occasionally they closed. Everyone was tired.

All of a sudden, Ms. Octavia's eyes flew open wide. She sat up. "Alex, look." She pointed. "The eel is back."

Alex scrambled over to the other side of the skylight and watched the eel slither up to the glass cage. Its back half was wrapped around its latest catch. "What's it got this time?" Alex muttered. "It had better stay away from the fishing hatch."

Sky sat up, alarmed. "What if it comes over as Lani and

LISA McMANN

259 « Island of Legends

Henry and my mother are escaping?" She couldn't hide the panic in her voice. "What if it attacks them?"

Alex glanced worriedly toward the spiral staircase. He didn't see anybody ascending. No one by the fishing hatch either. "So far so good. I hope they'd see the eel in time to stay inside until it's gone," he muttered, knowing it wasn't likely since the water was so murky that far down and the only light was coming from inside. The sea itself was dark just a few feet outside the glass walls.

They watched, breathless, as the eel used its tail to press something, which sparked in the water just as it had the last time. The door slid open, the eel backed into the cage, and it deposited its latest victim inside with the others.

Alex squinted, trying to see what it was, but it was hidden from view behind the giant squid, who this time tried without luck to escape. Instead the squid merely succeeded in getting one tentacle stuck in the door as it closed. The squid's eyes reacted, widening in pain. But it was stuck fast. "Oh no," Alex whispered.

"Poor thing," Sky said. "I wish we could do something!"

"It's too dangerous," Ms. Octavia said. "It'll hurt, but he'll be okay. We can try to help him later when we spring Florence free. But first we need Lani and Henry to find your mother. Where are they? What's keeping them?"

"I don't know." Alex's eyes were fixed on the cage, wondering what the new creature was and why the eel was so intent on collecting them.

Just then he heard a growl from Simber.

Without looking up, he asked, "What is it, Sim?"

"I just felt a trrremorrr."

Alex turned sharply, the cage forgotten. "I didn't feel it. Are you sure?"

Simber's look told him yes.

"Oh no," Alex said. He felt the blood drain from his face. "Lani . . . Henry . . ."

"Mother, hurry," begged Sky.

Everyone felt the next tremor. A few pirates appeared out of nowhere as the wall seats dropped. They slipped into the seats and buckled up.

"Crud," Alex muttered. Dread filled his heart. He strained to see the staircase, but no one was rushing up it. "Where are they?" Alex looked all around, wondering if maybe they'd come up a different way. He bit his lip hard, trying not to panic. "Come on, guys," he murmured. "Get out of there."

But they didn't come.

"Sky, get on Simber's back. You too, Ms. Octavia." The volcano shuddered hard, sending Alex running to get on the statue's back after the others. Simber lifted off the volcano, staying low so they could watch through the skylight.

Lani, Henry, and Copper were nowhere to be seen.

"Oh, come on," Sky urged. She gripped Simber's neck.

As Simber circled, Alex saw something bright flash out of the corner of his eye, but he kept his focus on the spot where they last saw Lani and Henry. When Simber turned, three heads turned with him. "There!" Alex cried. "See them? They're coming up the stairs!"

The volcano trembled as Lani, Henry, and Copper raced to the top of the steps and bounded past the display case, around the greenery, and toward the fishing hatch. Behind them something flashed again. It was coming from the glass cage. Alex looked. And what he saw nearly caused him to fall off Simber's back.

"Spike?" he said, in the midst of Ms. Octavia and Sky crying

LISA McMANN

out for the others. "Spike Furious!" The eel's latest capture was none other than Alex's shiny blue whale, swimming up and over the squid. Her diamond-like horn caught the light.

But Alex didn't have a second to think about his creature, because Lani, Henry, and Copper were running at top speed for the hatch, and a man was chasing them. Alex, Sky, Simber, and Ms. Octavia watched in horror. "Run!" Alex cried, even though he knew they couldn't hear him.

Lani reached the hatch first. She slammed her hand on the first button as the volcano shuddered and seized, knocking her to the floor, and then Alex lost sight of everything as the volcano plunged down into the sea.

LISA McMANN

A Change of Plans

The water crashed over the site where the volcano had been and churned in an angry boil until the waves organized themselves once more, giving no indication that anything had ever been there. Once it was calm, Ms. Octavia leaped from Simber's back and dove into the water to see if Lani, Henry, and Copper had made it out or if they were trapped.

Sky, sitting behind Alex on Simber's back, gripped Alex's arms in fear and worry. But Alex didn't feel anything except pain in his stomach at the thought of his friends being sucked down deep under tons of seawater, trapped inside a hidden, hostile, and dangerous world.

Sky and Alex scanned the waves. "Should we go down?" Sky asked. "We should go down. Shouldn't we?" Her fingers drummed Simber's back, and she couldn't sit still.

"No," Alex said. "I want to as much as you, but it won't do any good right now. Ms. Octavia will be back soon." He shivered with nervous energy. "I don't think they made it out. That outer door opens so slowly. . . ." He trailed off, unable to think straight enough to finish the thought.

They flew in silence as the minutes ticked by.

There was nothing else they could do but hover and wait. Eventually Simber asked, "What did you yell earlierrr, Alex? Just beforrre the island sank?"

Alex pulled his mind from his worries. He had to think about Simber's question for a moment before he figured out what the cat was talking about. "Oh!" he said finally, and then his face clouded. "Oh, that's right—Spike," he said, remembering, which only added fuel to his worries. "Spike Furious. Um, yeah. Remember my whale sculpture from the Museum of Large that I brought to life the other day? I know you were watching. Anyway, she swam away, and that stupid eel captured her, too. That's who he put in the glass cage earlier."

Simber's gaze never left the water, but his body tensed. "Does she brrreathe?"

Alex nodded. "Yeah, but she's a whale, so she needs the water—"

"She'll die in the cage, Alex. She's going to need airrr."

"What?" Alex asked, confused. "She nearly died from too much air in the museum. I had to . . ." He glanced at Sky, who stared at him, mouth agape, and the terrible feelings of failure became fresh all over again. "I had to put her to sleep and transport her to the water first."

"You what?" Sky asked, incredulous.

"No, no, no!" Simber said, frustrated. "Whales need to be in the waterrr to surrrvive because they can't move on land. Theirrr bodies arrre so heavy, they'll crrrush themselves and overrrheat. So if you crrreated herrr as a brrreathing crrreaturrre, which it sounds like you did, she can only live a shorrrt time without any airrr." Simber ended his sentence in a growl of frustration. He swished his tail.

Sky shook Alex's shoulders. "Why didn't you tell me you brought her to life? All this time I've been wondering, and you never said anything."

Alex looked from Simber to Sky, feeling helpless about what to do now. "I don't know," he said anxiously. "I was really sad about it. And embarrassed. I nearly killed her by accident before she got away. I didn't feel like telling everybody, okay? I didn't want to let you down."

Sky stared at him, speechless. She shook her head. "So that's why . . ." She trailed off. There was no time for this conversation. "I can't even deal with this right now."

Alex gripped his knees and leaned forward, his head next to Simber's neck, straining to see through the water. "Now what? How much time does Spike have?"

"I don't know," Simber muttered. "Maybe thirrrty or forrrty minutes. We need to get herrr now . . . while she still has a chance." Simber dropped lower, just above the water, and stared down, trying to see if Ms. Octavia was coming back. "Alex?" he prompted. "What's the plan?"

"Just let me think!" Alex couldn't look at Sky. Where could Ms. Octavia be? Spike couldn't wait. But what was happening down there? What if Ms. Octavia needed help? He dug the heels of his hands into his eye sockets and wished that someone else had to make the life-or-death decisions for once. After

LISA McMANN

a measured breath, he spoke. "Okay," Alex said quietly. "We're going in. I need everybody on the ship standing by. Now."

Simber soared back up. "Coverrr yourrr earrrs," he said to Sky and Alex. When they did, he bellowed at the top of his voice, "Ahab! Brrring forrrth the ship!"

Alex, still stunned by the news of the time-sensitive threat to Spike, grew more fearful about Ms. Octavia's lengthening disappearance, because *she* could drown too. He knew there was only one choice . . . but how best to do it?

"All right, then," he said, ripping his fingers through his tangled hair and looking over his shoulder at Sky. "It's happening. Are you ready?"

"What's happening?" Sky asked.

Alex hesitated. He was still figuring it all out himself. "Okay, so . . . Simber, I say we send one team down to find Ms. Octavia and the others, and another team to rescue the sea creatures and Florence. We do it simultaneously. Maybe it'll cause confusion and we'll be able to pull it off."

Simber nodded. "You think like a leaderrr," he said. A grim compliment.

Sky was quiet. Waiting.

Alex sat up a little straighter and peered into the darkness. "Is Ahab coming?"

"Yes," Simber said.

"Tell him to call all hands on deck and be prepared for rescue. Send the squirrelicorns here now."

Simber did so. When he was done, Alex looked at Sky for a long moment, and that's when the last piece fell into place. He knew how it would go now.

He offered a small smile. "We're going in. Sky, I want you to lead Operation Copper. You're the only one besides me who has been through the hatch, you know the workings of those doors the best, and you'll be the best one to convince your mother to leave the island at that depth. Can you do it?"

Sky's eyes crinkled with worry. "What about you?"

Alex looked down. "I need to right a wrong," he said. "Artimé's statues and creatures are sacred—as sacred as its people. I may have lost Florence because of my stupid mistake. I can't lose another one." He glanced at Simber, who stared hard at the water.

Sky gulped. "Okay," she said. "Okay." She sucked in a few deep breaths. "So what do you want me to do?"

LISA McMANN

269 « Island of Legends

Alex looked her in the eye. "I want you to take Samheed, Crow, and Kitten down to the volcano. We don't know how deep it is. It's going to be very difficult if it's far. Just take your time. You may need to go in and fight—you have your component vest."

"But I'm terrible with spells!"

"No, you're not. Well . . . okay, you are kind of terrible with them, but never mind that. Just stick with the ones you know, and use the strengths you do have, like your clever brain." Alex pulled extra spells out of his pockets and gave them to her, just in case. "Ms. Octavia, Samheed, Lani, and Henry are all excellent spell casters. Just do what you can and rescue your mother, and be wily and quick about it. That's your top priority."

Sky's chin quivered. She pressed her lips together. "Okay. I can do this."

"Yes, you can."

"Just . . . rescue my mother." Sky swallowed hard.

"Exactly. You were going to do it all by yourself once before, remember?" Alex teased.

Sky narrowed her eyes. "You be quiet about that."

The squirrelicorns arrived and soared around Simber's head, making sure they avoided his flapping stone wings, which could send any of them sailing into next week.

"Team," Alex said, addressing the squirrelicorns, "I need you to circle this area. If anyone pops up from the water, pull him out and fly him over to the ship. Simple enough?"

"Sir, yes sir!" The squirrelicorns were always somewhat militaristic. It made Alex wonder what words Mr. Today had used when creating them. He watched as they organized themselves and began circling the area.

The ship appeared out of the darkness, bringing a hint of pink at the edge of the sky and an early morning fog to go along with it. Alex frowned. The fog would only make it harder for the squirrelicorns to see. Not something they needed right now. He hoped it would burn off quickly.

"Okay, crew, we've had some new developments." Alex quickly filled in the others on what had taken place with Copper and with Spike. He assigned the teams and explained the two missions.

"We don't have much time. Sky, take your team down. Hopefully, you'll find Ms. Octavia and you can get our Artiméans out

LISA McMANN

of there. It worries me . . . ," he said, thinking of Ms. Octavia, but he didn't finish. Everyone else was worried too.

"Sean, Carina—I need you to come with me. We're going to release the creatures. And, Ahab, take the ship back a safe distance so you don't capsize when this volcano resurfaces. Got it?" He looked all around. "Is everybody ready?"

A cheer rang out, followed by a small voice from the ship.

"What about me?"

It was Fox. He stood on a box at the bow.

Alex's lips parted. "Aw, I'm sorry, Fox. I don't have a job for you. You float."

Fox blinked his big eyes. He looked down at the water.

Desperate, Alex flashed a pleading glance at Sky. He didn't have the time or patience for hurt feelings right now—his whale was running out of air.

"What Alex meant to say," Sky said gently, "is that he needs you on board the ship to take care of the rescued ones." She leaned toward the fox conspiratorially and put her hand by her mouth to shield her words from the captain's ears. "After all, we can't have the crazy one helping my mother—he'll scare her to death! Which is why you have the most important job."

Simber grumbled. "That's pushing it a bit farrr."

"I'll say," muttered Alex.

Fox perked up. "Then I will be the best welcomer ever."

"Think I'm going to throw up now," Carina said cheerily. "Can we get on with this?"

"Not a moment too soon," Alex said. "Okay. Be safe and be wise, everyone." He poised to dive and added, "And watch out for that blasted eel."

The Big Cat's Worst Nightmare

Into the water they went. Alex dove straight down, with Sean and Carina behind and Simber circling above. The three looked around, trying to find the underwater island. Alex figured they didn't have more than fifteen minutes to find and release the creatures before the whale would run out of air. They had to get it right.

Deeper and deeper they swam, knowing they could only go so far before too much time had passed and they'd have to head back up again. But Alex knew that Sean and Carina could hold their breath as long as he could—Carina even a little longer.

After a long minute, with pressure building up around

Alex's ears the deeper they went, he felt something tugging on his sleeve. It was Sean, who pointed to an area a little farther down and to one side. The top of the volcano! Alex gave Sean a thumbs-up and followed him and Carina, who had gone on ahead. The three of them swam down the side of the volcano to where the glass cage was. They rounded the edge of the rock and found themselves eye to milky eye with the giant squid—only his eye was bigger than their entire heads. And luckily, he was behind glass. Or maybe not so luckily. The good news was that the squid's tentacle was no longer trapped in the door. Did that mean the eel had been back?

Alex kept himself from panicking at the sight of such an enormous creature, knowing that the stress would only cause him to use up his body's oxygen too quickly. Instead he swam for the door, where the eel had been, and searched for the button or lever that the eel had used. As he searched, his eyes glanced to Spike, who swam around wildly at the top of the cage.

Beyond the cage, Alex looked straight into the middle floor of the strange island. He could see some activity, but he knew he couldn't concentrate on it. A moment later Carina caught Alex's eye. She waved frantically to get his attention and pointed. Floating near the top of the cage, tiny and limp and seemingly lifeless, was Ms. Octavia. No wonder she hadn't come back up. The eel had gotten her, too! There was no time to waste.

Alex lit a blinding highlighter and pulled himself along the door until he found a round carving in the glass. Inside there was a wire. Was that the door opener? He pushed his fist into the space and pressed the wire as hard as he could.

Nothing happened.

He pressed it again, pushing and swimming against it, trying to get some force behind it. But it was no use. Desperately he searched for another button or lever or *something* that would trigger the opening of the door. But there was nothing.

He pounded on the door, trying to wake up Ms. Octavia, but her body looked wrung out, squeezed by the eel. There was nothing they could do. Alex, Sean, and Carina looked at each other, knowing they didn't have time for anything else anyway—their lungs were growing uncomfortable. They needed to get to the surface.

Alex took a single glance through the cage to the area where he'd last seen Lani, but there was no one there now. Had they made it out? Or had they been captured?

He pounded once more on the glass and then, giving up, pointed to the surface. As they rose, Alex saw a familiar flash of light. Spike had heard his tiny pounding and moved over to the glass wall where Alex had been. Alex hesitated, and then, motioning to the others to go ahead, he turned back and went to the glass where Spike was, putting his hands against the cage.

"Spike Furious," Alex said. They'd all practiced speaking underwater during their training time, and now he did his best to sound as clear as possible without using up too much air. The words sent bubbles floating upward. He stabbed a finger into his chest. "Alex." The whale pressed her side up against the glass where Alex's hands were, lining herself up perfectly with where his hands had been when he brought her to life.

She knows! His face lit up. "We're coming back. Hang on!"

Spike seemed to calm down. Her eyes followed him as he pushed back from the glass and began to make his way to the surface, carefully and deliberately, and, as always, watching out for the eel.

When he broke through the surface and waved the squir-relicorns away so they wouldn't pluck him out of the water, Alex knew they were running out of options. As soon as he caught his breath, he looked up at Simber, shielding his eyes now that the sun was finally coming up. Sean and Carina floated nearby.

"Big problems," Alex said, his chest still heaving in the water. "Ms. Octavia's in the cage. We can't get it open." He filled his lungs with air and let it out again. He had to catch his breath before he could go down that far again.

"Sean and Carrrina filled me in," Simber said.

Alex nodded his thanks. "I think the eel sends some sort of electric shock through the wire that it uses to control the door."

"Speaking of the eel, you guys keep talking. I'm going to be the lookout." Carina ducked down under the surface again.

"Has anyone returned from Operation Copper?" Sean asked.

"Not yet," Simber said.

"Sim," Alex said, "I hate to do this." He pushed his shock of wet curls out of his eyes. "I'm afraid we need you ... to ..." Alex pressed his lips together and looked down at the water.

Simber regarded Alex. He closed his eyes for a long moment. And then he opened them again. "I'll do whateverrr it takes. But I'm worrried I won't have the momentum I need. And I don't want to hurrrt anyone."

"We don't have a choice," Alex said in a low voice. "It's the only way. We're out of time."

Simber nodded. "I'll need to get sufficient airrrspeed. You head down firrrst and warrrn them. Push them to the norrrth end of the cage."

Carina popped up, catching the tail end of the conversation. "No eel," she said.

Alex looked at her. "Can you head down? Sean, you too. I'll follow in a minute."

A second later, Sean and Carina went back below the surface. Alex looked at Simber. "Is there any way you could be destroyed doing this? The glass is very thick."

"In waterrr?" Simber chuckled. "No chance. I'll just need something to push off frrrom to get back up again afterrr it's overrr. It might take a few trrries. Orrr I'll climb up on top of the volcano and rrride up with it the next time it goes. You don't have to worrry about me."

LISA McMANN

"Okay. That's a relief. I'm going back down. You're very brave."

"Orrr stupid. I'm heading up. See you shorrrtly." Simber lifted up, then looked back. "And stay farrr out of my way."

"I will!" Alex rolled his eyes as the statue ascended, and muttered, "Trust me. I will."

"I can still hearrr you."

Alex shook his head, sucked in an enormous breath, and swam back down toward the cage. It was now or never.

Half Over

When Alex made it back to the glass cage, he found Carina and Sean struggling with the door mechanism, trying in vain to make it do something. Sean cast one spell after another at it, but nothing worked.

Alex went straight up to the glass and began pounding again, hoping to get Spike's attention. Spike turned to look and swam over to Alex.

"We're going to smash the glass!" Alex said, trying not to use up too much air. He pointed to the south side of the cage.

LISA McMANN

"That wall. Move away! Tell them." Alex pointed to the other trapped creatures.

The whale looked startled for a moment, and then she went up to the long-necked sea monster and seemed to converse with it. The sea monster moved to the north side of the cage. Then Spike approached the giant squid. After a bit of hesitation, the squid looked at Alex and shot to the opposite corner from where he'd been, nursing his injured limb.

Then Spike pushed Ms. Octavia's floating body to the back corner as well, near the squid. The octagator seemed to move a tentacle or two, Alex thought, but he wasn't sure. The squid reached out and cradled Ms. Octavia with one tentacle to keep her from floating away. Alex pointed out the act of kindness to Carina, who gave a sweet, crooked smile at the sight of it.

Then Spike swam to the bottom of the cage and began poking Florence's shoulder with her spike, trying to tell the statue to move. Alex watched.

The whale poked Florence again and again, but Florence didn't budge.

Alex pounded on the glass. "Tell her Simber is coming!" If anything would do it, it would be that, he was sure.

The whale seemed to understand, and just as Alex caught sight of Simber torpedoing through the water toward them, he thought he saw Florence open one eye. But he couldn't be certain.

"Look out!" Alex yelled, not sure how far his words would carry in the depths of this watery world. But Sean and Carina heard, and so did the whale. Sean, Carina, and Alex pushed away from the glass as fast as they could, and everyone inside flattened against the north wall. When the squid saw what was coming toward him, he wrapped his enormous body around all his strange-looking prison mates, shielding them just in time.

Simber hit the glass at full speed and broke through. The impact shook the entire underwater island—it was like an explosion. Alex covered his face as giant chunks of glass flew in slow motion through the water and Simber came to rest on the floor of the cage, like a perfect fire-breathing origami dragon coming in for a landing. Sean and Carina closed in, waiting for the debris to stop flying. Alex joined them.

Inside the reverse aquarium, there was a sudden flurry of movement, enough to make Alex look over. There, pirates began running about, pounding on the walls, trying to pull the seats out so they might secure themselves. At first, Alex didn't understand what they were doing, but then he realized that they thought the tremor was a signal from the volcano that it was about to move again. When no seats dropped into place, chaos broke out. People began running every which way, trying to find a place to strap themselves in for the ride, but to no avail.

It was during this that Alex saw the tiniest movement from within the glass island. A little white dot, jumping up and down, waving her little paws. Alex could see her pink tongue as she no doubt cried out, "Mewmewmew!"

Alex poked Sean with his elbow. "Kitten," he mouthed.

They watched as Kitten ran away from them, straight toward the fishing hatch.

Alex looked at Simber, who had gotten to his feet by now, though slowly.

"Okay! Get sea creatures out," Alex mimed. "I go help Kitten."

Sean and Carina nodded. They went around to the hole and inside the cage. Sean darted up, grabbed Ms. Octavia, and headed to the surface, while Carina spoke to Spike the way

Alex had, telling Spike to tell the sea monster and the giant squid and the other creatures to escape. While Alex swam toward the fishing hatch, the sea monster and squid darted out at Spike's urging and headed west. The last thing Alex saw was Carina, hopping onto Spike's back and riding toward the sky.

Alex rounded the glass island, running too low on oxygen, he could tell. His lungs burned. His eyesight dimmed. He pressed the door to the fishing hatch, and when it slid open, he moved into the box of water, then pressed the second button and fell into the island, gasping for breath. There was so much chaos inside, nobody even noticed him.

Except Kitten, of course. "Mewmewmew!" she cried. "Mewmewmew!"

Alex didn't have a clue what she was saying. "Show me," he said when he could catch his breath.

Kitten pranced through the chaos with a soaking-wet Alex on her heels. He dodged and weaved, keeping his arm near his face so he wouldn't be noticed. An alarm sounded, and pirates everywhere were becoming hysterical trying to find safety seats before their sickening ride upward. If Alex hadn't been so overwhelmed with everything else, he might have thought this was

LISA McMANN

the most inconvenient and annoying island he'd ever seen. He never wanted to see it again.

Kitten darted down the spiral staircase, jumping from one step to the next, and raced up a hallway past a few panicked people wearing the brown uniforms of slaves. Kitten stopped at a door. "Mewmewmew!" she cried, throwing herself at it.

Alex grabbed the handle and pushed open the door. He nearly fell inside when he saw the scene before him.

Fear Replanted

It didn't take long for Aaron and his new governors to make up a variety of atrocities to pin on the unsuspecting people of Artimé, painting them as a looming threat to the people of Quill. Aaron worked and reworked his speech, knowing he needed to be alarming yet appear totally in control, and also instill trust in his new team of leaders so that when Aaron wasn't around, the Quillens would listen to the governors.

When it came time to address the people, Aaron, his three new inductees, and Secretary, of course, rode to the Commons of Quill, arriving just slightly late as Justine would have done.

LISA McMANN

Aaron knew it was the little, consistent details that proved to gain the trust of the people of Quill. Being late was one of them.

Flanked by guards and wearing one of Justine's robes, Aaron stepped out of his car, followed by Secretary. The crowd in the amphitheater murmured and then was quiet. The next car pulled up, and Gondoleery, Liam, and Strang got out.

Aaron nodded to them and began walking to the amphitheater. They followed. When the high priest approached the podium, he didn't smile or frown. He looked over the crowd. The Wanteds stood in the front as usual. Behind them were the Necessaries in their assigned spots, and beyond the Necessaries were a small group of tattered-looking Unwanteds who had come crying into Quill when Artimé disappeared. Aaron had quickly turned them into slaves. The high priest narrowed his eyes in their direction, seeing a boy who had been in his own class in school, Cole Wickett, standing there. He wondered how Cole was liking the little deal the high priest had made with the returning Unwanteds. Not that he cared.

As usual, Aaron's eyes sought and found the spot where his parents always stood. The sun beat down on them now.

The last time Aaron had seen his parents, his mother was very pregnant. Now his mother and father each held a baby girl with dark brown ringlets. One of the girls squirmed, while the other sat pacified, looking in Aaron's direction. Aaron frowned and looked away. It was strange to know he had sisters. Identical twins once more.

When all was silent and the governors stood behind him, Aaron focused on a very different spot in the crowd and began his address.

"People of Quill, I come with news," he began. "As your high priest, I must tell you that our neighbors in Artimé are plotting to attack us." He let the words sink in and the murmurs die down.

"We don't know how or when, but we do know that they have been plotting this for some time. They wish to take over Quill, get rid of us, and expand their hideous world. And"—he paused for effect—"they are using *you* to do it."

Again Aaron waited in the thick silence.

"Those of you who have been visiting Artimé or accepting Unwanteds as visitors in your homes here in Quill—you are our weak link. I am asking you to cease these visits immediately

LISA McMANN

without letting on to Artimé that we know about their plans. If we tip them off, they may change tactics and put us into more danger. As it stands now, there is nothing to fear in the near future. We are watching them very closely. But we can also use your help."

Aaron flicked away a bead of sweat that dripped down his cheek. "In addition to ceasing your contact with Artimé, I'm asking each of you to watch your neighbors to make sure they are not sneaking off to visit the Unwanteds or inviting them into Quill. If you suspect someone is making contact with the people of Artimé, please come to the palace with your information and you will be rewarded with Favored Farm food for your efforts to make Quill a safer place to live.

"In addition, I have appointed three new governors to help protect you and serve our land." Aaron stepped aside to point them out. "Liam Healy, Gondoleery Rattrapp, and Septimus Strang." The governors bowed when their names were called. Aaron continued. "They are your advocates, and together we are working tirelessly to eliminate the threat from outside our walls. We will not let the people of Artimé try to control us! We will not let the Unwanteds take over an inch of our world!

People of Quill, we must come together for the sake of our land and our traditions. We need to act as one body in opposition to the enemy who is out to destroy us. And together we will become a stronger society, eliminating once and for all the enemy that has plagued us since they killed our beloved High Priest Justine."

Aaron pressed his lips together and leaned forward. "People of Quill, vow with me now to work only for the best interests of our land." He paused for effect and then said with a flourish, "May Quill prevail with all we have in us!"

The people gathered there did not cheer, but if they looked deep within their hearts, almost everyone present could feel something strange welling up inside them—something that felt like anger and loyalty and courage. They used the courage to beat down the anger, saving it for another day and knowing instinctively that they would need a large supply when the time came.

Aaron stepped back, spent. The seeds were sown. The reaction was exactly as he had wished it to be. He sent the three new governors out into the crowd to greet the Wanteds. They would be the temporary face of the palace. For a short time, anyway. Long enough for Aaron to build and grow his secret weapons.

And then all manner of war would be released alongside the collected anger of the people of Quill, and the Unwanteds would be gone and Artimé would be his.

Just Keep Swimming

In the dark room on the lowest floor of Pirate Island, Sky, Samheed, and Crow were frantically tending to Henry, Lani, and Copper, who were covered in bruises and blood.

Sky looked up. Her breath caught. "Alex, thank goodness." She waved her hand at the injured. "They weren't strapped in when the island plunged," she said. "They went flying."

Samheed looked at Alex. "They're all conscious now, at least. Henry was still out cold when we got here, and he's bleeding pretty badly. We'll have to sneak out in the middle of the night when we can go slowly."

Alex looked on in alarm. "No, we can't wait. They know we're here. That tremor you felt wasn't the island about to go up, it was Simber breaking through the cage glass. The eel got Ms. Octavia and, well, another creature, and we had to get them out or they'd die." He wiped the drips from his face with his sodden shirtsleeve. "Seriously, guys—we have to go now."

"I don't think we should move them," Samheed said, his stubbornness coming out.

"Sam. Listen. There's total chaos out there," Alex said. "Nobody will be paying attention to us. We can get out safely right now. I don't have time to explain, but we *have* to go. We have to." When Samheed hesitated and Sky didn't say anything to help, Alex repeated in a stern voice. "Now."

Samheed looked at Lani. She nodded and struggled to her elbows. "Alex is right. If they know we're here," she said weakly, "they'll find us."

Alex breathed a sigh of relief. He picked up Kitten and handed her to Crow. "Sam, take Lani. I've got Copper. Sky, you grab Henry. Let's get out of here. Don't stop for anything."

The three able bodies picked up their battered friends, Alex quickly yet politely introducing himself to Copper before he picked her up, explaining to her what his plan was. They left the room and made their way down the empty hall, then crept up the spiral stairs to where the chaos was.

Samheed reached the top first and waited for the others. Lani, despite her injuries, strained over the railing at the top of the steps to look inside the glass case nearby, which had caught her eye earlier. She struggled in Samheed's arms to see better as they waited for the others to reach them.

"Ouch. What are you doing?" Samheed whispered.

"Trying to see that drawing," Lani said, digging a knee into his ribs. "Boost me up!"

"No!" Samheed said. "Stop wriggling or I'll drop you."

Lani frowned and wriggled more, finally getting a long look at what was inside the case.

Samheed looked down the stairs as Sky struggled with Henry to reach them. He shifted Lani and held out a hand to assist Sky as Alex climbed past them all to take the lead with Copper.

"Everybody," Alex hissed, "keep your heads down and push on, no matter what. Do what you have to do to get out of here. Just stay close." He set off, with Sky on his heels.

Lani settled back down in Samheed's arms, spent from her efforts, and Samheed sped after Alex and Sky.

"My mother can't swim," Sky reminded Alex in a low voice as they dodged a wailing child who'd been separated from his parents in the confusion. "How will we get her all the way to the surface?"

Alex twisted left and right, moving through the crowd, his heart pounding. "I'm wondering the same thing about myself," he said. After two lengthy dives already today and little recovery time, he didn't have much energy left in him. And they couldn't afford to rest.

"Put a helmet on Sky's mother," Lani said, her head resting on Samheed's shoulder now. "I meant to tell you—there's air inside. She'll be able to breathe."

"Perfect," Alex said, relieved. So that explained how the fishermen could stay out in the water so long. Copper looked slightly relieved too, but Alex could still feel her shaking with fear. "Are you going to be okay?" he asked her.

She nodded, unable to speak because of the thornament around her neck.

"Okay. We're almost there."

Finally they made it to the fishing hatch. Alex spied the suits and helmets. He grabbed a helmet and placed it over Copper's head while Sky hit the button to the sliding door. As they made their way into the box, a shout rang out above the chaotic noise around them.

"Stop! Who are you?"

Alex looked up to find two men and a woman charging toward them.

"They're stealing my slave!" one of the men yelled.

"Get in, quick," Alex said. They scooted inside, having to squeeze to fit all seven of them. Alex pulled Samheed back so the door would close just as the pirate reached the first button and slapped it, holding it open.

"Grab them!" the pirate yelled.

Without a thought, both Samheed and Alex pointed and shouted, "Glass!"

Instantly not one but two panes of glass stopped the pirates in their tracks and walled the Artiméans in the chamber.

"Yikes," Alex said, sweating profusely now. "That was close." He ignored the pirates and looked at all his companions. "It'll take us a few minutes to reach the surface. Can everyone handle that? Copper," he said to Sky's mother, "Lani says your helmet has air inside."

"Right," Lani said. "And it'll seal up nice and snug around your jaw so no water can get in. You will be able to breathe normally."

Alex flashed Lani a grateful smile. "Just don't panic and we'll be fine, Copper. I promise I won't let you go."

"You can trust them, Mother," Crow said from Henry's side. The bandage on Henry's head had grown crimson with blood.

"Henry," Alex said, "can you make it?"

Henry nodded through half-closed eyes. "I got this," he said. His voice was weak.

"Lani?"

"Yes," she replied. "I'm fine. Really."

"Copper?"

The woman nodded her helmeted head. Alex could feel her hands shaking as she gripped his shoulders.

Alex breathed hard, trying to rebuild his depleted oxygen stores, though he wasn't sure how much oxygen was left in this little box—they had to get out of there. "Let's do this, then. Here we go. Everybody, gather your breath and stay close to me." He pushed the button. The outer door opened slowly, letting water in. The pirates behind them pounded on the glass, but Alex knew there was no way they'd be able to break through.

"Where's Kitten?" Henry asked, his eyes wide open in alarm now.

"I've got her," Crow said. He patted his best friend's arm as the water rose up around his chest. "Here we go."

Soon the water had reached the top of the box, and the door slid all the way open. Everyone looked for Alex to lead them.

Alex wasted no time. He floated out and pushed off the glass door frame to give him momentum in the right direction. He began kicking, and soon he and Copper were rising slowly through the water. Crow swam with Alex, holding on to his mother's hand. Samheed, with Lani wrapped in his arms, pushed upward on one side of Alex. Sky held Henry, who was clearly the most injured of the three. Alex urged Sky to go a little faster if she was able. Soon she took the lead.

Alex looked back through the murky water at the glass cage, which was nearly empty now. Only Simber and Florence remained. Florence was standing now, but Alex wasn't sure if Simber had propped her up that way or if she'd gotten up on her own. After a few moments, he couldn't see them any longer.

Soon the entire volcano island was out of sight and Alex could see a bright spot in the sky above. He couldn't wait to get everybody safely on board the ship.

When something flashed, Alex almost smiled. *Spike!* he thought. He looked around for the whale, hope surging— maybe they could get a ride to the surface.

But it wasn't Spike's faux diamond–encrusted horn catching the light.

It was the electric spark of the slithery eel.

And it was coming their way.

Flashes of Light

Alex grabbed Crow's arm and pointed at the eel, then up toward the surface. "Go!" he said in his garbled, watery voice. "Hurry!"

Crow's eyes widened in fear, but he always listened to Alex. He shot up through the water, swimming as fast as his little feet could kick.

When Sam and Sky noticed Crow, they looked at Alex. Alex showed them the eel, which came in and out of sight. It began to circle them. Alex pointed up, urging his friends to go faster, which they did. Alex tried too, but his arms and legs burned. He had the heaviest load and had spent way too many

LISA McMANN

minutes underwater today. It was exhausting, not to mention the fact that he hadn't stopped to eat anything in forever. He didn't know how much more strength he had in him.

Still, the presence of the eel was extremely motivating. Alex kicked through the pain and struggled onward. He could see the surface now. Everything was getting lighter. Alex pushed on, wanting to squeal in pain from the way Copper was gripping his arms. He kept telling himself that as long as she wasn't panicking, he could handle the fingernails digging into his skin. He began to wish he'd grabbed a helmet for himself.

He watched from below with great relief as Crow made it to the surface. Soon the boy was pulled from the water, presumably by two squirrelicorns eager to finally do something. Sky and Henry were next. Henry's legs disappeared first and then Sky's.

What a relief to know they were safe! Alex knew that Samheed and Lani would have to wait for the first pair of squirrelicorns to come back from dropping off Crow. Too bad Simber was still down in the aquarium with Florence.

Which made him wonder: Just how was Simber supposed to pull Florence up to the surface when he could barely propel himself there?

He closed his eyes briefly. One more obstacle. He kept kicking.

Copper's grip grew even tighter on his arms, until he felt like she was cutting off his circulation. He opened his eyes to the sight of the slithering eel closing in at his feet. Copper had seen it.

Alex didn't have time or energy to reassure her. His hope was that the eel wouldn't want anything to do with humans—after all, it had thrown Carina out to sea after it had grabbed her off the ship. In fact, the eel seemed to be pretty strict about collecting only weird sea creatures. Well, and Florence. But here it was, surrounding them, and it didn't look disinterested in the least. Alex kicked faster and watched Lani's and Samheed's legs disappear from the water. He was almost there.

The eel wouldn't stop circling. Alex wouldn't stop swimming. With a final burst of energy, he shot upward, pushing Copper above him until she reached the surface. He treaded water until he felt her weight being lifted from his arms, and then he broke through and gasped for air. He wiped the water from his eyes and looked for squirrelicorns, but they were all retreating, delivering Samheed, Lani, and now Copper to the ship. Alex flipped on his back, knowing he should go back under and watch the eel, but also knowing if he didn't catch

LISA McMANN

his breath for a second, he just might die anyway, without the eel having to do anything at all.

As he gasped and floated and waited for the first pair of squirrelicorns to return, his body spent and muscles trembling, he felt something wrap itself around his legs. Alex sprang to life, kicking and yelling. "Help!" he cried, hoping it would bring the squirrelicorns faster. He flailed about, just barely sliding out of the eel's grasp again and again, shouting when he could get a breath, until finally the eel rose up out of the water and wrapped around Alex like kite string around a reel.

"Aah—!" Alex's yell was cut short by the eel yanking him underwater.

Immediately he sucked in a breath of water and started to choke. The eel squeezed him and slithered around through the water, gaining momentum until it was moving at a maniacal speed. Alex's vision grew hazy, and he couldn't struggle anymore. He tried desperately to hold his breath, but the intake of water had messed up everything. Just before he blacked out, a flash of light caught his eye.

And this time, it wasn't the eel.

Spike Furious

The shiny, blue-painted whale with a faux diamond–encrusted spike shooting out from her forehead came zipping toward Alex and the eel at top speed. Even though she'd been captured by this same eel once before, she was not afraid. She had learned the eel's tricks. Compelled by a voice inside her, she swam at a furious pace, aiming her spike without fear at the enormous electric eel.

That voice inside—she'd heard it before, at the beginning of everything. But the voices of the sea had been louder back then, calling her to play. She hadn't been able to resist them.

LISA McMANN

Today in the cage she heard that voice again, coming from the boy. From the Alex.

At the beginning, during the terrible time, the Alex was there, feeling terrible too. It reminded her of something. Of someone. Of a man, a very long time ago, who remained by her side until the end. And even though it hurt, she felt comfort knowing that the man was there, feeling terrible with her.

When she heard that voice, the voice of the Alex, and saw his eyes and understood his words, she believed in him. And when the Alex's personal monster came to break the cage and set everyone free so they could breathe again, Spike Furious knew that she would want to stay near the Alex forever. The thought made her happy.

Now, with the Alex in grave danger, there was only one thing Spike could do to stop the bad eel from hurting him and everyone else.

She sped toward the giant eel and stabbed her spike into its side.

The creature recoiled. The Alex slipped out of its grasp. Spike Furious yanked her spike out of the eel's side, slipped her tail under the boy as he fell lifeless through the water, and lifted his body above the surface to the air, because every creature of the sea knows that the Alexes can't hold their breath as long as whales can.

When Spike heard the noises from the ship, she got scared, but then she saw that the people on board were smiling and cheering. Spike smiled back and cheered with them as two creatures of the air picked up the Alex from her tail and brought him to the ship.

"Thank you, Spike! You saved Alex!" said the girl with short fur who had been near the cage with the boy.

Spike bobbed in the water, tail and snout sticking up. She liked the girl with short fur. The whale ducked her head underwater to fill her blowhole so she could speak, and repeated, "Thank you, Spike!" And for some reason, just like when she had spoken to the sea monster and the squid and the dead stone woman, it didn't seem strange.

"Oh, you can talk," said the girl. "How excellent. I am Carina. Do you understand what I'm saying?"

"Of course I can," Spike said. She blew, and water shot up, hitting the Carina in the face.

The Carina laughed and wiped her eyes. "Lovely! Alex did an excellent job with you."

Spike nodded, somehow knowing this to be true, but not knowing quite how she'd learned of it. She submerged once more. "Where is the Alex?"

"He's here on the deck, coughing up a lungful of water—do you hear him? But he'll be okay, I think, because you rescued him in time."

"It is always good to be in time," Spike said, as if it just occurred to her. She was learning new things every minute.

"Indeed it is." Carina glanced out to sea, a worried look on her face. "I'm wondering if you can do me a favor while we wait for Alex to feel better."

"Oh," Spike said, and she closed her eyes as a wave of . . . something . . . passed over her. "You want me to check on the monster with wings." Again, Spike had no idea how she knew what The Carina wanted, but the knowledge was there. She could feel it, anticipate it. "And the dead stone woman."

"Yes, if it's not too much trouble."

"It is not." Spike dove down and barreled through the water

like a bullet in the direction of the cage. There was no sign of the eel, she thought with smug satisfaction.

On board the ship, Alex felt like he might never stop coughing. As soon as he was able, and despite the outcry of those surrounding him, Alex got to his feet and stumbled over to the side of the ship. "Where's Simber?" he demanded. "Has anyone seen him?"

For Alex, this scene was all too horribly familiar. Simber, lost underwater again. It was unnerving.

"Spike is checking on them," Carina said, joining Alex at the railing. "Our whale friend is quite intelligent and seems extra intuitive. She guessed what I was about to ask her."

Alex looked at Carina. "She spoke to you?"

"Yes—didn't you make her that way?"

"I did, yes," Alex said, a grin spreading over his face. "I made her to be able to communicate with all humans and creatures. But I didn't think it would actually work."

"She seemed to have no trouble speaking to that long-necked sea monster and the squid, and definitely no problems talking to me. That's a lot already. She calls you 'the Alex.' It's very cute," Carina teased. "As if you are your own breed."

Alex smiled and shook his head a little, lost in thought. "Can you believe it? I actually made a creature and brought her to life," he murmured. "That's crazy."

"And she's fully devoted to you. I don't know what she did to scare that eel off, because when I saw that slimy evil thing pop out of the water and grab you, I thought it was all over. But then she was right there, jumping through the air, chasing after you, her body shining and her spike sparkling in the sun—she's the most beautiful creature I've ever seen, Alex."

Alex, a bit overwhelmed by Spike and still worried about Simber and Florence, couldn't think of anything to say. And then he whirled around, remembering. "How's Ms. Octavia? Is she okay?"

"She's resting belowdecks, but we think she'll be okay once her body has time to reshape and heal. The eel squished her pretty hard. Luckily, she's flexible. She'll bounce back." Carina began updates on everyone else. "Copper and Henry have wounds we can treat. Lani's already up and about." Carina pointed to Lani, who was poring over a wrinkled paper and apparently having a terse discussion with Samheed. Carina gazed out over the sea once more. "It's Florence I'm worried about."

Alex nodded. "Me too. If I had any energy left, I'd go down there myself. But I'm afraid I've reached my limit on sea breathing for the day, and I'd only have to be rescued again."

"None of us, including Simber, would want you to attempt it at this point."

They stood side by side, not talking. After a while, Sean joined them, and then Samheed came over, leaving Lani alone with her precious paper. They stood in stoic silence: hungry, exhausted, aching. Waiting. Hoping that soon all the questions that plagued them would be answered.

When they saw the water rippling in a line toward the ship, they thought at first it was yet another sea creature. But soon they could see the ripples were coming from the tip of a sparkling spike, as well as from two enormous feet sticking slightly out of the water.

"It's Florence!" Carina cried. "Spike's got her, see?" She pointed as the whale moved toward them uncharacteristically slowly yet steadily. Behind them, in an explosion of water,

Simber appeared, his wings flapping wildly as soon as they hit the air, bringing him up and out of the water.

"Simber!" Alex shouted.

The enormous stone cheetah shook in midair, trying to rid itself of the horrid droplets, and he roared when the spectators laughed at the sight.

But the laughs died away when Spike and Florence approached. Spike sidled up to the ship with Florence, who was lying on Spike's back just under the surface. Everyone leaned over to get a look at her. Simber, still trying to rid himself of the water, flew over and joined them.

Alex looked at Florence. Her face was serene, arms folded over her stomach, eyes closed. She even had thin ebony eyelashes—Alex hadn't noticed them before. He bit his lip and looked up at Simber. "Is she . . . Is she dead?"

Simber's mouth opened, and then it closed. He looked away.

A wave of cold fear passed through Alex. He turned back to Florence.

And then Florence sat up on the whale's back. "HA!" she yelled, scaring everybody half to death.

LISA McMANN

Everyone screamed in fright. Simber cracked up—figuratively, of course—roaring with laughter. And before their hearts had stopped pounding, Florence grabbed the side of the ship while Simber touched down on the other side to keep balance, and in a rather undignified manner, with a little shove from Spike, the warrior hefted herself over the side of the ship and rolled nicely to the center, then sat up on the edge of the hole she'd made earlier and let her legs dangle through to the deck below. She looked at Alex, who was still gripping his robe, staring at her.

"Now," she said, grinning, "where did we leave off? And what enormous grunt left this big hole in your deck? How rude."

As everyone caught their breath and Captain Ahab and the other statues came running over to see Florence, Spike Furious jumped high into the air, unable to overcome her delight in saving the day.

The captain stopped short and stared at Spike, his eyes wide.

Spike blew the water from her spout in glee.

Ahab clutched his jacket. He whispered, "Deceitful eyes,

LISA McMANN

can you deny this scene before me? The splash and spout reveal her . . . but bedecked as such? Bejeweled? Nary a white speck upon her . . ." His face clouded over, and then it cleared. "'Tis the elusive beast disguised!" He shook his fist as Spike surfaced and jumped again, trumpeting water from her blowhole high into the air. Ahab ran to the ship's wheel. "Thar she blows!" he cried. "Thar she blows—the great *blue* whale!"

The Tale of the Sacrifice

When the crew had calmed Captain Ahab enough that he was merely shaking his fist and muttering at the whale whenever she surfaced, and preparing the ship to sail once more, Alex called everybody together. As on their last journey, the injured were triaged in one area, and even Ms. Octavia had managed to make it back up to the main deck, looking as wrung out as a tattered dishcloth but happy to see everyone alive all the same, most especially Florence.

After they had all greeted one another, Alex called things to order to introduce Copper. It was clear the woman was Sky's

LISA McMANN

mother—not just because of the orange eyes or the thorny necklace she wore, but because Copper looked like an older version of Sky, only with lighter hair and skin.

"I've talked to my mother about taking the thorn necklace off. She'd like you to do it, Alex. If you don't mind."

"Of course not." Alex didn't hesitate. He went to Copper's side and sat down to explain the procedure. Once she nodded her consent, Alex gathered up his concentration and cast the spell, and soon the horrible metal dissipated into the air.

Everyone watched anxiously as Copper tried to speak. It took her some time to get even a bit of her voice back, but it was better than nothing.

"It'll take a while, but I think you'll have it eventually," Sky assured her.

Copper nodded. "Thank you, Alex," she managed to whisper.

"Yes, thank you, Alex," Sky echoed. She looked at him.

Alex nodded. "Sure," he said in a quiet voice, holding her gaze for once. "That's what I'm here for." After a minute, he broke the connection and busied himself with other tasks.

Copper relaxed, eager to have everyone take their eyes off

her and go back to whatever they usually did after a rescue. Only her eyes darted every now and then to the spot where the island would surface.

While Sean and Samheed began to assist Ahab with the sails, Alex said, "Lani, tell us what happened to you guys. You must have freaked out when the island sank."

Lani held her head, remembering. "I thought we could make it. But when the volcano plunged underwater, Henry and Copper and I all went flying. At least I was in the hatch, so I didn't get battered as much. But Henry hit his head pretty hard."

"As you can see," Henry said, proudly pointing to his bandage.

"Yes, it's terribly serious," Lani said. She rolled her eyes. "Anyway, we all took a hit."

"Daxel, too," Copper whispered.

"Who's Daxel?" Alex asked.

"He's the other slave who worked with Copper," Lani explained. "He wanted to escape with us, but when we didn't make it out of the hatch, Copper signaled to him to act like he was trying to stop us so he wouldn't get in trouble."

"Instead," Henry said, "he distracted everybody so we could hide on the lower floor."

"I don't know how we made it down there," Copper rasped.

"Daxel saved us," Henry said.

Lani stood up and began to act out everything that had happened to them. "The island had this sickening drop, and then it jerked and shook for a while. We were falling all over the place, down the stairs and everywhere, trying to get to safety."

"Maybe if you hadn't wasted time in the beginning looking at their dumb drawings, you would have made it out in time," Samheed muttered.

Alex tilted his head. "How did you know she—"

Lani, ignoring Alex, retorted, "Will you stop, already? I'm telling you, it was important."

"We were there to rescue Copper, not nose around in some stupid ancient book. You put yourselves in danger."

"It *wasn't* a *book*," Lani said, jaw clenched.

Alex, Sean, and Carina glanced uneasily at each other. It felt like old times with Lani and Samheed bickering again.

Samheed sighed loudly. "Whatever. Sorry, everyone. Go on with your story."

Lani lifted her chin. "I'm trying to. Anyway. We were falling all over the place—"

"And I was getting gravely injured," Henry interjected.

"And yeah, Henry got a little bump on his head. Luckily, only a few people saw us. When we were hiding in that room, I saw two pirates take Daxel away. They didn't bother to hunt for us. I don't think they'd realized yet that Henry and I didn't belong there."

"And then I kept bleeding and bleeding, and we realized just how *very* badly hurt we were," Henry said, milking his injuries for all he was worth.

"Poor boy," Copper whispered. "Your mother will nurse you back to health when you get home." She smiled.

Henry dropped his eyes. Everyone was silent. "She died," he said at last. "I'm stuck with *her*." He pointed with his thumb at Lani. Alex and Samheed hid their grins.

"Oh—I'm sorry. About your mother, I mean."

"It's okay, Copper. You didn't know," Lani said. "Lots of us don't really have parents. It's different from Warbler in that way, I suppose." She reached over and patted Henry's hand and then put an arm around her brother and looked at him. "I guess you are hurt pretty bad," she conceded.

A small smile tugged at Henry's lips. "Yes. I might need some extra snacks to make me feel better."

Carina leaned over and opened a crate next to her. She pulled out a basket of treats and handed it to Henry. "That about right?" she asked him.

Henry pawed through the basket in delight. "I think this might work," he agreed.

Across from them, Sky smiled and reached out to hug her mother, silently grateful she had hers back.

"What happened next?" asked Carina. "Come on. We're anxious over here."

"We sent Kitten to explore," Henry said, "and hung out in that slave room until she brought Alex back. Good work, Kitten!"

Kitten emerged from Crow's pocket, her eyes sleepy. She smiled and arched her back. "Mewmewmew!"

Fox opened his mouth and took a breath, and then glanced at Simber. He closed his mouth again and pointed his nose at the deck.

"Before we go on to hear Florence's story," Alex said, "I

have an unrelated question." He noticed they were floating to the west, and that they were precariously close to where Pirate Island would appear when it next chose to surface. He felt strongly about getting out of there in case the pirates decided to come after them. But he didn't necessarily want to lead the pirates toward Artimé if they did decide to come after them. Still, he knew everyone was tired, and he wanted to see how the Unwanteds were feeling.

When Alex had everyone's attention, he asked, "Is everyone set on heading home? We're all present and in relatively good shape—except for Henry, of course, who is near death over there. But I guess I can't think of anything else to do but head straight back to Artimé." He lifted his eyebrows innocently. "Can you?"

The thought of doing something else beyond the rescue hadn't crossed anyone's mind. They shrugged and looked about. "I guess we should just go home," Sean said. "In case they need us." But he sounded a little disappointed.

Lani looked up. "They know how to send a seek spell if they need us. I think we should keep going west."

Samheed rolled his eyes.

Alex had had quite enough of their obscure argument. "What is going on with you two?"

They both began talking at once, so fast that neither one could be understood.

"Stop!" Alex shouted. "Stop it!"

They became silent.

Alex shook his head at them, his mouth open to speak, but he had no words for their ridiculous behavior. They hadn't fought like this since their early days in Artimé.

"Ahem, ahem," came a voice from the bow. "Excuse me, please."

Alex turned to look, glad for the distraction. It was Fox who had spoken. "What is it, Fox?" Alex asked.

"There is another island. I saw it last night when the sun went down and the moon was rising. I wanted to howl, but as I am a cat, I would never do that."

"You'rrre not a cat," Simber said to Fox through clenched teeth.

Alex knew there was one more island in this direction. He looked up at Simber. "Can you see it?"

"Yes, it's therrre."

The fox licked his lips and resisted the urge to pant.

From alongside the ship, Spike said, "That is where the squid went."

Alex rushed to the railing. "Really? I've been wondering about her crushed tentacle."

Spike looked up. "Oh, hello." She paused, as if realizing something. "The Alex. You are finished with the coughing."

Alex grinned and saluted. "Hello again, Spike Furious. Yes. Thank you for saving me."

Spike considered that for a long moment. "Yes, and thank you as well." She dove down and circled back. "The other big one went that way too, I think."

"What about the eel?"

The whale frowned. "The eel moves around. It doesn't live at the island. But the squid . . ." The whale trailed off, swimming just below the surface. "Oh no." And then she sped up and jumped into the air, landing with a splash, and with a swish of her tail she was speeding to the west.

Simber sampled the air and stared hard after the whale. "I'm going to follow herrr," he said. "Something strrrange is happening."

Alex looked at Simber, who pumped his wings and flew

off, following Spike. Fox stood at the bow of the ship, eyes like slits against the wind, and began yipping excitedly. Alex wasn't sure what was happening, but he was very sure he didn't want to miss it or go home, especially with two of Artimé's finest creatures heading in the exact opposite direction.

"Captain," Alex said with a decisive air, "follow that whale."

The Tale of the Statue

Captain Ahab couldn't have been happier to take off after a whale. Sean helped the captain adjust the sails, and soon the pirate ship was sailing at a brisk clip, following Simber and Spike. After a time, Simber slowed and waited for the ship to catch up.

Alex went to the stern of the ship, where he and Simber had often talked privately. Soon the cat pulled back even more until he was flying just over Alex's head. Alex wasn't sure if things were still off between them. He felt like they might be, and it troubled him greatly.

"I can't stand this anymore. I'm sorry, Simber," Alex said,

LISA McMANN

looking up. "I messed up. I should have known more about Florence—I got distracted, and I never thought to wonder about it. Can a giant warrior made of ebony swim? Does she breathe? I mean, I come from a very different world, where no one questions such things because they don't exist. But I've been in Artimé long enough to know I have to think harder, and differently, and I need to act more . . . more responsibly now that I'm in charge of so much. And I will." He thought again of Sky, and his heart twisted. "I will. Again, I'm sorry."

Florence, who was sitting near enough to hear, narrowed her eyes but remained quiet.

The cheetah harrumphed a few times. "All rrright," Simber said. He harrumphed again.

"Is something stuck in your throat?" Florence asked him. She wore a stern look. "An apology, maybe? What happened here, anyway?" She looked at Alex. "What's going on?"

Alex shoved his hands in his robe pockets. "We— I didn't know if you could swim. And I didn't know if you needed to breathe in order to live. And I should have known that before we set out. If I'd known, I could have had Simber do something more to help you against that eel. We were so worried—"

"Wait a second," Florence said. She looked at Simber. "Both of you seem to have forgotten that I am the Magical Warrior instructor. I command our army. And I was fully aware of the risks I was taking. If I had needed or wanted help, I would have asked for it! That eel couldn't hurt me, and I knew it. It was crucial—*crucial*, Simber, that you got everyone out of the water as quickly as possible, because that eel could hurt *them*." She paused. "I'm a little bit angry that you didn't trust me to know what I was doing."

"But you could have been stuck on the bottom of the ocean forrreverrr," Simber muttered, clearly not happy about being called out.

"You don't think I can walk home just because I'm under-water? Simber, please." Florence folded her arms.

"You werrre in a cage until I rrrescued you."

"Come on. I could have broken that glass just as easily as you. I was waiting for you to carry out the mission first so I didn't mess anything up!"

Simber was completely silent. He glared out over the water.

Alex sat very still, trying to disappear, as a few others over-heard and edged a bit closer to hear the argument.

LISA McMANN

"But, Florence, why didn't you move at all?" Carina asked, skirting around the hole in the deck and joining in. "We thought you were dead."

Florence tilted her head. "I'm sorry. I considered that. I truly did. But think about it. If you lived in that underwater island and you saw something like me *moving*, wouldn't that be a little bit alarming? Alarming enough to draw a lot of attention, and maybe have a band of pirates actually do something to me, and hinder your rescue efforts? I had to play statue so I didn't look like a threat."

Carina nodded. "That makes sense."

Alex silently agreed. Florence was a brilliant warrior. She'd done what she had to do for the sake of the mission. She'd let the eel take her away to save the rest of them, and she was fully aware of her own capabilities. She was a hero.

Florence turned to look at Alex. "I know you're the mage, Alex," she said, "and I will do whatever you command me to do. But I don't expect you to know every detail about my abilities and my weaknesses. I expect you to trust me, as a leader of Artimé, to know what I'm capable of and to ask for help if I need it." She glanced at Simber, who remained silent above

LISA McMANN

them. "I know it's hard when things like this happen. It's pain-ful. Sometimes we make sacrifices. Sometimes we lose dear friends whom we love deeply, and that makes us want to hold our other loved ones closer so we don't lose them, too."

Lani glanced at Samheed, who stared stubbornly at the deck. Sky smiled at her mother and flicked away a tear. Carina's face was melancholy as she gazed out over the sea toward home. Sean watched her for a moment, then looked away.

Alex was silent. Florence didn't take her eyes off Simber's face.

Finally Simber looked down at her. They held each other's attention for a long moment. "Shut up, Florrrence," grumbled the cat.

Florence's laughter rang out across the sea.

Back to the Jungle

Aaron had a hard time sleeping these days. Thoughts, ideas, and plans raced through his head. He hadn't been this excited in a long time, yet he kept his penchants hidden from the intrusive Secretary. But now he had Liam living at the palace too, adding another watchful eye on the high priest's daily activities.

"Why not give Haluki's house to Liam?" Secretary asked innocently one morning. "No one is using it."

"No," Aaron said a little too quickly. He shifted in his chair.

"But why? I don't understand. You don't even like Haluki."

"I despise him," Aaron said. "But that doesn't mean I'm

going to give his house away. Besides, I don't think Liam would want it after all the time he spent there."

Secretary sighed. "Well, that's probably true."

"We'll have one of the old governors removed. Liam can have their house."

Eva Fathom feigned confusion. "But not Haluki's, which is already empty." Then her face cleared. "Oh. Is this about the tube? I thought you destroyed it."

"The . . . the what? Oh, that," Aaron said, trying to sound nonchalant. "Yes, well, I tried to destroy it, but it's too big and solid. We certainly don't want anyone living in that house with such a dangerous thing in it." He paused. "And, by the way, the house was all wet inside the other day."

Eva appeared to be surprised. "You were there the other day?"

"To try to destroy the tube."

"Oh, right. Wet? Did you say wet?"

"Yes, the floor was wet, and water was dripping from the ceiling. I, um, I forgot about it until just now."

"Oh my. That's very strange."

"Yes, isn't it?" Aaron tapped his fingers on his desk. "Well, then. Off with you. I've got a very busy day. I'll be gone for a bit, so don't worry if you can't find me."

Eva nodded and headed toward the door. "Strang and Liam are already out there handling complaints and taking in information from our good citizens today."

"Keep an eye on Gondoleery," Aaron said.

"If she shows up," Eva said lightly. "Maybe we should consider keeping *her* in the palace." She disappeared into the hallway, leaving Aaron alone.

After a minute, Aaron opened his drawer, picked up the two heart attack spells, and put them in his pocket. He stood up and went to the window, wondering if anyone was hanging around the driveway. When he saw it was clear, he headed out of the palace, down the driveway, and past the guards at the portcullis, where a short line of Wanteds waited to tattle on their neighbors to the new governors in exchange for food. Aaron slowed, thanking them for coming to share their concerns or information. "You're making Quill a safer place to be," he said. He continued on down the road.

As Eva Fathom went outside to call in the next visitors, she saw Aaron in the distance turning down the governors' road. "Now what's he up to?" she muttered.

She went back inside and looked around Aaron's desk, checking the drawers. "He took the heart attack spells? Whatever for?" She looked up toward the closet and called out in a soft voice, "Matilda."

The gargoyle peeked out.

"Has Aaron been seen in Artimé?"

Matilda shook her head.

Eva frowned, then walked over to the gargoyle. She retied the bow around her horn and wiped some dust from her shoulders. "Poor thing, stuck in here all this time without Charlie. Are you holding up all right?"

Matilda smiled and nodded.

"I suppose it's a bit easier for statues," Eva admitted. "Anyway, tell Charlie that if Aaron shows up in Artimé today, to beware that he's got heart attack spells in his pocket."

Matilda nodded once more and climbed back into the box in the closet where Aaron had dumped her and forgotten her long ago.

» » « «

Arriving in the jungle once more, Aaron stepped out of the tube. He didn't see anyone at first, but soon he could just barely feel the earth vibrate below his feet, and when he turned, the enormous rock was right there. Aaron sucked in a startled breath. The rock's ability to sneak up on him was uncanny.

"Hello," Aaron said.

"Welcome back," the rock replied in his soft, rumbling voice. "I'm surprised to see you so soon." He seemed pleased.

Aaron smiled. "I wanted to make sure Panther was all right."

"She's fine."

Aaron started walking, venturing into the jungle down an obvious path that was just wide enough to fit an enormous moving rock. "And how are you?"

"I—I suppose I'm well too." He moved along with Aaron. "Would you like a tour?"

"I think I have time," Aaron said. He was dying for a tour, but he didn't want to seem too eager.

"Stay close to me, or your life could be in danger," the rock said.

"I will," Aaron said. "But won't everyone out here obey me?"

"Not everyone."

"Not even if you tell them I'm the new head mage?"

"No."

Aaron pursed his lips. He didn't like hearing that. He fingered the heart attack spells in his pocket, which he'd brought along for protection even though he hadn't thought he'd actually have to use them. Now he wasn't so sure. "This really is a dangerous job, isn't it?"

The rock seemed to nod. "This path," he said, "leads into the deepest, thickest part of the jungle, where no light can penetrate. The scorpion lives at the end of the path in a pitch-black cave of branches and vines." He paused. "Don't worry. We won't be going that far."

Aaron slowed. "Um, we could turn around now if you like."

"In a moment. Just ahead is where Dog lives." The rock pulled up to a small hollow in a large tree.

Aaron looked inside. He didn't see anything. Then slowly the outline of the dog appeared—it had blended in with the rich brown background of bark and dirt. The dog looked peaceful, sleeping there. But Aaron still had the teeth-size scabs on his arm to prove otherwise.

The little dog opened one eye, saw Aaron, and jumped

LISA McMANN

to his feet. His tail wagged. Aaron stepped back, but the dog didn't attack. He barked a few times.

"Hello again," Aaron said. "Just passing through. I didn't mean to wake you."

The dog's pointy teeth gleamed. He barked again.

"He's happy to see you," said the rock.

"Oh," Aaron said. "That's nice." He waved and then felt stupid about waving, so he folded his arms over his chest. He really had no idea how to communicate with animals. Or . . . statues. Or people, for that matter.

Aaron and the rock said good-bye to the dog and went back the way they'd come, toward the tube. When they reached the clearing, the rock switched directions and headed down another path.

"Where does this one lead?"

"This leads around the outside of the east wall of Quill. The only other way to access that end of the jungle from Quill is through the secret passage."

Aaron stopped in his tracks. "The . . . what?"

"Marcus didn't tell you about that either?" the rock thundered.

"No."

"Well." The rock stopped moving. "I'm sure he's blocked it off by now. He always meant to." He stayed still. "There's not much down there, anyway." Abruptly the rock turned, nearly running over Aaron's toes to get to the clearing once more and travel down a third path.

"This is the way to Artimé. It's a long walk. My path takes you as far as a stream. You'd have to cross the stream and travel quite a distance to go the rest of the way."

"Where do you end up?" Aaron asked.

The rock looked at Aaron for a long moment, and then he said in a skeptical voice, "Are you sure you're qualified to be doing this job?"

Aaron felt his face heat up. "Mr. Today died very suddenly," he said, getting defensive. "He didn't have time—"

Just then a furry gray creature dropped from a nearby tree onto Aaron's head. It bared its fangs and hissed. And then it chomped down hard on Aaron's shoulder. Aaron screamed and fell to the ground.

Aaron Hatches a Plan

R elease him!" the rock thundered.

The furry gray creature paused mid-chomp.

"Release!" screamed Aaron. Pain ripped through his shoulder, and he tried to shove the thing off of him. "Agh! Release!" He couldn't think.

The creature withdrew his fangs and hopped out of the way of Aaron's flailing arms, ran down the path to the nearest tree, and scurried up it.

Aaron flopped to his back in the dirt. "Ugh," he cried out. "What was that?" He squirmed, gripping his shoulder. "Why does everything here have to stinking *bite* me all the time?"

LISA McMANN

The top of the rock leaned over, peering at Aaron. "Are you okay?"

"No, I'm not!" Aaron said. He rolled to his good shoulder and rested there for a minute before he got to his feet. "What was that thing?" he asked again.

"That was actually not one of Marcus's creations," the rock rumbled. "There are a few of those around. Dropbears. They drifted to Artimé many, many years ago on some wreckage from a ship, or at least, that's what I remember from Marcus's story. But they are carnivores, so Marcus sent them here to the jungle. They're quite cuddly and fun-loving . . . if you're not edible."

Aaron lifted his hand to check his shoulder. "At least it let go of me."

"Yes. The dropbears aren't magical creatures, but Marcus did train them not to eat him by bringing them food."

"Perhaps you should have mentioned that to me last time," Aaron grumbled.

"I'm continually surprised at how little you know about us." The rock's cave-mouth closed. He rolled back to the clearing where the tube was. "You can clean your wound by the creek if you'd like."

"Sure, and wait for something else to attack me? I think I'd better go." Aaron pressed his shirt against the puncture wounds.

"Panther will be sorry she missed you. She's rather taken a liking to you. I don't think you'll find her attacking you anytime soon. Your work on her tail has made her loyal to you. If she'd been here, she'd have put that dropbear out of commission."

Aaron looked up at the rock. "Really?"

"Yes."

"Where is she now?"

"Out hunting, I suppose."

"Oh." Aaron looked at the rock.

"I hope you'll come back again."

Aaron didn't quite know what to make of such language. Nobody he knew actually said such . . . such emotional things, or expressed themselves quite like this rock was doing. Well, besides Alex. To Aaron, it didn't seem logical to *hope* anyone would do anything—did it? Either Aaron would come back or he wouldn't, and the rock would have to be fine either way. Hope was a waste of time.

"I will, I suppose." Aaron's shoulder throbbed, and his mind turned back to what the rock had said a moment before. "So, about Panther. You're saying she'd attack others if they seemed like they were trying to hurt me?"

"I think so, yes. But I don't know her thoughts."

A new idea was forming in Aaron's mind. "Actually, yes," he said slowly, "I'll definitely be back. Soon. Tell Panther I'd like to see her. I'd like that very much."

The Apology

Those who needed sleep slept. Those who didn't need sleep spent the hours conversing quietly or contemplating in silence. Namely, Simber.

In the morning, when Alex awoke, Simber approached.

"Will you come forrr a rrrride with me?" Simber asked, his voice more gruff than usual.

Alex resisted the urge to say, "I thought you'd never ask," and instead played along with Simber's game, knowing the proud cat found it extremely difficult to admit failures of any sort, even the smallest kind. He climbed aboard, and the two of them soared ahead of the ship.

Alex could see the new island in the distance, and it gave him a little thrill of fear and excitement. The island had a deep red outline. It was almost perfectly rounded, like a soup bowl floating upside down on the water. Trees grew on it, taller and more concentrated in the center.

"It looks quite nice from this far off, doesn't it?" Alex ventured after a bit.

"It does," agreed Simber. "Therrre's something odd about it. I haven't figurrred it out quite yet, though."

"Odd how?"

Simber didn't speak at first, and then he said, "Odd like Warrrblerrr, when we rrrealized therrre was no sound." He paused again. "It's not that, though. I can alrrready hearrr things. Bits of things. Nothing clearrrly, of courrrse."

"Life?"

"Yes."

Alex nodded. He could see Spike a short distance ahead of them, her spike cutting through the water. She hadn't let up her pace, and Alex had a feeling she could go much faster if she wanted to. He was so glad they'd found each other once again. It was interesting to see how she learned things.

"What do you think of Spike?" Alex asked after a bit.

"She's verrry smarrrt," Simber said. He clamped his jaw shut.

Alex felt the cat tense underneath him. "Yes, she seems to be picking up on things at lightning speed." He frowned, puzzled by the cat's reaction to the question. "I imagine she'll be a big help to us in the future," he continued.

Simber was silent. Alex could see him working his jaw.

"I would have told you more about her, really," Alex offered. "Eventually. I felt foolish, is all. About bringing her to life and losing her immediately."

"It's not a prrroblem," Simber said. "You don't have to tell me everrrything about yourrr plans."

"I almost always do, though," Alex said. He had no idea what was happening with this conversation. Simber seemed almost hostile.

"Well, now you won't have to."

"What?" Alex exclaimed.

"I assume you intend to rrreplace me."

Alex nearly fell off the giant cat's back. "Don't be insane!" he cried. He flung his arms around the giant statue's neck and held on. "Simber, you've gone completely bonkers if you think I would ever want to replace you! Is that what you've been thinking?"

Simber growled, but his neck and back relaxed a bit. "It crrrossed my mind."

Alex closed his eyes and held the beast, pressing his cheek against the smooth stone of his neck. "Oh, Simber," he said in a quiet voice. "I wouldn't want to live without you by my side. You're my best friend. I . . . I love you."

Simber was silent as they soared through the air toward the red island. After a while, he cleared his throat and said in the gruffest voice Alex had ever heard, "I'm sorrry about the way I trrreated you." The cat swallowed hard. "I was wrrrong to speak to you that way in frrront of everrryone. I won't do that again."

A smile tugged at the corner of Alex's mouth. He knew how hard it was for Simber to say that. He stroked the cheetah's neck.

"And . . . ," Simber said.

Alex waited a beat. "And?" he prompted.

"And . . . I love you, too. Harrrumph!"

Alex's smile spread across his face.

The Island of Legends

When Spike began to jump through the water, Simber turned his ears toward her. A moment later, he slowed. "Hang on," he said to Alex.

Alex hung on. Simber swooped around and headed back toward the ship. "Ease up, Ahab," Simber called out.

The captain adjusted the sails and the ship began to slow.

To Alex, Simber said, "Spike noticed something strrrange about the island too. We'rrre going to apprrroach with caution."

"Good call," Alex said. "Did she say what was strange about it? I can't hear what she's saying."

LISA McMANN

Simber swooped down near Spike so that Alex could speak to the whale directly.

"Spike, what's happening?" Alex asked.

"It is moving."

"What is? The island?"

"Yes. But not up and down like other islands do."

Alex squinted at the island, which wasn't far off now. "Simber, do you notice that?"

"I'd thought it as well but wasn't surrre. It's verrry slow, like it's floating. It's just . . . strrrange."

They continued on. Spike disappeared beneath the surface to check things out from below, while Simber and Alex flew back to the ship to update the others. As the ship drew close to shore, they could begin to see details on the lush plants and trees grow-ing both on the mainland and also along twin reefs that jutted out into the water. The reefs formed a large lagoon where the water was calm. Captain Ahab guided the ship into the calm water.

Soon Spike surfaced alongside the ship. "The squid is here. He's in a lot of pain."

Carina looked over the railing. "I can help him." She glanced at Alex. "Is it all right if I go?"

Alex knit his brows together, thinking. He was extremely wary about this island, based on his past experiences with the other islands. But Spike was there. "Spike," Alex called.

The whale surfaced.

"I want you to stay close to Carina, and if we retreat, I want you to take her and follow us right way."

"And me," Sean said. "I'd like to go too."

Alex nodded. "That's fine. You guys see if you can help out the squid. I'm going to take a team on shore. If you see any danger, get out of there."

"Aye, aye, boss," Sean said.

The squirrelicorns lifted Sean and Carina and lowered them to Spike's back.

"Hold on. We can zoom together. The Alex made me very fast," Spike explained.

Sean and Carina exchanged amused looks and grabbed on. Soon they and Spike disappeared.

Alex turned his back to the island and surveyed the group that remained, looking first to the injured. "Ms. Octavia, Lani, Henry, Copper, you're staying here. Sky and Crow, now that you have your mother back, you're not allowed to risk your lives for at least a week, so you stay too."

Sky didn't smile. She didn't even look at Alex.

He hurried on with his announcements. "Squirrelicorns, stay put for now. Ahab will stay with the ship as usual. So who . . . ," he said slowly, as if he were thinking very hard, "am I going . . ."—Fox scrabbled to his feet—"to bring with me?" Alex gazed at the remaining Artiméans.

Fox began hopping, one front leg raised.

Alex pretended not to see him. "Let's see, so that leaves Samheed, Kitten, Simber . . ."

The fox hopped higher.

"And Florence."

Fox deflated.

Alex grinned. "And Fox, of course."

The fox beamed.

Simber rolled his eyes. "Perrrhaps I'll sit this one out."

"Alex," Samheed interrupted. "Everybody. Check it out." He pointed to land, where the sea monster from the Pirate Island aquarium was climbing onto the sandy shore. Her short, stout legs and flippers made her waddle from side to side as she walked.

"So she's a land monster too," Alex mused. "She looks a little like a girrino, only with shorter legs and no fur."

"And her face is more horselike," Lani added.

Alex didn't really know what a horse looked like—he'd only ridden on invisible ones. But he took Lani's word for it. And he hoped the monster was friendly.

As Alex and the others went about planning the safest way to visit the island, Carina and Sean surfaced for air. Spike circled around, her spike catching the light and sparkling as she turned.

"We're getting the squid's tentacle all fixed up," Carina reported.

"Spike talked to the squid a bit more," Sean said. "I guess the eel has been terrorizing all the water creatures who live around this island."

"All the water creatures?" Alex asked. "Are there more than just the squid and the sea monster?"

"There are a few more," Carina said. "And some land creatures too. We're trying to get the scoop. But the important thing is that this island seems to be safe for us to approach—especially since we saved two of its inhabitants."

"Yeah," added Sean, "Spike saw the sea monster and told her that you guys were going ashore, so she went ahead to tell some guy named Talon that you're friendly."

Alex felt a surge of excitement. It was a relief knowing there were some nice places out here. And people, too? He couldn't wait to meet this Talon guy.

Carina and Sean went back underwater to work on the squid some more, and Alex had Ahab swing the ship around and pull up along the reef so that Florence could get out.

As the small group disembarked and Florence carefully stepped one foot out of the ship, something glinting in the sun caught her eye. She looked up.

Standing on the shore was a gorgeous, shirtless giant. He had wings on his back. And he was made entirely of bronze.

Florence gasped. Her foot clipped the edge of the ship. She lost her balance and fell, grabbing on to the reef with one hand as her lower half hit the water.

Without a second's hesitation, the reef curled around her. The end of it opened up like a giant claw. It grabbed Florence around the waist, lifted her up into the air, and set her effortlessly on the shore next to the man.

The bronze man observed Florence for a moment, and then he bowed before her and offered his hand. "Greetings, beautiful stranger," he said in a deep, musical voice. "I am Talon. Welcome to the shell of Karkinos the crab, known to some as the Island of Legends."

A Brief Respite

Once Florence had gotten hold of her senses, she introduced herself, Alex, Samheed, Fox, Kitten, and Simber to Talon.

As they were greeting each other the sea-and-land monster from the Pirate Island cage waddled over to Talon's side. "This is Issie," Talon said. He reached out his enormous hand and scritched her long neck. Issie bobbed her head in greeting and continued walking to the edge of the island. She slid into the water, her head above the surface, the humps on her back rippling as she emitted a mesmerizing, forlorn call, looking this way and that.

"What's wrong with her?" Alex asked in a hushed voice.

Talon gazed after the beast. "She's looking for her foal."

Fox hopped. "Kitten and I can help her look for it."

Talon looked down at the fox, a sad smile on his face. "That's very kind, but I doubt you'll find it. Issie has been looking for her foal for quite a long time."

"How long?" Florence asked. "Was it captured by the eel as well?"

Talon turned his gaze to Florence and made no attempt to hide his admiration of her sleek muscles. "No. It's been seven hundred years," he said.

Alex and Samheed exchanged a glance. Was this guy joking? They didn't think so. And what was the deal with the crab?

Simber walked gingerly over the island, sniffing and checking things out. The colossal crab was obviously alive but had clearly been here for a very long time, floating on the sea. Its shell and its claws—the twin reefs—were covered with sand and plants and trees, though the deep red color of the crab's shell dominated along the edge of it.

Suddenly Simber growled and crouched, his ears flattened against his head.

Alex whirled around, pulling components from his robe. "What is it?" he said.

From behind a clump of trees came two majestic creatures. A furry white lioness with blue accents, who seemed to be floating just above the ground, and a white deer with stunning golden horns.

Talon held his hand out to Simber and Alex. "We are peaceful here, friends," he said. "We wish no harm to anyone who comes here. May I introduce Lhasa the snow lion? She is our queen. And this is Bock."

"Hello," Lhasa said. She smiled brightly. Bock was silent, but he nodded politely.

Alex greeted the creatures with caution. Simber remained skeptical. "Wherrre arrre yourrr enemies?" Simber asked. "Surrrely you have some."

Talon smiled. "Our enemies are all dead except for one."

Lhasa stepped around some delicate-looking plants and made her way toward the Artiméans. She hovered just above the sand nearby, content to observe.

"Dead?" Simber's interest was piqued.

"We killed them," Talon said matter-of-factly, as if he were describing what he ate for breakfast.

"I see," Simber said. He rose from his crouched position and sat. "And the one?"

"You've met him. The eel. He eludes us. I've chopped his tail off twice, the slimy worm, but he simply grows it back. He's caused quite a lot of grief for our sea creatures."

"Then it seems we sharrre an enemy."

"Indeed. Which is why we ought to be friends."

Ever cautious, Simber kept his guard up. "Perrrhaps."

Talon turned to Alex. "Issie and the squid were gone for many weeks. We feared the worst. But Issie tells me your group saved her."

"Simber did, actually," Alex said modestly. "And Spike, our whale friend." He turned to look out to sea, feeling a bit uneasy. "Spike stabbed the eel, but it got away."

"It nearly capsized our ship," Florence said.

"Florence saved all of us that time," Samheed said.

"I do not doubt it," Talon said.

If Florence could blush, she most likely would have.

Lhasa the snow lion, rose to her feet. "We would like to thank you for rescuing our friends. Won't you all come explore—your injured friends too?" She pointed to the ship, where Henry, Lani, Sky, Crow, and Copper all stood watching them. "We shall prepare a feast to celebrate the return of Issie and the squid."

Alex looked at Simber. Simber raised an eyebrow at Florence. Florence nodded.

"We'd love that," Alex said. "Thank you."

Within the hour, everyone except Ahab was either resting in the shade on the edge of the crustaceous island or preparing to explore the various paths. Ahab desired to remain with the ship, which was really better for everyone, Alex decided. Sean and Carina had finished working on the squid and were thrilled to catch their breath and enjoy a cool drink.

Lani, who was feeling quite good now, joined Samheed, and thankfully they refrained from arguing. They stood beside Alex and Simber in front of Talon and waited for instructions.

"If you reach Vido the golden rooster," Talon said, "perched high in the tallest tree, you will know you are at the center of the island. Beware of dropbears when walking through the most forested parts of the island," he told them. "They won't hurt you, but they might frighten you. They like to play tricks."

"Dropbears?" Lani asked under her breath. "Now I can't wait. Let's go!"

"What are dropbears?" Samheed whispered back.

"I have no idea, but they sound adorable. I bet they're tiny little bears."

"Drop-size?"

Lani smirked. "Exactly. Or at least I hope so."

"If you see the hibagon, try not to stare or you might fall in love," Talon said with a smile. "He's about Lani's height. Brown fur. Kind of . . . blurry."

"Blurrry?" Simber asked.

"Not in focus," Talon said. "You'll see what I mean if he makes an appearance. It's hard to describe. But for the most part he keeps to himself. You'll smell him well before you see him." Talon looked around. "Does anyone have any questions?"

They all did, but no one voiced them, preferring to find out the answers for themselves.

The Tale of Talon

While half the Artiméans explored the Island of Legends, the other half rested on the beach near the lagoon. Florence, who could see quite a bit of the island just by standing, opted to check in with Spike, who had been swimming around the lagoon chatting with Issie in a language Florence couldn't understand.

"Any sign of the eel?" Florence asked.

"No. How did you come back to life?"

"What? Oh. I wasn't dead. I was just pretending to be."

"Oh. Why does Issie have legs and I do not have legs?"

Florence blinked. "You'll have to ask Alex. But you do have a very lovely spike on your head."

"I did not know that until I ran into the glass wall."

"You can't see it?"

The whale scrunched up her face, eyes crossing to get a look at the spike. "No, but I saw it in the glass after I hit it. Where is the Alex?"

"He's exploring the island."

"This island is alive, you know. It is named crab. It is much, much bigger than the squid."

Florence smiled. "I noticed that."

"The shiny man is behind you."

"What?" Florence whirled around, hands in the air and ready to fight or cast any number of spells.

Talon held up his hands and took a step back in defense. "My humble apologies, Lady Florence," he said. "I didn't want to interrupt your conversation. The whale is very beautiful. I haven't seen anything like it."

"Thank you," said Spike. She darted away.

Florence held her pose for a moment and lowered her fists. "Sorry."

LISA McMANN

Talon smiled warmly. "I believe you must be a tremendous warrior. I'll have to tell the dropbears that it wouldn't be wise for them to drop down on your head."

"If they know what's good for them, they'll steer clear," Florence agreed.

Talon sat down, folding his wings in closely. He didn't seem to use them much.

Florence hesitated, and then sat next to him. "What is your role here?" she asked. "You seem to be in charge, though you called Lhasa the queen."

"No one has any more power than anyone else here. I like to think that I am the protector of the island," he said. "I . . . I look after Karkinos. For now, anyway."

"The crab," Florence said, remembering. "I suppose a crab so large must need a lot to eat."

"The squid helps."

"Does the squid have a name?"

"I would imagine so, but I don't know what it is."

"Why would he help the crab at all? Two large carnivores seem like they'd be unlikely allies."

"Yes," Talon agreed, "but the island offers vegetation that

grows over the side, attracting fish. The crab's claws offer protection from the eel. The crab allows the squid to stay protected if the squid brings it food. As long as the crab survives, the squid survives."

"Unless the squid moves too far away from the crab's claws and gets captured."

"A mistake he's not likely to make again, after what he's been through."

Florence drew her knees up and clasped her arms around them. "And what about Issie? You said she's been searching for her foal for seven hundred years."

"At least," said Talon. "That's about when she arrived here. She might have been searching before."

"Where did she come from?"

"We don't know. Our communication is limited. She says she's from another world. Perhaps she means another island. Could she be from yours? She came during a storm."

"I—I don't think so. We are all very young compared to you and Issie and Karkinos."

Talon gazed out over the water. His face was troubled. "Sometimes I think Karkinos was here before the sea."

His simple, profound words made Florence feel things she'd never felt before. She didn't notice his troubled look. "And you?" she asked. "Have you always been here?"

"As long as I can remember. One day I woke up here, saved by the crab as you were, though being alone and without a ship, I imagine my circumstances were a bit more dire." He ducked his head. "Not to minimize your near-tragic stumble, of course."

Florence laughed. "If that was the worst I'd been through, I'd have no stories to tell."

"Even if you made them up, I'd listen to all your stories until there were no more and then demand you begin again."

"I— Oh my." Florence shifted in the sand, her mind grasping for something, anything, to say. She blurted out, "How long have you been here?"

He flashed a teasing smile but grew serious once more. "I don't know. Thousands of years."

Florence could hardly imagine it. "Thousands," she repeated.

Talon nodded. "It's nice to have visitors."

Florence looked at him. He caught her gaze and held it.

"Do you get many visitors?" she asked finally.

"Only a handful in recent years." His gaze drifted to Pirate Island, a mere dot on the horizon. "Pirates came a few times. They stole some of our plants and trees during the night and escaped." He scratched his chin. "If only they had asked, we would have given them whatever they wanted. We have more than we need. There was no reason for their stealth. But because of their actions, we'll never trust them." He looked at the pirate ship. "I feared you were from there when I first saw your ship."

"This ship wrecked on our island some years ago with two dying pirates aboard," Florence said. "Our leader restored it and made it sound again."

"Alex?"

"No, the one before him." She grew thoughtful. "Do you suppose we've stolen the ship from the pirates if we've made no attempt to give it back?"

Talon thought about it for a while. "Sounds rather to me that your ship was trying to escape them. My verdict is that you've done the ship a good deed."

"I'd like to think so," Florence said. She couldn't imagine

LISA McMANN

what shape the ship would be in if it had stayed docked at Pirate Island when the volcano sank. "The pirates—they steal people too, and keep them as slaves. That's why we had to pay them a visit. And now they're stealing your sea creatures."

"So it seems, and I know not why. From what you've recounted, it appears the eel is under their command." He shook his head. "I don't understand their motivations."

"I don't either." She thought about Quill and Warbler. "I don't understand many things about the evil people in our world."

"I can tell you've seen more of them than I have, Florence. I hope you believe me—you have nothing to fear here."

Florence dropped her gaze. "It's a relief to know it. And you have nothing to fear from us . . . unless your sinister dropbears make a false move." She smiled and looked out over the sea to the east, toward home, feeling strangely melancholy. "We'll need to go back soon. We won't trouble you for long."

Talon was silent for a long time. And then he sighed and said in a soft voice, "Never have I desired trouble more."

The Tales of Vido, the Dropbears, and Lhasa

He's so hot!" Lani whispered. "Seriously—I almost burned my arm when I bumped into him. I thought Florence was hot after a day in the sun, but Talon, being metallic, is even hotter. I bet he sizzles when he goes in the water." Lani, Samheed, Alex, and Sky sat around a campfire while Talon served them dinner.

"I can fry an egg on my biceps," Talon agreed. "Would anyone like an egg? I can ask Vido if his hen friends have any." Then he shook his head in disgust. "Chickens," he said. "Foul creatures. I don't understand them at all."

LISA McMANN

Sky and Lani erupted into laughter. "No, thank you. We're so full already. Everything was delicious!"

"And speaking of Vido," Samheed asked, "what is up with that golden rooster guy? Does he ever come down from that tree?"

"No, he never does," said Lhasa, a mischievous smile on her face. She float-walked over to the fire and sat just above the ground nearby. Florence, Simber, and Bock, the golden-horned deer, gathered as well. "Vido doesn't leave his post. He's waiting for the gods and spirits to return." Lhasa waggled her furry head. "I keep telling him we are here already, right, Talon?" She tittered.

Talon, who had finished serving his guests, sat down across the fire from Florence and smiled at her. "Yes. In the meantime, he has plenty of advice, whether you desire it or not."

Alex spoke. "He told me that when I look in the mirror, a stranger looks back." He scratched his head. "I'm afraid to ask what that means."

Sky sat up. "He told me a girl with eyes of fire has a heart of ice." She gave Alex a long look. "So don't mess with me."

He grinned uneasily.

Talon watched all this with a smile on his face. "I wouldn't worry about anything Vido says."

"He *opined* that a beast without furrr has narrry an hourrr to live," Simber drawled. "I told him that a birrrd without featherrrs has about ten seconds." He licked his paw and began working a claw with his teeth. "That shut him up."

The snow lion laughed. "He's harmless. Very spiritual and superstitious."

"I don't blame him forrr finding the tallest trrree to sit in, though. I almost had a few drrropbearrrs for lunch."

Florence grinned. "What happened? What do they look like?"

"They're not tiny," Samheed said with a wry grin. "About the size of a really fat baby. They look soft and cuddly. Gray and white and furry with long arms, cute round ears, and black button noses. They sit in the trees eating leaves and being all cute—cute enough that you think, 'Hey, I should get one of these down for the girl I like, and maybe she'll forget we're fighting.'" He glanced at Lani, who started laughing. "But I do not recommend that."

Florence's eyes widened. "What happened?"

"As soon as he started climbing the tree," Alex said, "about a hundred of these things started dropping out of nowhere and onto our heads. They grabbed our hair like reins and rode on our backs like knapsacks. They clung to our arms and legs until we were completely covered with them."

"And then there were the fangs," Lani said, still laughing. "If we tried to get the dropbears off, they opened their mouths and showed us their giant fangs, and then they started growling and hissing! It was so weird to see these cuddly-looking creatures turn into your worst nightmare." She wiped her eyes and sighed. "But you were right, Talon. They didn't hurt us. After a while they got bored and climbed the trees again."

"Where did they come from?" Florence asked.

"They were here when I got here," Talon said. "None of us understands their language, but they seem to understand me, at least a little. In the early years, when it was just Vido and me, they would attack and try to bite me, but it didn't hurt and eventually they stopped. I think it has something to do with the metal," he said, rapping on his chest. "It's a bit hard on the teeth. They are tame now and stick to eating plants. Too afraid to try to take a bite of anything that moves."

Alex was fascinated. After a moment, he looked at Lhasa. "When did you arrive?"

"I was born here," the snow lion said. "My father was kidnapped by sailors, and my mother drowned chasing after them." She didn't seem bothered by this. "Talon was too heavy for the sailors to carry, so they tied him down. The dropbears bit through Talon's ropes and set him free, and Talon found me and took care of me."

"How is it that you seem to float just above the ground?" Ms. Octavia asked from the shadows. She didn't like to sit too near a fire because it dried out her skin.

The snow lion laughed merrily. "I should ask the same of you."

"Oh, me—it's just an optical illusion," Ms. Octavia said. "I sort of roll along on several tentacles, but each only touches the ground for a short time, so it looks like I'm floating."

"I have always been this way." Lhasa lounged to one side dramatically. "Talon says it is because I am a queen, but Vido thinks it is because my mother's spirit is inside me, lifting me up." Her laughter filled the air again.

"And who do you believe?" Ms. Octavia asked.

LISA McMANN

"Both, of course." She got to her four paws and shook a tiny bit of sand out of her fur. "One day I shall get revenge on those sailors." She smiled the sweetest, most unassuming smile imaginable and, seeing all eyes on her, pranced to the edge of the island. "I shall thunder around the world! Skate across the sea! Find those evil sailors and bring my father home with me!" She teetered at the edge of the island, then flounced over the water and hovered there, too, not even getting the least bit wet in the process. "Ha! Tricked you." She grinned and shook her head from side to side, her fur flying joyously.

"Wow!" Lani said. "You can float above the water, too? Ms. Octavia can't do that." She looked at Ms. Octavia. "Wait. You can't, can you?"

Ms. Octavia tapped her lips. "I might be able to think of a way to do it with magic," she said. "But no . . . if I walk off the edge, I'll fall in the water."

Samheed, who couldn't take his eyes off the snow lion, felt like applauding. He ran over to the edge. "You were born to act on the stage, Lhasa," he said, with the deepest admiration in his voice.

"The stage, the stage," Lhasa sang. She pranced over the water. "What is the sta—"

But she didn't have time finish her question, because the giant eel burst from the water, curled around her belly, and pulled her under.

The Return of the Eel

What? Stop!" Talon's wings unfurled, and he flew like the wind to the water, his hands gripping his head in shock and disbelief. "Where is she?"

Samheed, who had come to his senses, turned back to the group and shouted, "It's the eel! Get back!" He ran to help Henry and Copper move away from the edge.

Florence and Simber thundered over. Sean and Carina kicked off their shoes and dove into the water. Alex whipped off his robe, throwing it at Lani. "Stay here!" he yelled. "Move everybody to the center of the island!"

The crab's reefy claws began clicking out in the darkness.

"Get back, Alex!" Simber roared.

But Alex didn't listen. He grabbed a blinding highlighter and dove in after Sean and Carina into the cool, silent darkness of the sea. Above him, Florence plunged her face into the water, and next to her, Talon did as well, both of them straining to see.

The eel wasn't far off. Alex did a double take—the eel seemed much bigger than it had been before, nearly twice the size. Was it even the same one? If so, it must have been eating a ton to have grown so large. It swam lazily just below the crab's reach, with Lhasa dangling like a rag doll inside the curl of its tail. There wasn't much time before she'd be dead, Alex knew. He began firing spells, knowing they probably wouldn't work but not having many other alternatives. Sean and Carina tried the same, but soon all three of them gave up. Their only hope was to get Lhasa to the surface, and there was no spell for that.

Sean pointed frantically at Lhasa and then upward, trying to tell Carina and Alex to go to her and attempt to push the eel's tail above the water. They nodded and swam over while

LISA McMANN

Sean grabbed a blinding highlighter and went straight for the eel's head.

The eel struck. Sean dodged, then grabbed on to the creature, sliding around to the back of the eel's head. He reached around with the highlighter and stabbed it in the eel's eye socket.

The eel writhed and screamed. Sean hung on for dear life. The crab snapped its pincers at the eel, but it was still out of reach. Alex and Carina watched in horror as Sean stabbed at the creature again.

This time the eel dodged the blow. It rose up and out of the water at a dizzying pace, Sean still clinging to its head, and flung its front half onto the island. It began twisting and rolling, hitting everything in its path, destroying plants, trees, and the campfire, and bowling over Simber and Florence.

Talon grabbed the middle of the eel, draped it over one shoulder, and heaved with all his might, trying to pull it onto the island, no doubt hoping to find Lhasa at the end of it. As the eel squirmed, Talon pulled, using his wings to help gain momentum. Florence got to her feet and ran to join him. But as soon as the eel lifted Lhasa out of the water, it let go of her, leaving her floating motionless just above the surface several yards off shore. Simber charged and sprang into the air, flying out over the water to rescue Lhasa. He grabbed her by the scruff of her neck and flew up, out of reach of the eel, then over the trees toward the center of the island.

The eel whipped its now empty tail around Talon, pulled him off his feet, and slithered over plants and trees, screeching and rolling, and slamming Talon into the ground.

Sean couldn't hang on any longer. After a violent shake of the eel's head, he let go and went flying through the air, landing with a sickening thud.

Simber returned from dropping off Lhasa, shouting, "Spike! Find Alex!" He lunged at the eel, sinking his claws into the slippery skin, while Florence grabbed on to its head, trying to hold the creature still. But the eel slipped out of her grasp and knocked her over.

Dangling in the air, wrapped in the eel's tail, Talon managed to pull his sword from his belt. With all his strength he struck the eel, slicing clean through it. The eel screeched as

LISA McMANN

its tail fell to the ground with Talon still wrapped inside.

The eel began to flail even more, rolling and twisting its way toward the center of the island, bucking Simber off and swatting Florence aside.

Talon, stunned from the fall, fumbled free of the still squirming tail and bounded after the creature. The tail wiggled its way to the water's edge and fell into the sea.

In the water, Spike rushed to the shore, towing Carina and Alex, breathless and trying to figure out what was happening.

"Holy smokes!" Carina yelled. "The eel is on the island. It's destroying everything!"

They pulled themselves ashore and ran toward the horrendous noise.

When they reached the destruction, all they could do was watch in horror. The eel had twisted around, and with a violent slap, it sent Simber soaring into the air once more. Simber came roaring back, his jaw not quite wide enough to grip the thicker parts of the beast, and his claws doing little to stop the eel from terrorizing everyone in its path.

The slimy creature batted Simber away and lunged at

Talon, grabbing the bronze man in its mouth as it snaked its severed end around Florence, rolling her up in it. She managed to free her hands just as Talon began to push up on the eel's jaw, trying to pull his body free.

The eel screeched. Suddenly a bright, blinding light sparked all around. Talon cried out in pain, his entire body lighting up like a fireball. Smoke poured from around him. Florence shuddered with the jolt of electricity, unable to move. When it was over, she reached behind her and pulled an arrow from her quiver and the mighty bow from her shoulder.

"Talon!" Florence yelled.

As the eel shook her all around, Florence painstakingly nocked the arrow and waited until the eel had curled her around to face its head once more. When it did, she drew back the arrow and aimed. "Talon, don't move!"

She released the shot with a powerful *thwack* that resonated across the island. Florence's arrow soared straight and true, missing Talon's neck by inches and burying itself deep between the eel's eyes.

The eel's scream died in its throat.

LISA McMANN

With a loud crash, its head flopped to the ground, throwing Talon hard into the brush. The severed end followed, slamming Florence into a copse of trees.

On the second impact, there was a thunderous snap of tree trunks, followed by an eerie silence. The eel quivered and was still. And then a hundred dropbears descended onto the creature and covered it.

The First Life of Lhasa

Alex, Carina, and Simber rushed to where Florence lay on top of several felled trees. One arm and her bow rested a short distance away. Alex and Carina scrambled onto the tree trunks and ran along them to Florence's side.

"Florence, you did it!" Alex shouted. "You got the eel!"

"Are you okay?" Carina asked.

Simber pushed gently on the trees from the other end and peered at Florence's face. "Florrrence?" He wore a look of concern.

Florence stared up at the sky. She turned her head gingerly

LISA McMANN

from side to side and checked the joints and fingers of her still attached arm. Then she sat up and looked down at her other shoulder. "Well, that's a bit inconvenient. Not as bad as when my legs got lopped off at the knees, though. I'll manage."

"Can I give you a *hand* out of that trrree?" Simber asked.

"Har har, Cat," Florence said. She eased up to a sitting position, checking her quiver first to make sure she hadn't lost any arrows, and then her back, her legs, and her feet. "I think I'm all in two pieces."

She grasped Simber's neck and he helped pull her to her feet. "I got 'im good, eh, Alex?" she said with a grin.

"Right between the eyes," Alex said. "I've never seen you use your bow before."

"I only have one quiver of magical arrows. Once they're spent, they lose their magic. So I only use them if I really, really need them." She looked around, worried. "Is everyone else okay?"

She heard a step behind her and whirled around to see Talon coming toward them. "You used a precious arrow for my sake," the bronze giant said, his voice full of wonder, but it turned to despair when he saw her missing limb. "And you've lost an arm—" He clapped his hand to his head in horror.

"Don't worry," Florence assured him, "it doesn't hurt, and Ms. Octavia can fix it." She looked at Simber. "Besides, we have bigger things to worry about. Where's Lhasa?"

"I left herrr with Lani and Sky in the centerrr of the island."

"Was she . . . alive?" Talon asked fearfully. "Oh, how foolish . . ." He began to run toward the center of the island, not waiting for an answer.

Florence looked at Simber.

"Go," Simber said. "We'll get yourrr arrrm and meet you therrre."

Alex and Carina picked up Florence's arm and bow and hoisted them onto Simber's back, balancing the items between them. Simber trotted a few steps and leaped into the air, weaving through trees, avoiding dropbears and other creatures they hadn't heard about yet, until they came to the gathering under the golden rooster's tree. The rooster peppered the silence with his occasional whimsical advice.

Simber hovered above the circle of humans and creatures and then found a clearing nearby where he could land. Henry, his head still bandaged, and Ms. Octavia, not quite back to her

LISA McMANN

plump self but making a steady recovery, worked over the snow lion.

Talon slipped through the crowd to Lhasa's side and knelt down. "How is she?"

Henry shook his head. "Not good." He pried open the snow lion's mouth and shook the contents of a small vial into it, but almost nothing came out. "Is it safe to go back to the ship?" he asked, looking up. "I have more medicine there."

"I'll go," Alex said. "Where is it?"

"In my healer's kit near the ship's wheel. Hurry."

"A wise man sacrifices speed for accuracy," squawked the rooster.

Alex hopped onto Simber's back, and the cheetah galloped toward Karkinos's head, to the lagoon where the ship sat completely unharmed by the eel. Simber jumped from the edge of the shore and sailed straight to the ship, flapping his wings backward to stop the momentum and letting Alex slide off.

"Everything okay?" Alex hollered at Captain Ahab.

"A sourer day this life has never seen!" the captain roared back. "Complete misery."

"Good to know," Alex muttered. He found Henry's kit and

raced back to Simber, grabbing the cat's wing and letting him flip him onto his back. They flew to the shore, where Simber took to the ground once more, speeding across the land, going so fast the dropbears missed them and landed on the path instead.

Simber skidded to a halt as Alex tossed the kit to Henry. Henry ripped it open and administered the liquid between Lhasa's lips. Carina came up to Alex and whispered, "She's not breathing. It doesn't look good."

"A life is but a small turn in time," remarked the rooster.

"Please, Vido. Not now," Talon said. The strain showed in his voice and on his face as he turned back to the snow lion. "Come on, Lhasa. Who will be the queen?" His voice broke.

Henry put his ear to the snow lion's heart. He raised a hand to her muzzle and held it there, hoping to feel her breath while everybody else held theirs. But there was nothing.

After a long minute, and then another, Henry bit his lip and looked up at Talon and Bock. "Our medicine didn't work," he said. He lowered his gaze. "I guess . . . I guess the eel just hurt her too badly. I—I'm sorry. She's . . ." His lip trembled.

"Is she dead, Henry?" Florence said gently.

Henry nodded.

No one spoke. Slowly Talon bowed his head and rested it in Lhasa's fur. Ms. Octavia dabbed her eyes. Samheed wrapped his arms around Lani's shoulders and hugged her. Alex stood numb, alone. Sky hesitated, then went over to him and rested her hand on his arm. Florence watched Talon for a moment and dropped her eyes.

From Crow's pocket, Kitten emerged and ran over to the fallen snow lion. She climbed up onto the beast and hopped up and down on Lhasa's chest. "Mewmewmew," she cried. "Mewmewmew."

Simber sat up. "What?" he asked, his face filled with concern.

Kitten stopped hopping and stared at Lhasa's face. "Mewmewmew!" she said again.

Fox, too forlorn over the death of the flopsy animal, didn't even try to translate.

"Arrre you surrre?" Simber growled at the kitten.

Kitten didn't respond. She stared at Lhasa for a long moment.

"What's happening?" Alex asked. "Doesn't she understand about Lhasa?"

"Mewmewmew!" Kitten cried again. She stared a moment

longer, and then she froze, tipped to one side, and fell over, a tiny, lifeless porcelain statue. Her body slid off the snow lion's slick fur and landed in the dirt. She didn't move.

But Lhasa did. She gasped and opened her eyes. She sputtered and coughed. She heaved and sighed. "Talon," she said weakly.

"Lhasa!" Talon exclaimed.

"Kitten, no!" Alex yelled. He ran to her, sliding on the dirt, and picked her up, clutching her with shaking hands. She was cold. Alex whirled around and stared at Simber. "What just happened? What did she do? What did she say?"

Simber just stared from Kitten to Alex in shock. He tilted his head slightly, as if he didn't know what to say. And then he blinked and shook his head. "Kitten is dead."

"What?"

"Let me think," he growled. Simber wore a distressed look Alex had never seen before. The statue began pacing, as if trying to figure something out. Suddenly he stopped and looked at Alex. "You have to brrring herrr back to life."

"What?" Alex exclaimed. "I can't! Not if she's dead."

"You have to trrry! Trrrust me, Alex. I'll explain in a minute.

LISA McMANN

I hope to, anyway. Just do it beforrre I have a hearrrt attack."

Alex's jumbled mind scrambled to think of the spell. Did he need the live spell or the restore spell? He looked around wildly at all the eyes, including Lhasa's, on him. And then Sky squeezed his arm. "I'll get the robe," she whispered. "You— just breathe."

She picked her way to Lani, who slid out of the robe and handed it over straightaway. Sky brought it back and helped Alex on with it. "Okay?" Sky asked him. "Just turn around and don't worry about them. Concentrate."

Fox began to howl. Even Simber didn't have the heart to quiet him.

Alex let out a breath. "Thanks." He was feeling better now after his moment of panic. He'd try the restore spell first. But he still didn't know if it would work—if either of the spells would. How did she just *die* like that? What kind of statue could just die on command? He cradled the cold kitten in his hand, trying to warm her, and began to concentrate on the words of the restore spell. He closed his eyes.

"Imagine," he whispered, imagining the adorable kitten racing around and hopping joyfully again. "Believe," he said, forcing himself to believe without a doubt that whatever had just happened, she could come alive again. "Whisper," he said, picturing his whisper swirling around and through Kitten, encouraging her to come alive once more, and then, "Breathe." Alex took in a deep breath and let it out, passing life to the porcelain creature. When he was quite sure everything was in place, he uttered the final word. "Commence." And then he began again from the beginning, two more times, ignoring the restless shuffling of feet and whispers and Fox's howling behind him. This spell was not one to be rushed.

When at last he was finished, he opened his eyes and opened his hand, and looked down at the kitten. Kitten didn't move.

"Kitten?" Alex said, his heart pounding.

Kitten remained still, her face serene, her eyes closed.

"Oh no," Alex breathed. What had he done wrong? What was going on?

And then Kitten jumped to her feet, shouting at the top of her tiny voice, "Mewmew*ha!*"

Alex gasped. And then he felt like throwing Kitten at a tree. "Ugh!" he said. "You statues need to stop! Don't ever do that to me again." He clutched his heart. "That trick is officially no longer funny."

"Mewmewha!" Kitten said, laughing.

The crowd around Alex exploded in relief, with Kitten chattering over and over again, "Mewmewmew!"

Alex raised his hand over the joyous noise. "Now somebody please explain to me what just happened."

Just then somebody grabbed Alex's arm. He turned, surprised at the strong grip. It was Carina, her face awash in fear. "Alex," she said. "Where's Sean?"

A Setback

Alex looked at all the faces. Sean wasn't there. "Hey!" he shouted over the noise. "Has anybody seen Sean?" Simber and Florence turned sharply to look at him. Samheed and Lani craned their necks to see what was happening.

"Sean!" Carina yelled. She gripped Alex's arm tighter. "Oh, Alex, where is he? I haven't seen him since the eel pulled him out of the water, and then everything happened and I didn't notice he wasn't here—"

"I didn't see wherrre he went once the eel landed on the island," Simber said. "Did you, Florrrence?"

LISA McMANN

"No, I was getting steamrolled with you."

The two looked at each other, as if speaking without making a sound.

"I'll organize on the ground," said Florence.

"I'll searrrch frrrom overrrhead."

"I'll help," Talon said.

Simber and Talon rose from the ground together and then split up, flying in separate directions over the island. It was easier for Simber in the dark, because he at least had his sense of smell and could see quite well without much light. The rest of the Artiméans, along with Lhasa—who was feeling fine again—and Bock, began searching the island on foot.

It took an hour before a shout rang out. "He's here!" Samheed yelled, not far away from Alex, Carina, and Sky. "Tail side of the island!" Word spread from one group to the next, and everyone headed in that direction.

Carina broke into a run when she saw Samheed waving people over to the location where Sean lay. Alex stayed right behind her. When they got there, they knelt down on the ground next to the lump.

Sean's face and body were covered in sweat. Sand stuck to

his skin. Lying on his side, he breathed in jagged bursts, every now and then a moan escaping his lips. His eyes were open, but glassy. He was covered in scratches.

Carina pushed his hair off his forehead. "Sean," she said softly.

He attempted a smile and then winced. "Hey," he managed to say. "Thought you'd never come."

"I'm so sorry," she said. Hurriedly she began checking him over. "What hurts?"

"Leg," he said. "It's pretty bad."

More help arrived. Alex cleared out of the way, making room for Ms. Octavia and Henry to see what they could do for Sean. Henry looked inside his kit.

"Don't give me . . . ," Sean wheezed, "that crud . . . you gave Alex . . . that one time . . . when he puked all night." His breath was shallow, yet he grinned as he tried to manage the pain.

Carina smiled. "You know firsthand that we've improved a lot since then. None of us wants to see you puke." She reached out and took his hand in hers, and with her other hand she smoothed his hair back again, gazing down at him. "Hang on, darling," she said with a wry grin. "Florence is going to help set your leg. This is going to hurt. So just look into my eyes."

"Did you just . . . call me . . . AAH!" There was a sickly snapping sound as Sean cried out in pain and gripped Carina's hand.

"Don't be ridiculous," Carina said. "I would never call you that." She kept the smile plastered on her face, but her distress over Sean's pain was evident. She looked away and found Alex watching her, his hand to his chest. She put her hand over her mouth and stifled a sob, then sucked in a deep breath and blew it out. After another breath, the stoic smile returned and Carina turned back to Sean, locking eyes with him and keeping him focused as the others worked on his leg.

When they had finished stabilizing him and the medication Henry had given him for the pain began working, Simber stepped in, ready to carry Sean to the ship, where he could rest.

"Wait, Simber," Talon said. "Do you think he would be more comfortable on the island? He can take my bed. Please, it's the least we can do."

"Yes," Lhasa said, her happy demeanor subdued. "Karkinos is a bit more stable than your ship—and Talon's bed will be more comfortable than the ship's deck, won't it?"

Sean's eyes were closed now. Carina looked at Ms. Octavia and Henry. "I think that's a good idea," Carina said.

They nodded.

"May I?" Talon asked Simber, pointing to Sean.

"Of courrrse. Lead the way."

Talon picked up Sean in his gentle, giant arms. Simber, Alex, Carina, Henry, and Ms. Octavia followed, while the rest of the party headed back to the ship or to the beach to get some rest.

Talon's bed was a feather-stuffed mattress under a canopy of palms, whose leaves had knitted together naturally to form a waterproof ceiling and walls on three sides. The bronze giant set Sean gently on one end of the bed, leaving plenty of room for others to rest comfortably in other corners of it if they so desired, as it was quite the largest bed Alex had ever seen.

Talon showed Henry around his castle, as he called it, pointing out other things that would make the team more comfortable throughout the hours ahead. Henry, Carina, and Ms. Octavia went to work making things cozy for Sean. Carina shooed Simber, Alex, and Talon away to the lagoon, where the fire had been before the eel destroyed it.

LISA McMANN

They talked as they walked, Simber clearly warming up to Talon after all that had happened.

"We'll help you sorrrt thrrrough the wrrreckage once we've all had a good sleep," Simber said to Talon.

"It's very kind of you to offer, thank you."

Something told Alex that Talon wouldn't actually mind having to do all the cleanup work himself. He seemed like he might get bored at times.

Talon added, "I'm just grateful that Karkinos wasn't hurt. The eel could have cracked his shell. Oh, Karkinos . . ." He hesitated, like he wanted to say more, but closed his lips instead.

"That would have been terrible," Alex agreed. He turned to Simber. "Did you think the eel seemed bigger, Sim?"

"Rrremarrrkably so."

"And then everything that happened with Lhasa," Talon added, shaking his head as if he were trying to understand it all. "Simber, will you explain what happened? How did that tiny kitten bring Lhasa back to life? I have so many questions. Is she a god?"

Simber offered a rare grin. "She is not, to my knowledge, a god. Though it turrrns out she is a most unselfish feline.

Perrrhaps she'll tell herrr storrry. I see she's gatherrred therrre with the otherrrs." He looked at Alex. "You know I don't need to sleep, but I am prrroperrrly bushed rrright now. Arrre you holding up all rrright?"

Alex nodded. "I'm fine. Just tired and sore. I think it'll be nice to sleep out here tonight. Look," he said, pointing, "Sam has our fire going again. I bet he used an origami dragon to start it. He's always looking for reasons to use those."

Talon listened to their conversation with a curious look on his face. "Your magic is very strange and interesting," he said. "I should like to know more. Our dragon, Pan, can light fires too, but she doesn't come on shore, so her skill isn't very useful to us."

"You have a *dragon*?" Alex asked as they reached the fire. "A real one?"

"A coiled water dragon who rules the sea," Talon said. "She comes around now and then."

Alex couldn't believe it. What else was here? He didn't want to leave.

They sat down. After the long, eventful evening, Lani and Samheed, bickering once more, said good night to the others

LISA McMANN

and headed back to the ship, where Sky, Crow, Copper, and many of the others already had gone.

Alex leaned up against Simber's side. Fox dozed, curled up but quite far back from the fire—he didn't want to become kindling. Kitten played pounce with a tiny sand bug, while Lhasa lounged just above the ground nearby, watching Kitten play. Florence stoked the fire, and Talon settled in. It was time to hear Kitten's story . . . as told by Simber.

And Fox.

The Tale of Kitten LaRue

Talon watched the playful kitten with amusement. "I should ask Vido the rooster how such a tiny thing can do such a large deed. Tell us your story, Kitten."

The kitten looked up from the bug she was chasing and saw that all eyes were on her, except for the sleeping Fox's. "Mewmewmew," she said.

Immediately Fox jumped to his feet, bleary eyed. "She says she is so happy to be here with you all today, and you are her very special friends—" Fox stopped abruptly when he saw Simber. He lay down again and put his paws over his nose. "Sorry. I forgot."

Talon tilted his head, looking from Fox to Simber. A smile played at his lips. "If it's all right with you, Simber, I'd like to hear Fox's interpretation and then yours."

Simber stared at Talon, saying nothing.

"There, there," Alex said, reaching back to pat Simber's neck. "Just close your eyes and pretend it's not happening. Just this once."

"Good grrrief," the cat growled, but didn't object.

"You are kind to humor me, fine cheetah," Talon said. He turned to Fox. "Continue, if you please."

Fox pushed his nose up from the sand. "Me?" His fearful eyes darted from Talon to Simber and back again.

"Yes, of course," Talon said.

"Go on, Fox," Alex said. "Simber's not going to do anything."

Fox cautiously got to his feet. "Well." He cleared his throat. "As I was saying, Kitten is so happy to be here with you all, her very special friends." He glanced at Simber, who lay with eyes closed, a pained expression on his face, and then continued. "She feels especially thankful for, um, the shiny guy, whom she considers to be her best friend, except for Fox, of course. Ahem."

Kitten hopped. "Mewmewmew!"

"Aaand she would like to announce that she, like others in the past, namely Carina, has taken on a new name and would like you all to call her that from now on, but only if you feel like it, as she will also continue to answer to Kitten. The new name is . . . henceforth . . . or not—as she said, it is up to you—Kitten James Bob LaRue." He sucked in a breath and paused dramatically. "The 'James' part is in honor of Jim the winged tortoise, and the 'Bob' part is because Bob is the best name, and because it is what I do in the water. The 'LaRue' part is because it is her mother's name, and, um, *also*, secretly, it just happens to be Mr. Today's nickname, which only those who knew him best would know, which would be her. And, ah, me, who is named Fox . . . Bob. LaRue. Which are also the names," he added slowly, almost as if he were just thinking it, "for if you are a cat of some sort. Yes." Fox smiled politely, and then with a nod prompted Kitten to continue.

Simber groaned. He listened to Kitten's "Mewmewmew" and then put his paws over his ears.

"Yes, our dear Kitten had a mother, quite unlike all the rest of the statues. Her mother's name was Glenda Morris Bob

Cat LaRue, and she could play the pipe organ like an absolute dream." Fox gazed over his audience's heads for a moment as if he could hear the music. "You see, when Kitten was born, she was a real human kitten, but Mr. Today loved her so much that he decided to make her into a statue so she could live forever, which is what he does with all his favorite humans."

Alex blinked. Lhasa wore a puzzled expression and turned to Talon. "That's not at all what the kitten is saying," Lhasa whispered, which Talon found highly entertaining. He hid his grin and they both turned back to hear more.

Fox leaned on his elbow in the sand and closed his eyes halfway for effect. "You see, Kitten's mother lived a long, lonely life, until one day she got hit by a bus, which, according to Mr. Appleblossom, is something that you ride on, kind of like a cheetah. Only it wasn't a cheetah, because a cheetah would never hit a cat, or hurt it in any way. Only dogs. Of which I am not one. Of." Fox slid his eyes to the side to check on Simber. All appeared safe, so Fox nodded at Kitten once more. "Continue, cousin."

Alex elbowed Simber, who uncovered his ears to hear Kitten's next statement.

"Mewmewmew! Mewmewmew!" said Kitten.

Fox nodded intently at his friend, and then he rose on his haunches and put his front paws out toward his audience, setting the scene. "Imagine it, friends. A real, live human kitten loses her mother to a tragic bus accident. Left alone and in the wild, a kindly mage named Mr. Today . . . *LaRue* . . . takes her in, saving her from starvation and other things human cats have, like fleas and litter boxes and icky things like that. He transforms her sickly body into a statue—and not just any ordinary statue like that freak Ahab, or Florence here, but one of his *top* statues who actually get to play in the lounge band." He nodded enthusiastically. "It's a rags-to-riches story for one cool Kitten and her friend, coincidentally also a cat, named Fox—Fox LaRue—who is in no way a member of the Cananadada family, because those are what dogs are made of."

Fox paused for effect, or to see if Kitten was going to mew again—no one was quite sure. "And that," he said finally, bowing, "is the very true story of Kitten LaRue and how she saved the snow lion queen named Lhasa. Thank you, thank you all. Thank you very, very much." Fox blew kisses to everyone but Simber.

LISA McMANN

Almost everyone clapped. Kitten beamed at Fox, clapping her paws together so that they made a tiny *tink tink tink* noise. She hopped on top of Fox's head and settled down in his fur.

"But Fox didn't explain how Kitten saved me," whispered Lhasa.

Talon chuckled and applauded harder, clearly tickled by the Fox's strange, senseless story. "Bravo, friend Fox," he said. "You are a masterful storyteller and a very fine cat." He turned to Alex. "That was most entertaining. Does Simber have a version to tell?"

Alex looked over at Simber and tapped his shoulder. "He's done now. Your turn."

Simber slid his paws off his ears and sat up, clearly trying to wipe the look of disgust from his face. "Verrry well," he said. He bowed his head once, regally, in Kitten's direction. "I shall hope to do this story the justice it deserrrves."

Alex smiled. It wasn't common for Simber to verbalize his respect for anyone, so he knew that Simber must really think highly of Kitten. He sat forward in anticipation so he could capture every word.

Simber began. "When Mrrr. Today was a boy, a little olderrr

than Alex, he set out frrrom Warrrblerrr Island on a jourrrney with his sisterrr to discoverrr a new island. They took few items with them. Likely some food and waterrr. A rrrope, perrrhaps, and some tools and textiles. As they pushed off frrrom the shorrre, theirrr motherrr called to them. 'Stop!' she said. 'Take this, and rrrememberrr me.' She tossed something to Marrrcus, and he caught it. It was a tiny white porrrcelain kitten, no big-gerrr than a marrrshmallow."

Fox looked at Simber like he was crazy.

Simber ignored Fox. "Yearrrs passed, and Marrrcus kept the kitten safe in his pocket, taking herrr out often and thinking of his motherrr. One day, afterrr he'd made otherrr crrreaturrres and statues come to life, he looked at the kitten and thought, 'This kitten should be alive.' And so the mage brrreathed life into the tiny porrrcelain statue. As he perrrforrrmed the spell, he thought, 'Therrre was one thing that I did not do with Simberrr that I wish I had done. I grrrant to this kitten nine lives, forrr cats arrre in constant dangerrr, and she should live a long and prrrosperrrous life. What I did not do beforrre, I will do now. Kitten, you shall live nine times beforrre yourrr end comes. And,' the mage added, almost as an afterrrthought,

LISA McMANN

'you shall have the ability to give up one life to anotherrr cat in need if you so choose.'"

Simber paused for a moment. Everyone was silent, realizing that this was a very different story from the one Fox had told.

"When the mage was finished casting the spell, the kitten's body warrrmed and she sprrrang to life, mewing instead of talking—in his quest to give Kitten nine lives, Marrrcus forrrgot to grrrant it the ability to speak to humans." Simber chuckled, his eyes growing misty.

"He was a forrrgetful mage, indeed. But, luckily, Kitten could underrrstand Mrrr. Today. He told herrr about the special gift many years ago, but she neverrr had a need to give away the life until today. Which she did, I must add, without a moment's hesitation." Simber looked at Lhasa, who had tears in her eyes.

Kitten stood up on Fox's head and hopped. "Mewmewmew," she said.

Simber hesitated. "And now she says she is glad to be herrre with you, and she considerrrs you verrry grrreat frrriends."

"Mewmewmew!"

"She says please don't die again, Lhasa, because she is afrrraid she has no morrre lives left to give."

Lhasa smiled, knowing Simber had interpreted perfectly. "I shall keep that in mind and be very careful from now on, dear Kitten."

"Mewmewmew."

Simber frowned at Kitten. "Please don't make me say that."

Kitten gave Simber a stern look. "Mew. Mew. Mew."

Simber's jaw dropped open. "Oh, come on."

"Mew!"

Simber rolled his eyes. "All rrright." He sighed, and then mumbled, "She says she is changing herrr name, and would like to be called Kitten LaRrrue, if you please, but only if you want to—it's totally up to you."

Palace Discord

Aaron could easily hide his bandaged shoulder under a fresh robe, but that didn't make it hurt any less. And the pain definitely affected his ability to concentrate and make good decisions. This particular evening he found himself staring out the window at the forty-foot wall where the opening used to be, contemplating the removal of just a block or two, when Secretary came in.

Eva updated Aaron on how Quill had been reacting to his latest address.

"It's all very favorable," she said, almost puzzled. "No one is pushing back. It's like they all really wanted this sort of extreme structure again."

"It's not extreme," Aaron said. "It's comfortable."

"Well, whatever you want to call it. They're welcoming it."

"Obviously I know what I'm doing."

Eva sighed. Sometimes Aaron's arrogance was just a little too much. "Don't let the power go to your head. You need to take it slow," she said. "Whatever you're planning on doing, stop and think a bit first, will you? If you're going to take over Artimé, be calculated about it. Get everything in order before you start a war."

Aaron gave her a chilling glance. "I know what I'm doing," he said again.

She stared at him. He was so naive. "So does Gondoleery," she blurted out. "Only she's doing it right. You'd better watch out."

"Please. Don't be ridiculous," Aaron said. "Gondoleery is a crazy old woman who burned off her own eyebrows. She's not a threat to anybody but herself. Besides, I'm watching her. She's working for me, after all."

"Keep thinking like that," Eva said, fuming. "You'll get us all killed."

LISA McMANN

"Now *you're* the one acting crazy," Aaron said, his voice cold.

Eva stared. "I'm the one trying to help you be more like Justine, but you're too busy being an ignorant, arrogant child to listen to me." Eva Fathom turned on her heel and strode out, muttering under her breath.

"You may not speak to me like that!" Aaron yelled after her. "Come back here!" He waited, his face puckered and getting redder by the minute. But she didn't return.

After a while Aaron went to bed, but he tossed and turned, unable to sleep. Secretary infuriated him time and time again—he really didn't know why he put up with her insolence. She was constantly picking at him. Telling him he was doing things wrong. Trying to take his power away. And now she was insulting him to his face. He'd never quite trusted her, and now he once more questioned his decision to keep her on.

Slowly his anger fizzled and his thoughts turned back to the jungle and the half-formed idea he'd had after his conversation with the rock. *Panther would do anything for me.* That's how the rock had made it sound, anyway, and Aaron was eager to test it out. With Quill paying close attention at the moment, maybe it was time to let Artimé get a taste of what was to come.

He couldn't get the crazy idea out of his mind—let *them* live in fear for once. Let Artimé see who was in charge on this island, and whom they should be scared of. Because everybody needed to face the truth. Aaron was tired of people not respecting him. His brother had to be taught a lesson. And so did Secretary. He'd show her that her constant undermining was only going to serve as incentive for him to do exactly the opposite of what she told him to do. And he'd be right every time.

By the time he finally drifted off to sleep, Aaron Stowe had hatched a surefire plan that would get him the attention and the respect that he deserved. And Artimé would get the smallest hint of what would become their nightmare.

While Everyone Slept

LISA McMANN

Before long, Fox and Kitten curled up on Lhasa's furry side to sleep. Alex dozed off near the fire, and Simber did too, since there was nothing else to do. Florence went out on the claw reef to check on the ship, finding everyone dead asleep, including her detached arm—it didn't move a muscle. Ms. Octavia would have to reattach it in the morning. In the lagoon she spied the tip of Spike's spike as the whale floated near the surface, sleeping as well. And then she saw a long tentacle herding a squirming eel's tail toward the crab's open mouth. All was good.

Florence wandered over to Talon's castle of palms to check

on the patient, and there she found everyone sleeping as well, even the octogator. Sean moaned quietly in his sleep, and Carina reached out to comfort him with a touch. Peace had come, finally, but not without a price.

Florence walked back to the fire to find Talon waiting for her.

"Do you sleep?" he asked.

"Not often, but I've been known to doze off every few weeks. Do you?"

"I do, but sleep eludes me tonight. How is your arm?"

"It's . . . fine. It's just lying in the ship."

Talon chuckled. "What I mean is, do you have any pain in the place where it should be?"

"No. It's inconvenient to be without it, but I'm lucky—I have no pain. Which reminds me of something I've been meaning to ask you about. That eel lit you up like a fireball. I was afraid for you."

Talon looked at her with a crooked smile. "Were you? Afraid for me?"

Florence felt her face grow warm. "I was afraid for everyone," she said. "Do you feel pain?"

"Some." He didn't elaborate. Instead he looked at the fire and

LISA McMANN

said, "To be honest, I've had days when I wished I could let myself be killed, for I have had a lifetime of lifetimes. My body is not invincible, and that eel could have taken me from this never-ending monotony and into the next life. I would be lying if I said I didn't consider letting it. Or taking your arrow meant for the eel."

Florence tried to think what it would be like, living thousands of years, caring for the life and accessories of a giant crab. "But you didn't."

"Taking the arrow was only a fraction of a second's thought before I realized how it would make you feel, so that was never a true consideration. And I have others who depend on me. Lhasa, Karkinos. Bock. Even the hibagon, to some extent. But they would survive without me if they had to. Though the crab . . ." Talon trailed off.

"What is it?"

Talon looked at her. "I don't wish to trouble you."

"Tell me, Talon. Please. Perhaps we can help."

Like any great leader in tune with the needs of others, Alex's eyes popped open at Florence's words. He turned to face the fire and began to listen to the nearby conversation, unnoticed by Florence and Talon.

"I don't know," Talon said, his voice full of doubt. A shadow passed over his face. "I don't think there's anything you can do." He looked out at the crab's claws, silent and floating before them. "I'm afraid Karkinos is dying."

Florence sat up. "Oh no," she said, dismayed. "I'm sorry. How horrible for all of you."

He didn't deny it. "He's not in pain, thank the gods. But . . ."

"But what?"

Talon sighed deeply. "I don't know what will happen once he's . . . gone."

Florence wasn't sure what he meant. "You mean what will happen to his body?"

"Well, that, yes, but to his shell, too. And to us."

Florence's mind raced. "What do you think could happen?"

"I don't know. When the bottom-feeders finish off his body, will this shell remain intact? Will our island move about at the whim of the currents? Will our vegetation die too? If it does, Bock and the dropbears will starve. And what of the squid and Issie? They'll lose their protector." Talon closed his eyes, defeated. "I don't know what to do."

"But—" Florence began, her thoughts whirling. "How long does he have to live?"

Talon opened his eyes again, but he didn't look at her. "It's hard to say. He's in a slow decline. We may have years left, but I believe that could change at any time. I'm doing my best to give him the care and comfort he needs." He frowned. "That thrashing eel didn't do him any favors."

Florence's expression was one of deep concern. "Is there any way I can convince you and the others to come with us?"

Talon afforded a small smile. "I'm afraid I cannot abandon the crab. And after so many hundreds of years together, I doubt the others can abandon me. But I suspect you knew that."

Florence was silent for a long moment. Then, in a soft voice, she asked, "What will happen to you?"

Talon stared at the fire. "Perhaps it will be the end of me. Perhaps . . . perhaps Karkinos's death is the answer to my predicament."

The silence was overwhelming. Alex stared at the flames, his heart in a clutch over what he'd just heard.

Florence glanced sidelong at Talon. "Do you still wish to be done with this life, then? If we were to journey this way in the future and find the carcass afloat, are you saying we might not find you here? Not anywhere?"

Talon looked down and murmured, "That you would think to search for me is an unexpected treasure I shall cherish." He touched Florence's hand, making a clinking sound, and said in a low voice, "I must admit, dear lady, that the hope of seeing you again erases every morbid thought from my mind. I would indeed live on for the chance of that."

Florence looked down at Talon's hand on hers. "It might not be often," Florence found herself saying, as if she had been planning their next visit already. Beneath her six-pack warrior abs, an entire host of butterflies swarmed.

"If only once in a hundred years you find me, stranded and alone upon this rotting carcass, I should not complain," Talon said. He swallowed hard and dared turn to look into her eyes.

Florence met his gaze and held it. In her mind, she reached over to touch Talon's cheek, but she couldn't actually do it because that hand was attached to the arm on the ship. Instead she said, "I was actually thinking more like once a year."

Talon pressed his bronze lips together, then replied, "That would be even better, Florence."

The Line of Possibility

Alex tried not to gag at the mushy words between Florence and Talon. Sure, he was glad they were crushing on each other, but he couldn't exactly unhear their conversation, no matter how hard he tried to block it out.

After a while, tossing and turning to the lull of conversation as he tried to get back to sleep, Alex began to wonder if he could actually learn a move or two from the bronze gentleman. But then he remembered his promise to Simber and to himself. And he knew he wouldn't be needing any smooth moves with the ladies anytime soon.

He also knew he needed to talk to Sky about it, and explain why he was being so aloof. It wasn't fair to her not to. And even though she was busy with her mother, he could tell she knew something was wrong. If he could only find a little time alone with her . . . but it had been nearly impossible this entire trip. Maybe when they got back home he'd have the chance to explain. That would give him time to figure out exactly how to say what he was feeling, because at the moment, he certainly didn't understand it himself. All he knew was that his heart ached when he thought about her. But it ached even more when he thought about the mistakes he'd made because he'd let himself fall for her.

When Florence and Talon grew silent, Alex's thoughts reverted to the island's predicament. Poor Karkinos. Poor everybody who lived on Karkinos. There had to be a way to help. Perhaps Henry could make an enormous batch of medicine that would heal the crab. . . .

Alex dozed off. In the morning he walked down the reef toward the ship. There he found Lani swinging from a rope tied to the ship's bow. She gained momentum, leaped, and landed on the reef a few feet in front of Alex.

"Oh, hi," she said with a grin. "Didn't want to bother the squirrelicorns for a ride."

"I was just coming to talk to you. Is Sam up? I need him, too."

Lani scowled. "Yeah." She turned to the ship and hollered, "Sam! Alex wants you."

Alex gave her a quizzical look. "You don't look very happy. What are you two always fighting about, anyway?"

Lani shrugged. "I'm not fighting. He's just being dumb."

Alex squelched a grin. "Right. Okay. So what is he being dumb about?"

Sam appeared at the railing with two squirrelicorns, who clutched him by the arms and carried him to the reef. "Hey, Al," he said.

Lani folded her arms.

Alex looked from one to the other. "Well?" he prompted. "Why so much fighting?"

Samheed shrugged. "Tell him, Lani."

"Fine." Lani pulled a folded piece of paper from her pocket and opened it. "See this? It's called a map. Well, it's half of one, anyway—it's ripped. You find them in books. They're supposed to show you where things are."

Alex looked at it. "I know what a map is," he said. "Ms. Octavia had me draw one of Quill once, since she's never actually gone to see it."

Lani nodded. "Well, look at it." She shook the paper a bit to add emphasis.

"Okaaay . . . what about it?"

Lani sighed, frustrated. "Don't you see? There's all these dots here, and this giant land over here." She flicked the paper. "We're the dots."

"We're the dots?"

Samheed rolled his eyes. "You see what I'm telling you?"

Alex was becoming more confused by the moment. "I don't think I get what's happening here."

"We're the seven dots. The islands. Quill, Warbler, Pirate, Legends, and the other ones we haven't seen yet on the east side of Quill. And this big massive thing to the west? It's more land. A giant island." She tapped the paper. "At least, that's my theory."

Samheed shook his head.

Lani smirked. "Sam thinks I'm nuts."

"That's because you are."

LISA McMANN

"And you're obtuse." Lani folded up the paper and put it back in her pocket, and the three started walking toward the island.

"Where did you get it?" Alex asked her.

"From that vessel thing that landed near Artimé. I found it floating in the water."

"Well, how do you know it's not just a drawing of something pretend, like you find in books sometimes?"

Samheed slapped Alex on the chest. "See? That's what I said."

Lani frowned. "It could be, I suppose."

"After all, the map doesn't say that those seven dots are islands," Samheed said. "And even if they are, it doesn't say the names of any of them. You just think they are because there happen to be seven of them."

"Be quiet," Lani said. "Alex, what do you think? Don't listen to him."

Alex shrugged. "I really don't see it, Lani. I mean, if there was a giant island farther to the west, why wouldn't Simber and Mr. Today know about it?"

"This is exactly what I'm saying!" Samheed said. "Lani thinks she knows more than Mr. Today and Simber."

"Oh, you be quiet!" Lani said again. "I do not."

"Um, it's pretty obvious—"

"Come on, Sam," Alex said. He looked at Lani. "Look. It's a cool theory and all, but . . . well . . ."

"Wait, Alex—I didn't even tell you everything. I totally understand you being skeptical about it. I didn't even start thinking this was a map of the islands, or that there could be more beyond these islands, until I saw this same exact map inside Pirate Island." Lani's eyes shone.

Alex grinned in spite of himself. He never got tired of seeing Lani all fired up over an idea. Her face got so animated. She could tell a complete story with her eyes—now, that was true art.

"What are you grinning about?" she demanded.

Alex sobered up. "Nothing. So you saw the same map in Pirate Island."

"That's what I just said."

"Like there would never be a duplicate," Samheed said sarcastically. "Even Mr. Today has multiple copies of all our books—in the library and in the Museum of Large. It's not unheard of."

"Anyway," Lani said, ignoring Samheed, "in the glass case

inside Pirate Island, there was a full map, not just this torn-up part."

By this time, they had reached the fire, where Sky sat alone, enjoying a giant plate of breakfast that Talon had apparently cooked for her. She looked up at them, mouth full. "Talking about the map again?"

Alex nodded. "So you've heard?"

Sky swallowed her food. "You hear a lot of stuff you wish you hadn't when you sleep on the ship."

"What do you think?"

"If I said what I thought, Samheed's head might explode."

"So you think it's possible?" Lani asked. She sat down. "See, Alex—I'm not the only one."

Sky took another bite and chewed thoughtfully. "Sure, lots of things are possible. I mean, it does seem strange that nobody would know about land being right there—even Queen Eagala says there are only seven islands. It's in the handbook and every-thing. But hey, I don't know. We're on a floating crab right now, and we were on an underwater island just a few days ago. Who's to say there's not some sort of invisible island out there?"

Alex, Samheed, and Lani stared at Sky.

"What?" asked Alex.

"Are you kidding me?" Samheed exclaimed.

"Now *that's* just crazy," said Lani.

Sky just laughed and shook her head. "Well, I think we found the line that separates possible from impossible." She shoveled another bite of food into her mouth and said, "And Lani's theory falls on the possible side."

A Breakup

The four of them stayed by the fire, Talon bringing more food and leaving again to take care of Karkinos. Alex steered the conversation to the issue of the dying island, telling Samheed, Lani, and Sky everything he'd heard the previous night. Well, almost everything. He left out the mushy parts.

"So what are we supposed to do about it?" Samheed asked.

Lani shrugged. "What *can* we do? This crab is huge. I mean, we can see if Henry and Carina can get to work making medicine, but it could take forever to mix up a dose big enough."

"We don't even know what's wrong with the crab, so

how would we know what kind of medicine to make?"

They stewed over it for the better part of an hour, and in the end, they had no solutions. Eventually, Samheed and Lani left the fire, not fighting this time. Alex watched as Samheed slipped an arm around Lani's shoulders and Lani slid hers around Samheed's waist, the two exchanging spirited grins as they called a truce . . . for the moment. Alex smiled wistfully. He turned to Sky, and the smile faded. They were alone.

"I miss you, Alex," Sky said in a quiet voice. "Where have you been?"

Alex looked into her eyes and was immediately captured, his heart thudding all over the place, out of control. "I'm right here," he said. "I've been here."

"You know that's not what I mean."

Alex dropped his gaze. "Yeah," he admitted.

"You've been avoiding me."

"It's not like I want to," Alex muttered. "It's just that . . ." He sighed deeply. He didn't think he was ready for this conversation.

"It's just what?"

Alex sighed again. This was really hard—harder than he'd

LISA McMANN

thought it would be. He pressed his thumbs against the bridge of his nose, trying to figure out how to say what he was feeling.

Sky waited.

Alex looked at her once more, and his stomach fluttered. "See, you're doing it again."

Sky blinked. "I haven't moved."

"You don't have to move. You just— You're always— Ugh. I hate this."

"Clearly."

"I mean, I don't hate *this*, like, this thing we have. I mean . . . trying to explain . . ."

Sky just watched as he struggled for words. "Well, I do."

Alex paused. "You do what?"

"Hate this thing we have."

Alex stopped breathing. "Y-you what?"

Sky's face was pained, her voice calm. "I hate this thing we have, Alex. Because it's not really a thing, is it? It's just uncomfortable and awkward."

Alex was silent. A blast of pain seared his gut. He dropped his gaze.

"It's not fair to keep me in the dark. You're so brave when

you're leading Artimé, but when it comes to me, you can't even talk." Sky bumped her elbow into Alex's arm. "Hey. See? Say something. Tell me what's happening. Please. I'm begging you."

He looked up. He wished he could explain to her how miserable he felt. He wished he could just talk to her and tell her everything he was feeling, but the problem was so confusing he didn't understand it himself. How could he explain something he didn't understand?

"You're right," he said. He knew it wasn't enough, yet it was all he could get out. How could he tell her the truth? How was he supposed to say that he made too many mistakes when she was around? That he couldn't concentrate when she was nearby? That he thought about her all the time, when he should be thinking about more important things, like keeping everybody alive?

And now she was looking at him with such deep disappointment in her eyes.

"That's it?" she asked. "That's all you've got?"

He wanted to reach out and take her hand. He wanted to kiss her. He wanted to tell her everything he was feeling in a way that she would understand, and he wanted the two of

LISA McMANN

them to be okay again. But every second that went by, things became less and less okay. And he knew they'd reach a point soon when there was no fixing it. "Yeah," he said weakly. "I guess that's all I've got."

Sky didn't flinch. She didn't show any emotion at all. She just stared at Alex.

Alex shook his head. Her reactions never stopped surprising him. "I can't believe you're not crying or yelling at me right now," he said.

She allowed a small laugh to escape. "Don't you know me by now, Alex? Every time somebody hurts me, I just get stronger. Eyes of fire, heart of ice—just like the golden rooster said." She stood up. "Maybe you should think about what Vido said about you."

She turned then and walked toward the crab-claw reef and the ship.

Alex watched her go. "I'm so sorry," he said, but she was too far away to hear him. He dropped his head in his hands and thought about all the things he'd just messed up so that he could be a better mage.

The way he felt now, he wasn't sure it could ever be worth it.

A Final Tale

The Artiméans stayed on the Island of Legends for a few more days. Ms. Octavia reattached Florence's arm and declared it to be as good as before, perhaps better. Simber, Florence, and Talon cleared the trees that had been toppled by the eel. They split the logs into planks, and Alex, Samheed, and Lani used the wood to repair the ship's deck.

Sky, Crow, and Copper helped the others replant things that had been uprooted, trying to make Karkinos beautiful again, and maybe even a tiny bit healthier. And when the work was done, many of them spent their time lounging by the sea,

LISA McMANN

telling stories, and taking walks together. Kitten and Lhasa were seen deep in conversation from time to time, with Fox trying, as always, to join in.

Florence and Talon stayed up late talking every night until Talon drifted off under the stars, and Florence did too, just to be polite. It was sort of, almost, quite perfectly, a little glorious holiday for most of them. Even Sean began to feel better, and he joined the others on the beach once Florence made him a special chair to sit in. It was big enough for Carina to lounge next to him, as she had taken it upon herself to care for her friend. Lani kept her eye on the two, wondering if there was a little something more than friendship going on. She had a lot to tell Meghan already.

Alex and Sky barely spoke, and when they did, it was only out of necessity. Both of them tried to pretend they weren't hurting inside. And it was working . . . for now.

The group spent a quiet last evening around the fire. The ship was packed and ready to sail at first light. And while everyone wanted to stay longer, they were all growing curious about how Ms. Morning, Mr. Appleblossom, and Meghan were getting along with the new group of children from Warbler.

When it came time for stories, it was Florence's turn to tell her tale.

"Many years ago," she began, "in the early days of Artimé, Marcus Today was out wandering deep in the jungle. There he found an enormous rock. Marcus brought the rock to life and put it in charge of the jungle, and the two became friends."

Talon, Lhasa, and Bock were getting used to feeling shocked by the strange things that were alive on their new friends' island, but they weren't the only ones sitting up in anticipation. Most of the Unwanteds were deeply curious too, for they had never heard this story before.

"The rock's mouth was a cave," Florence continued, "and Marcus spent hours exploring inside. One day when Marcus visited, the rock asked Marcus if he would extract something from his mouth because it was causing him pain. Of course the mage agreed to help his friend, so he went inside and found the source of the rock's discomfort—a large piece of ebony was embedded in his throat, and a portion had broken off and fallen away, leaving a sharp corner.

"Marcus marked the outline of the ebony stone and began chiseling, going deeper and deeper around the perimeter. Soon

LISA McMANN

he discovered that the stone was much larger than he had initially thought, buried far into the wall of the rock mountain's throat. With his friend's permission, Marcus set out to recover the fine stone whole. The rock mountain was happy to be rid of it, as it had been a source of discomfort for years."

Florence shifted in the sand. The firelight danced on the sheen of her body. "After weeks of work," she went on, "he found the end of the black stone. He chipped away at the rock surrounding it until finally the enormous piece of ebony was freed. Once it was loose, Marcus realized it was way too big for him to move. So he used the transport spell to bring the ebony stone to the mansion."

"Wow," Alex said under his breath. He caught Samheed's eye, and the two shared a moment of amazement as Florence's story unfolded.

"Marcus wanted to keep as much of the stone intact as possible. He'd never seen a piece of ebony so large before, and he wanted to respect its grand size. He envisioned a giant warrior to complement Simber inside the front door of the mansion, and began carving ever so carefully. Once he had chiseled out my shape, he began the painstaking work of sanding and smoothing hundreds of rough edges to give me this sleek, polished look. It took him years to finish me."

She smiled. "He always called me his most frustrating project ever, and he told me he'd thought about giving up on me several times. But then he said, 'Florence, every night, when I wanted to give up on you, and give up on my art because it was so difficult, I always told myself that if I still felt like quitting in the morning, I could quit. But I had to sleep on it first.'

"I remember feeling really strange that he'd admitted this to me. But then he said, 'But, Florence, every time I looked at you after a night of sleep, I could only see how beautiful you were, and how much progress I had made. And that kept me going.'"

Florence paused, a bit choked up. And then she continued. "When he finally finished me and was ready to bring me to life, he said, he wrote out everything he wanted me to be, so he could read it as he was casting the spell. He didn't want to mess up or forget anything after all that work."

She smiled and looked at Alex. "I miss Marcus. We all do. And I'll never forget everything he sacrificed to make me. But we continue on with our memories of him, and you are a worthy successor, Alex. I wouldn't want anyone to take your place."

"Hearrr! Hearrr!" Simber said.

Those around the fire murmured in agreement.

Alex looked down at his hands. He didn't feel very worthy. "Thanks, everyone. I'm just trying to do my best to not make mistakes. It's hard not knowing all the secrets. But I'm getting there."

"Well, Alex," Ms. Octavia said, her pride for her student evident on her face, "you did a fantastic job bringing Artimé back from ruin and rescuing Samheed and Lani from Warbler. *And* creating Spike." She beamed. "I can't wait to see what you do next. You have my full support."

"That's very generous of you, Ms. Octavia," Alex said. She'd taught him so much, yet he knew she could teach him so much more. "I hope you all will tell me if you think I should do something differently. I'm really still learning, and I count on everyone to help me figure out this job." He turned to Florence. "I'm so glad to know how he made you."

Alex looked at the others who had shared stories over the past days. "It helps so much to understand what he was thinking and how you all came to be. I wish I'd thought to ask before. Talon, you are really cool for introducing this storytelling thing to our evenings by the fire. Thanks."

Talon reached out to shake the boy's hand. "It is nothing compared to the service you and your people have done for me," he said. He looked at Lhasa, and then at Florence, and spoke from the heart. "You have given us new life and new reasons for living. There is not enough thanks in the world for that gift." Talon's words were positive, but Alex couldn't help but notice the tinge of sadness that went with them. It made him more determined than ever to figure out a way to save the giant crab island.

By and by, the tired creatures, statues, and humans made their way to their resting places for the night, until all who remained by the fire were Alex, Lani, Samheed, Sean, and Carina. Alex lay on his back on one side of Sean's chair, Lani and Samheed on the other, looking at the stars.

Alex wished Sky had stayed by the fire. Just having her nearby seemed to take some of the ache away. But she stayed away from him. He couldn't blame her at all. He'd been a total jerk to her, not giving her any explanation at all for his distant behavior after the Spike and Florence incidents. Here, under the stars that he'd so often shared with Sky, it was all he could

LISA McMANN

do to stop dwelling on it and try to make conversation, just to keep the misery at bay.

"Are you sure you're feeling well enough to sail home?" Alex asked Sean.

"I'm ready for anything, really," Sean mused. "Anything that doesn't require fighting an eel, that is." He yawned. "It's been nice resting up on this island, but I'm getting a little bored. Isn't there something exciting we can do before we head back?"

Alex narrowed his eyes. "Like what?"

Carina looked at Sean in much the same manner. "Yeah, like what? It sounds like you have an idea."

"Oh, I don't know," Sean said. He looked off over the water to the west and began to whistle a slow tune.

Lani propped herself up on her elbow. "What—you want to see what's out that way? Let's do it! I'm in!"

Samheed groaned. "There's nothing out there. It says so in the Warbler handbook."

"So you trust Queen Eagala?" Carina said. "Her word doesn't mean anything."

"Simber said it too," Alex offered. "But I don't know if he

meant there are only seven islands in the world, or just seven in this chain."

Sean grinned. "I happen to know that Simber said there were seven in this chain. He doesn't know if there's anything beyond it."

"I can hearrr you," muttered Simber from somewhere in the darkness. But he didn't deny the claim.

"And?" Carina prompted Sean. She turned on her side next to Sean in the chair, wearing a playful grin.

"And so I was thinking that we could maybe just go that way and see if anything appears on the horizon. Head west for a day, and if Simber still can't detect anything, then we'll turn around and head back home. Whaddya think, Al?"

"Come on, Alex. Please," Lani said. "We're right here—when will Samheed ever have this chance to prove me wrong again?"

Samheed laughed and tugged at Lani's hair. "Hey, you're cute *and* funny," he said. "I like you. Even if you drive me crazy."

"Same to you," Lani said. The two affectionately touched their foreheads together, grinning.

Alex thought about going farther west. It seemed like a fine time to check it out, since they were out this way anyway. At most it would only add two days to their trip home, and they really hadn't been gone long, though it felt like a lifetime with all that had happened. "I think it sounds good," Alex said. "I'll check with Simber to see if he has any concerns. If he feels good about it, we'll do it."

"Sounds fine," came Simber's response.

"Hooray!" Lani said.

"Do what?" said a voice from behind them. It was Florence. She and Talon came walking toward them. "What are we doing?"

"We'd like to go west to see if there's anything else out there," Alex told her. "If we don't see anything by the end of the day, we'll turn around. But I thought it would be nice to check since we're out this far already."

"Hmm," Florence said with a grin. "Interesting. I've always wondered too."

Lani beamed at Samheed.

"Stop already," he said, feigning annoyance this time.

Florence turned to Talon. "Do you know if there are any more islands in that direction?"

"I have never explored it," Talon said. "Nor have I seen any ships coming from that way—only from the other direction, as you came."

"Which doesn't mean there aren't civilizations that way," Carina mused. "They might be like you—having no means or desire to leave their island. And maybe not even knowing anyone else exists, like the people of Quill thought for so long." Her growing excitement for the adventure was clear in her voice.

"Well, then," Talon said, "I see no reason why you shouldn't explore it. If anyone is well equipped to handle any situation, it is your team from Artimé."

It was a melancholy departure on a cloudy morning. Best wishes were exchanged between the inhabitants of Artimé and Karkinos, and both Florence and Alex stooped down near Karkinos's face to say good-bye and thank you, silently wondering if they'd see him again.

When they could think of nothing more to do, Alex called, "All aboard!" and everyone assembled on the ship and stood at the railing, except for Florence, who stood centered on the new portion of the deck, and Simber and the squirrelicorns, who flew above. Captain Ahab directed the ship out of the crab-claw lagoon and into new waters to the west, with Spike alongside. Lhasa blew kisses from shore, while Talon, stoic, held one hand on his bronze chest. His eyes were locked with Florence's.

Florence put her hand up to signal her farewell, while Simber made sure to fly off to the side so he wouldn't block her view. At last, with Talon but a speck on the red-rimmed lump of an island, Florence lowered her hand. She looked down at the deck and emitted a sigh, and then sat down carefully and stared straight ahead. Alex stood next to her and, after a moment, reached up and put his hand on her shoulder, vowing once more to himself that he'd do anything in his power to help the Island of Legends survive.

A Chilling Turn

E va Fathom, who had made herself scarce recently even though she continued spying on the high priest, stopped Aaron in the hallway on his way down the stairs.

"Where are you going?" she demanded.

"It's not your business," Aaron said.

"What happened to your shoulder?"

"What? Nothing." He shifted it and barely winced at the pain.

"You've been holding it funny for days."

"I must have hurt it putting the block wall back up."

LISA McMANN

Eva glared. She knew he was lying. She also knew he still had the two heart attack spells in his pocket. And that he'd been going into Haluki's house a lot lately . . . and most certainly using the tube to Artimé. But she didn't know why, or what he was doing during the hours he was away. All she knew was that Artimé was vulnerable right now and she had to hold Aaron off from doing anything there until Matilda let her know that the ship was back.

"I'm warning you, Aaron," Eva said, her voice hushed, "if you rush into . . . into doing something to harm Artimé, you will risk losing Quill's loyalty. You'll look like you've lost your head. It took Justine years and years to get everyone so thoroughly behind her. One false move for you, and it's—"

"Stop." Aaron clenched his jaw. "Not another word about it. And you'll address me as High Priest."

Eva closed her lips. The two of them stood facing each other in silence. Finally Aaron stepped aside and strode past her, down the stairs and toward the front door.

Eva whirled around and watched him go. As he closed the door, she hurried after him, hesitating briefly and then blindly rushing outside.

"High Priest, wait!"

Aaron didn't stop walking.

Eva ran to catch up to him as they reached the portcullis. "Listen to me, please!" she said. "Don't do anything to Artimé. Not just yet. We'll work together to figure out the right time. I'll help you, I promise. Just . . . *wait*."

Aaron stopped walking. He turned, his boots grating against the gravel road, and looked at her.

"Please," she said again.

Aaron held her gaze for a long moment. And then he looked at the guards who stood at the portcullis. "Guards," he said, wincing and clutching his shoulder, "take her to the Ancients Sector."

Eva's heart froze. "What?"

Aaron didn't look at her. "Get busy!" he barked. The guards jumped to attention, grabbing Eva Fathom by the arms.

"No!" Eva cried out. "Aaron, no!"

But Aaron Stowe, high priest of Quill, turned away from her pleas and continued walking through the open gate toward Haluki's house.

Eva, eyes wide with fear, strained her neck to watch him go,

LISA McMANN

remembering his remorse when he'd done this to his own father. But this time he didn't turn back. He didn't change his mind.

The guards nudged Eva toward the palace. When she refused to walk, they picked her up by the elbows and carried her to the Quillitary vehicle near the door. They opened the door, put her in the backseat, and instructed the driver on what he was to do with the woman.

Eva, silent, faced forward as the jalopy sputtered and chugged down the driveway. The shadowy lines of the barbed-wire ceiling of Quill crossed over her paper-thin skin, each one marking a year of her long life in service, many for the bad and fewer for the good.

When they passed the high priest on the road, Eva didn't look at him. And when he was left in the dust behind them, Eva looked at the driver and took in a short breath of recognition. She gathered her thoughts, then leaned forward. "Sir," she said in a quiet voice, "is there any chance you'll take a risk for me today?"

The driver slowed. He glanced over his shoulder at her. It was the driver Eva had given extra fruit and vegetables to. He hesitated. "There's a chance."

Eva closed her eyes for a moment, and then she opened them again and spoke. "Before you drive me to the Ancients Sector, could you please make one stop?"

The driver pinched the bridge of his nose and scratched his head. "All right, as long as it doesn't take too long."

Eva blew out a breath of relief and looked at her hands. "I assure you, good sir, that it won't."

Panther Goes for a Walk

From Haluki's house, Aaron took the tube to the kitchenette, where he listened briefly but heard no one. "Good," he muttered. "Perhaps they're out on the lawn." He pressed all the buttons at once, then found himself in the jungle.

This time he stayed in the tube until he located the rock. He spied Panther lounging on top of it. The panther sprang to her feet and made her way nimbly down the rock face, jumped to the ground, and bounded over to Aaron, mouth wide open and hissing.

Aaron stepped back, alarmed. This didn't look like affection.

"It's all right," the rock rumbled. "That's how she shows appreciation."

The panther pushed her face into the tube and bumped Aaron's hand, still hissing.

Aaron pulled back from the fangs. "Are you sure?" he asked, his voice shaking. "Nice panther." He patted the creature's back gently as she tugged his clothing, pulling him out of the tube and hissing at every move he made.

Aaron stepped out, trying to make small talk with the rock while also trying not to appear afraid of the panther, even though he was. Soon the panther bounded up a tree and showed off her ability to balance on even the thinnest branches.

"Interesting," Aaron muttered. He wasn't sure what he was supposed to do. Did the beast expect him to praise her or something? He didn't understand these creatures. "Anyway," Aaron continued, "I'm back, and I thought I'd take a walk. Maybe Panther can come with me so I don't get hurt this time."

The rock seemed to think about it. "That would be nice. Okay, Panther?"

The panther hissed.

"Well, I guess that's a yes," the rock said, chuckling.

"Don't go too far. I like Panther to stay nearby so she doesn't wander too close to . . . you know what." He pointed his peak toward Artimé. "Stay on the jungle paths and you won't get lost."

Aaron nodded. "Got it, chief."

The rock chuckled, pleased by the title.

Aaron and the panther set off into the jungle, Aaron trying to stop the anxious energy from boiling over. He also needed to put aside his thoughts about what he'd just done to Secretary. He could hardly believe he'd done it. But she had crossed the line so many times, and Aaron had been too lenient with her. He'd let it go too far, hadn't he? Once the insults began, there was nothing else he could do, no matter how she pleaded. She was dead wrong, and she wouldn't stop bugging him with her wrongness. It's not like she didn't know she was over the line. More than once.

But Secretary was useful. And perhaps, deep down, Aaron was a tiny bit fond of her. She'd helped him out of a jam more than once. He furrowed his brow and sighed. He could always stop at the Ancients Sector tonight and spring her out of there. They likely wouldn't put her to sleep until tomorrow at the earliest. Maybe having her spend a few hours there would be enough to scare her into behaving better.

That's it, he decided. *That's what I'll do. I'll just scare her.* "But it'll be her last chance," he grumbled, glad to have that issue resolved. "If she does anything else to defy me, it's over. And that's final." He continued on the path. Panther occasionally bounded ahead. As soon as they were out of sight of the rock, Aaron left the path and picked his way over fallen trees and vines until he reached the real path he wanted to be on—the path to Artimé.

"Come on, Panther," Aaron called, moving faster now.

The panther hissed, saliva dripping from her jaws.

Aaron began to imagine the scene: Alex, lounging on the shore with that pretty orange-eyed girl. Aaron and the panther entering the lawn from the jungle—no one would ever expect them. And if Alex wasn't out there, it didn't matter. He'd send Panther into whatever crowd there was—and there was always a crowd on Artimé's lawn. "We'll just scare them," Aaron said to the panther. "Show them that they aren't the only ones who can command a living statue."

Panther hissed.

LISA McMANN

451 « Island of Legends

Aaron picked up the pace when he saw the stream. The path ended there. Aaron called out to the panther to follow, and Panther did. They crossed the stream and continued on. Aaron began to look for brighter areas so he'd know where the forest ended.

With no path now, it was slow going, but Aaron could tell that the trees were thinning. Eventually he could hear birds and voices in the distance. He crashed through the brush to the edge of the jungle, where he could see Artimé.

"Come here, Panther," Aaron said, peering at Artimé's lawn from behind a tree.

The panther hissed and sat down near Aaron. He stroked the panther's head as he watched the people move about the property, still quite a distance away.

Aaron's heart raced. The Unwanteds would soon see how powerful he was. Yet, in the back of his mind, doubt crept in. Eva Fathom's words invaded his brain. "Don't move too quickly. Get everything in order first." But Aaron shoved the thoughts aside.

"We're just scaring them a little, okay, Panther? Don't . . . don't kill anyone. Not just yet."

Panther hissed.

"Scare them good, though, I mean. Then turn around and come back to me."

Panther looked at Aaron, and the two seemed to have an understanding. At least, Aaron thought so.

"Ready?"

Panther hissed.

"Go!" Aaron cried.

The panther bounded from the jungle toward Artimé at top speed, jaws open wide.

Surprise Attack

Eva Fathom got out of the Quillitary vehicle at the gate to Artimé. "Thank you," she said to the driver. "I'll be very quick."

He nodded and looked down. Both of them knew he could be sent to the Ancients Sector for this if anybody found out.

Secretary hurried into Artimé, greeting the girrinos by name. They narrowed their eyes at her but let her in. She walked down one of the paths to the mansion, but then she caught sight of Claire Morning on the lawn with a group of orange-eyed children, all with strange scars around their necks.

The instructor had been teaching the children how to sing.

Claire did a double take at the sight of Eva Fathom. She rose. "Excuse me for a moment, dear children," she said. "Talk about your favorite songs quietly. I'll be right back."

She stepped away. Eva met her in the grass.

"What do you want?" Claire asked. She folded her arms over her chest.

"Claire, I know Carina isn't around right now. But I need you to tell her something for me."

"How would you know she's not around?"

"It doesn't matter—it'll all come out one day, I'm sure." She hesitated. Her chin began to quiver, and she frowned, trying to stop it. She turned her face and gazed out at the sea, realizing it would be the last time she'd take in its beauty. "I'm being sent to the Ancients Sector," she said, her voice soft. "I was arguing with Aaron, and he got mad, and now I'm . . . about to go."

Claire's mouth twitched. "If you want me to say I'm sorry about your circumstances, I'm afraid I can't. Not after what you did to me."

"I don't blame you, Claire. Though when I spoke loudly

in Haluki's home about you and Gunnar, it was on purpose. I wanted you both to know the other was there. It's not much, I'm afraid, but it's all I can tell you right now." She pressed her lips together. "I'm on your side, though I don't expect you to believe me. I've been staying with Aaron so I could keep an eye on things."

Claire frowned. She glanced at the children, who were talking animatedly about their favorite songs. "What is it you want me to tell Carina?"

Eva focused on Claire. "Please, will you tell her I love her and little Seth? And that I'm so sorry . . ." Her hand flew to her mouth, fingers trembling. She took a deep breath and continued, stronger. "Tell her I'm sorry I didn't get a chance to say good-bye. And to explain."

Claire looked at the ground. "I'll tell her."

Eva pressed her fingers to her eyelids to stop the tears. "Thank you. There is someone who can vouch for me. But I can't say anything more. I have to go." She looked at Claire. "I'm so sorry, Claire. I hope you can forgive me someday. And . . . Liam, too. He's been appointed governor, but he's faking his loyalty. He's sick over what he did." She touched

Claire's arm. "Marcus wasn't supposed to die like that. He and I had a plan. . . ."

Claire recoiled from the touch. "How dare you?"

Eva faltered. "I've said too much. My driver . . ." As she stepped back and turned toward the gate, she added, "Aaron is plotting an attack. He uses the tube. Did Charlie tell you? Because I told Matilda." Now she was just babbling, and it didn't matter—Claire hated her, and Eva understood why. It was senseless to try to explain herself. She dropped her eyes. "Good-bye," Eva said.

Just then a shout rang out. And then another, followed by a piercing scream. Soon screams filled the air.

Eva turned to look. Bounding toward the group of children was a huge black creature with gleaming white teeth and a screech that chilled her blood. And behind the creature was a figure in a black cloak running toward them. It was Aaron.

"Aaron, no!" Eva screamed. She ran to the children and began to pull them to their feet. "Run to the mansion!" she told them. "Go!" She turned around and ran toward the screaming panther, trying to get between the beast and the children. With a sinking heart, Eva knew that she didn't have any magical spell components to stop the panther, and her elemental magic was of no help—neither rain nor ice would stop the beast, and fire out here in the open would only serve to put Artimé in grave danger.

There was only one thing Eva could do to stop the panther. Her legs weren't as strong as they once were, but with all her energy Eva ran and threw herself in front of the children as the panther opened up her mighty jaws.

Claire was scrambling to put up a protective glass wall and herd the children to the mansion. As they ran, screaming, Claire looked back over her shoulder to see Eva Fathom leaping, putting herself in harm's way. The creature pounced, knocking Eva's frail body to the ground, and the beast's fangs took hold.

In the distance, Aaron Stowe watched in horror. What was Secretary doing there? "Panther!" he yelled. "Just scare them! Come back! Release! Retreat!"

But it was too late. Secretary was down. And the Panther wasn't letting up. Aaron panicked. "Secretary!" he whispered. He shoved his hand into his pocket, pulled out the two heart attack spells, and sent them flying at Panther, yelling, "Heart attack!" as he did so.

The heart-shaped components sprouted wings and flew straight and true, hitting Panther in the side. The beast stopped cold, held her position for a second, and then toppled over to one side in the grass next to Eva Fathom.

Neither one moved.

A second later Artiméans streamed out of the mansion to defend their world. Aaron stared. And then he turned around and ran as fast as he could back into the jungle.

With all the children safe inside, Claire rushed back outside and pushed her way to Eva's side. The nurses were already there. But there was nothing they could do. Eva Fathom was dead.

For what seemed like an eternity, no one knew what to say. Eva Fathom had sacrificed her life for the sake of Artimé.

"We should summon Alex so Carina can come," Claire said quietly. She looked at Mr. Appleblossom, who nodded. "Eva threw herself in front of that panther. If she hadn't, it would have gotten the children." She shook her head, sickened by the frightening beast. "Where in the world . . . ?" she said. She'd never seen anything like it.

The nurses covered Eva Fathom's body, picked her up, and

brought her inside the mansion. Claire couldn't tear her eyes away from the beast lying still in the grass. Next to it were two used heart attack components. "Who cast these?" she asked, looking around.

No one claimed the deed.

"Whoever did it most surely saved lives," Claire said. But she felt uneasy inside. Had her ears played tricks on her, or had she heard Eva shouting to Aaron, of all people? Was *he* responsible for the creature's attack? Or for its demise? Claire hadn't seen anything in her haste to protect the children.

"Reluctant heroes in our midst, perhaps?" suggested Mr. Appleblossom, and then he declared, "May paybacks for a good deed never lapse."

Claire frowned, sizing up the creature. It was bigger than a man, but not nearly so big as Simber. "I'm pretty sure this panther's not dead," she said as Gunnar ran out to join them. "She took a double hit, but I believe the spell will wear off eventually even if we don't release it." She looked up. "What'll we do with her? She's actually very beautiful when she's not charging toward you."

"Look at those fangs!" Haluki said with a wistful smile. He

touched the panther's back. "I'm glad she's not dead. I know her. I'll take her back where she belongs."

Claire twisted her neck to look at him. "You *know* her? How is that possible? I don't remember ever seeing her before. Did my father make her?"

"Yes, he did," Gunnar said, nodding. "Call everyone to go inside, and keep them there until the panther and I are long gone. All right?"

"Are you sure she won't hurt you?"

"I'm sure." Gunnar touched her sleeve. "I'll be back soon."

Claire smiled, and then she turned and ordered everyone into the mansion. The people of Artimé lined the windows, peering out, ever so curious to know how Gunnar Haluki would tame this wild beast.

When everyone was safely inside, Gunnar held his hand toward the panther and released the heart attack spells. As the panther lifted her head, the former high priest spun around. His body blurred, and when he stopped moving, a giant gray wolf—with kind blue eyes—stood in Haluki's place.

The panther struggled to her feet as the wolf moved to help her. They put their heads close together for a long moment,

461 « Island of Legends

as if the panther and the wolf were old friends getting reacquainted.

When the panther had recovered enough to stand and move on her own, the feline and canine friends slowly trotted off to the jungle together.

To the West

The ship traveled several hours, Sean peering anxiously ahead from his chair on the deck and Lani asking now and then if Simber could see anything.

"Still no," Simber said. "It is endlessly the same. Waterrr and sky meeting at the horrrizon."

By late afternoon, Alex had grown restless. "Nothing new?"

"Nothing new," Simber said.

Samheed wisely held his tongue.

Florence kept a constant watch over the sea, forever uneasy on the open water since the eel had attacked. And while she was pretty sure Karkinos had ended up munching on the

LISA McMANN

squirmy tail end of the eel, no one really knew for sure if it was the same eel they'd encountered before, despite its increased size, or if there was more than one eel out there. And Florence wasn't about to take any chances.

"Simber," she asked suddenly, looking up, "have you seen Spike lately?"

Simber frowned. "I'm surrre she's fine," he said, but he dropped back anyway to look for the whale.

Alex watched him go. When the stone cheetah grew small in the distance, Alex turned to scan the horizon for any sign of land.

Some time later, when Alex went to check on the giant cat, a flash caught his eye. Spike's sparkly spike was reflecting some sunlight. A bird-size Simber flew in the air above, heading toward the ship at a lazy pace.

"They're coming," Alex told Florence. The statue seemed relieved to hear it.

At first, almost no one noticed that the ship had begun to go faster. Ahab gave a shout, but he was always giving shouts about something, and no one paid much attention to him these days. Lani glanced up methodically, then went back to her map.

It was Sean, from his comfortable perch near the ship's

wheel, who looked sharply at the captain after the old statue shouted again.

"What's that you're saying?" he asked.

"The ghost of the whale!" Ahab cried, reaching for the ropes that would lower the sails. "She's got ahold of the ship once more!"

Samheed rushed over to help Ahab. "What's happening?"

"That ghoulish monster has overtaken us," Ahab mumbled. He yanked at the ship's wheel.

"But Pirate Island is back the other way," Samheed said. "Are you sure?" He tied down the sails and looked at Sean. "Are we still speeding up?" he asked, incredulous.

"We are," Sean said, perplexed.

By now Alex had felt it too, and seen the flurry of activity. "Something's happening," he muttered to Florence as he passed by her. "Call everyone on deck."

Lani put away her map and strained to see what was happening. "Land?" But she soon realized the excitement had nothing to do with land.

The ship pummeled over the waves, and the sea turned choppy. Alex didn't understand it. It couldn't be a storm. In

LISA McMANN

front of them was the same sky they'd seen all day, except the morning clouds had all dissipated. Only the sea looked different. Whitecaps fizzed and churned around the ship as its speed continued to increase. Samheed dodged obstacles as he ran to the bow to see what was happening, while Florence began calling out instructions to everyone.

"Simber!" Alex called.

The stone cheetah looked up from a quarter mile behind them, where he'd been flying along with Spike. He and the whale began moving faster to catch up with the ship. "What's wrrrong?" bellowed the cat when he was close enough to be heard by the boy.

But Alex didn't have time to answer, because from the front of the ship, Samheed began yelling. "Holy moly!" he said. "Captain, turn it around! Turn it around!" Samheed whirled about, fear on his face. "Somebody lower the anchor—we need to stop. NOW!"

Lani rushed to release and unfurl the anchor. Alex ran to Samheed at the bow, slipping and sliding on the deck as spray splashed everywhere. "What is it?" Alex asked. "What's happening?"

"See for yourself," Samheed said, distressed. He pointed ahead.

The place where the sky met the sea no longer seemed like a spot far off in the distance as it always had in the past. There seemed to be an end to the sea now, and it had grown steadily closer. The ship was barreling toward that point. Alex sucked in a breath. "Buckets of crud," he said. "It's the edge of the world!"

"And we're about to fall off," Samheed said. "At top speed. It's pulling us to it."

Alex stared, trying to figure out what to do, what to tell everyone else to do. His eyes grew wider with each passing second. Spray and foam created an eerie fog that rose in front of them, distorting their view. A sound like the constant rumbling of thunder began, and grew louder. He looked over his shoulder and shrieked, "Simber!"

Alex and Samheed looked at each other as they both realized what the thunderous noise was.

"Waterfall!" they yelled together.

Alex turned to face the ship full of scared faces. "Everybody tie down and hang on," he urged. "Major bumpy ride ahead!"

LISA McMANN

Finally Simber caught up to the ship. He swooped in at top speed, with the whale not far behind. "Tie down a rrrope and thrrrow me the otherrr end!" he shouted. "One to Spike, too!"

Carina and Sky sprang into action.

Florence, who needed to remain planted on the deck or risk capsizing the ship, called out, "Give me the ropes when you've got them!"

Carina and Sky scrambled to untangle ropes and toss them to Florence.

Florence wound the first one around a tether on the deck, tying it tight. "Here, Kitty," she said, tossing it high. Simber swooped in and caught it with his teeth. Florence tied down the second rope, located Spike in the water, and tossed that one to her. Spike grabbed on.

Alex ran to Sean's side and began strapping him to his chair, and his chair to the ship. "Sorry, buddy. I've got to do this," he said. "I figure you can't swim real well right now."

Sean nodded. "Yeah. I wish I could do something."

"Don't be stupid." Alex gave him a wry smile and punched him in the shoulder. "Just hold on."

Alex watched as Simber's and Spike's ropes began to pull

taut. "Hang on, everybody!" he shouted. The ship jerked and shuddered, but it soon recovered and barely slowed at all as it continued speeding toward the precipice.

Alex looked up at Simber, desperate. "We're not stopping," he said. "What do we do? Squirrelicorns, assist!"

Rufus and the other five 'corns flew to take hold of the ropes and tried with all their might to pull the ship in the other direction.

Simber's face showed little expression, but his eyes were worried. Gripping the rope in his mouth, he strained and pulled, unable to speak as he tried to turn and fly in the opposite direction. The ship only dragged him backward through the air like a kite.

In the water, Spike held on with her razor-sharp teeth, but it made no difference. She was being dragged through the water as if she weighed as much as Kitten. They were doomed.

"Everyone—abandon the goods and tie *yourselves* to the ship!" Alex yelled. "Stay abovedecks!" His worst nightmare was to have someone get trapped belowdecks with water pouring in. At least out here, Simber and the squirrelicorns could rescue them. Down there . . . Alex shuddered. He whipped his head around as the ship began to tremble. The thunderous pounding felt like the mad rush of his beating heart in his ears. Through the mist he could barely make out the edge of the sea a hundred yards in front of them.

He had to say something to his people, but his magely words caught in his throat. They were going over the edge of something, and no one knew how far they'd fall. The ship full of people, the statues and creatures all battening down and taking cover, Simber and Spike hanging on without a hope of saving the ship—Alex had never had so much time to face the possibility of death before.

But he couldn't die. Not now. Not ever! Finally he found his voice. "Pull!" he screamed to Simber and Spike. "Hang on!" he screamed at everyone else. All his words were lost in the thunder.

"Alex!" Simber shouted, the rope loose in his teeth as he flew closer to the boy, a question in his eyes.

Alex knew what Simber wanted him to do. As the point of the ship's bow neared the edge of the world, Alex stared Simber down. "No," he said, hoping the cat could read his lips. "I stay with the ship."

"Then so do I."

Alex brought his hand to his chest and held the cat's gaze as Simber slowed and let the rope grow taut once more, pulling with all his might, his efforts fruitless, but not giving up. Alex sought Sky and found her at the top of the sails, just where he knew she'd be. Her mother and Crow clung to the ropes beside her.

For the briefest of moments their eyes met, and her look tore Alex's heart in half. And then, as the bow crossed over the edge and the ship neared the tipping point, something bright and fiery flew toward Alex, stopped in front of his face, and exploded into a picture of a spider painted on a stone.

It didn't register.

And then it did. It was a seek spell from Claire. Artimé was in trouble.

"Siiimber!" Alex cried, his voice lost in the thunder.

The ship tilted sharply. Alex's eyes met Simber's. And they all went sailing over the edge.

The Edge of the World

They plunged toward the thunder and into the mist, falling at a dizzying speed, dragging Simber and Spike and the squirrelicorns with them. Sheets of water slapped the Artiméans, batting them about and knocking them off their feet as they clung to or hung from the ship. "Hold on!" Alex shouted, but his mouth filled with seawater, which choked off the words.

The ship shook and bounced as it fell, pummeled by rapids. Florence's body slammed against the stern, squashing Ms. Octavia and pinning Fox. Sky, Crow, and their mother swung wildly from the sails, trying desperately to grab on to the mast

LISA McMANN

with their feet. Lani, Henry, and Carina hung on to Sean's chair for dear life. Ahab clung to the ship's wheel, while Alex and Samheed remained secured to the bow, certain to be the first to hit whatever was at the bottom of the drop.

Second after agonizing second passed as they dropped, their stomachs in their throats. Alex felt faint and sick. He couldn't see anything, couldn't do anything to help anyone except ride out the journey and hope to live through it, though the chances of that seemed tinier the longer they fell.

The ship slammed from one side to the other. The thundering grew so loud that Alex thought his eardrums would burst. His whole body shook and swung about, and it was all he could do to hang on.

Then everything shifted. The ship took a second right-angle turn forward, slamming everyone with water once more and yanking them wildly against their ropes. It took Alex several seconds to realize that they were now sailing completely upside down: The ship and the sea were above them, the sky below, and they dangled precipitously as a reverse sort of gravity seemed to want to pull them down into the never-ending sky. Their speed increased but the thundering noise decreased, and soon Alex

LISA McMANN

could hear the cries of his friends once more. He opened his eyes, and through splashes of water saw Florence holding on to the side of the ship with one arm while Simber attempted to wrap his rope around her leg.

"Stay strong and hold tight, everyone!" Alex yelled, relieved to know that at least some of them remained attached to the ship. "We are still here. Hold on! Take a fresh grip and wrap yourself in the ropes if you can!"

They continued upside down for an almost unbearable amount of time, and then, just as swiftly as it had fallen, the ship took an upward turn and the thundering noise increased once more. Alex and Samheed, hanging on to ropes, slammed into the deck and bounced, which gave them momentary relief until a few of their shipmates dropped on top of them, unable to hang on after the most recent shift in direction. Something furry scrabbled straight up the deck and sank its claws into Alex. Instinctively Alex held on to it, deducing that it had to be Fox, and then another body slid into his—human this time. "Sky!" he cried, but she didn't answer; or if she did, he couldn't hear her. Alex wrapped his arms around both of them, weaving the rope as best he could to secure them against him. Water poured over them now.

Alex held his breath, hoping against hope that Simber had secured Florence enough that she wouldn't come crashing into anyone, for she would surely crush any human to death.

The ship thudded and shook, smashing against Alex's spine. He wasn't sure how long he, much less any of the others, could hang on. The thunder pummeled his ears and rattled his head, and soon he couldn't tell which way was up. He grew disoriented and flustered. Waves of black washed over his eyes, and as the ship pounded over the water, Alex's shaking arms could hold on no longer.

Samheed shouted something near Alex's ear, but Alex couldn't make it out.

"What?" he cried.

Sam shouted again. It sounded like "Crow!"

Alex looked around, but he couldn't see anything. "Crow?" he shouted back.

Samheed shook his head. "Scroll!" he cried out. He drew a circle in the air and put his mouth next to Alex's ear. "We're scrolling! Like Mr. Today's scroll feature! In Artimé!"

Alex didn't understand. The term sounded familiar, but he couldn't concentrate long enough to remember what it meant.

LISA McMANN

He felt ill. "I can't . . . ," he said. Another wave of black crossed his vision. He fought to keep from passing out, thinking of Sky and how he couldn't let go of her. They had to get through this. Ms. Morning needed help. But how would they find home now? Where were they?

As they rounded a fourth sharp turn forward, bringing them upright at last with the sky above and the sea and ship below, Alex could stave off the blackness no more. The echoing thunder in his ears became silent. His arms fell slack; his head bobbled and sank to his chest. Fox slipped from his grasp and slid to the deck, and Sky crumpled to the floor at Alex's side.

Alex slumped to the deck, unconscious, arms and legs tangled in the rope around him.

Only a few ears heard the thunder slowly dissipate in the distance behind them; few eyes saw the sea slowly grow calm again around the tattered ship. Behind them, the horizon was close enough to touch. In front of them, the sea and sky stretched on and on.

When the second flash of light streaked through the air and exploded into a painted spider in front of Alex's lifeless face, it would only have taken one clever pair of eyes to notice it and follow the path from whence it came, which would point the way home. But the question remained: Had anyone seen it? Anyone at all?

Henry lay stiller than a statue near the stairwell to the lower deck, one foot twisted around the anchor rope. From his pocket, a white porcelain kitten emerged. She stretched and yawned. She licked a paw and brushed the sleep from her eyes. And then she hopped off Henry and onto the deck, looking over the destruction that had taken place during her nap.

She stepped around Sean, who moaned. She moved past the mast and sails, where Crow and his mother still clung for dear life. She climbed over Florence's leg and the captain's chest and a squirrelicorn's horn, sniffing her way across the deck until she saw him.

She bounded over to Fox, sodden from lying in a puddle and looking like a rat, but smelling like Fox was supposed to smell. She licked his face until he woke up, and then she hopped on top of his head. When he stood up, Kitten could see over the railing. Fox blinked and shook the water from his fur. He walked over to Alex and began licking the mage's face earnestly, trying to get him to wake up.

Kitten narrowed her eyes, tilting her head this way and that, finally noticing a fading streak of light going from Alex off toward the sunset. She sniffed it and sat up. She had seen one of those before and knew what it meant. She hopped once, as if it would help her see farther, and then hopped two more times.

When at last Fox had successfully licked Alex's eyes open and the mage lifted his head, the streak of light had vanished. Kitten could wait no longer, for she did not want to forget.

"Mewmewmew! Mewmewmew!" she cried. She lifted her paw out over the endless sea, pointing the way home—or at least the way to Ms. Morning . . . wherever in the world she happened to be.

Dear Readers,

Since you are the greatest fans ever, and since there would be no Artimé without you, I'd like to share a very special letter written by Mr. Today to his daughter, Claire Morning, when she was thirteen. I hope you enjoy this glimpse of the early days of Artimé.

Lisa McMann

An excerpt from
Letters to Claire: A Journal for My Daughter
By Marcus Today

Tuesday, 5 July. Artimé is coming alive!

Dearest Claire,

My dream of Artimé is finally taking shape. The mansion is nearly complete, and not a moment too soon. I'm running out of room to hide the Purged children, and I can't wait to awaken them all and welcome them to a better life than they could ever have imagined.

I've finally convinced Justine to send you here at your upcoming Purge—thank goodness you finally got caught singing. Without that infraction, you would have been stuck in Quill forever. You're a clever girl, hiding your music all this time.

I admit I am excited and a little scared to see you, for I fear you have no memory of me—I am only the dreaded Death Farmer to you. I hope you and the other Unwanteds are not too frightened . . . but of course you will be. I wish I could somehow let you know that you'll be all right, but the risk is too great. Justine must never find out what I am doing here!

Simber continues to grow, but I think he's slowing down. I do hope he stops soon, or he'll crack the ceiling with his head when he stands upright on his pedestal. He's a bit more vain than I intended him to be, but it's turned out all right since his antics are so amusing. This morning he informed me that he believes his pedestal should be carved with dire warnings so as to make him more imposing, but I told him that he was clearly imposing enough and that the written warnings would only be redundant. He seemed to like that, and proceeded to growl at himself in the hall mirror for three-quarters of an hour. What a racket. I was afraid people in Quill would hear, so I had to put up a magical sound barrier.

Simber also expressed that the entryway's balance seems slightly off with him stationed on one side of the door and nothing but open space on the other. I tend to agree. Perhaps I'll look into creating an equally impressive companion to stand in the open space. A panther, maybe. I've always been fond of panthers.

A few weeks ago during the dead of night, Simber and I installed magical cameras along the top of the wall. I put the corresponding monitors in my office so I can keep an even closer watch on what's happening in Quill. I am saddened that your aunt Justine has become more and more of a tyrant. I have so many regrets. . . . I should have paid closer attention to her true motivations when we first founded Quill. I should have trusted her less. Now I'm forced to keep up the guise of Death Farmer to retain her trust in me. If only I'd seen through to her evil heart from the beginning! Being a twin to a monster is truly heartbreaking. I wonder if anyone will ever understand the pain as I do.

Ah, but now is my chance to make up for my failings. I hereby dedicate my life to righting our wrongs against the people of Quill. I pledge to you and to myself that I will make Artimé into a most wonderful haven for all the Purged, and to teach Unwanteds to use their creative gifts in the cleverest of ways. I am eager to have this magical world perfectly functional for your arrival, Claire, and then together we shall awaken the other Unwanteds who have been under sleep spells these past years. We'll be grateful for that magical sound barrier on that day, for sure.

Now that the details of the mansion and the grounds are being finalized, there's one minor thing about Artimé that's still bothering me—the weather. While the breeze off the ocean makes Artimé far more comfortable than inside the walls of Quill, it's still too hot for my plants and flowers, and the grass keeps dying. I need cooler temperatures and occasional rain, especially if I'm ever to create that surrounding jungle I've been thinking about. Just imagine all the wonderful creatures I could make to fill it!

A few days ago as I was building the water fountain, I recalled secretly working with rain and ice spells as a child on Warbler, along with Justine and our friends Eva Fathom and Gondoleery Rattrapp. But it was so long ago that try as I might, I couldn't extract the spell components from my memory. I found myself wishing I could ask my old friends if they remembered, but obviously I couldn't do that. However, this very morning, after two days of experimenting, I had my breakthrough! In frustration, I'd flung a handful of water into the air and shouted, "Make it rain!" Lo and behold, a steady rain shower began. What luck! Now my vision of a soft green lawn and a lush jungle is becoming a reality. The steady drumming of the rain on the roof as I write this is a most welcome companion.

With a little more experimenting, I think I could decipher some similar spells to control other elements, like wind, snow, ice, fog . . . anything! Even fire. Though we'd need to keep fire far away from the cat, of course. Perhaps I could write the spells in a little book for my steadily growing library. I'll call it *Element-ary: A Guide to Elemental Magic*. Ha-ha! It's good I'm writing this down, as I'll have a better chance of remembering it. A book like that could really be useful someday.

But now my work calls to me. Today I must finish the marble staircase to the balcony and figure out a transportation system for Unwanteds to travel quickly and easily from place to place. The Unwanteds will need a way to get into the rooms without doors. . . . Hmm. That one's got me stymied for now.

Until next time, my dear daughter. I wait impatiently for you. If only I had a spell to speed the days. But if I did, alas!—I'd never finish Artimé in time.

Your humble father and servant, I am,
Marcus Today